MARS

HOSPITAL

A DOCTOR'S NOVEL

MARS
HOSPITAL
A DOCTOR'S NOVEL

LLOYD FLATT, MD

BookPress®
publishing

Published in Des Moines, Iowa, by:

Bookpress Publishing
P.O. Box 71532
Des Moines, IA 50325
www.BookpressPublishing.com

Publisher's Cataloging-in-Publication Data

Names: Flatt, Lloyd, author.
Title: Mars Hospital / Lloyd Flatt, MD.
Description: Des Moines, IA: Bookpress Publishing, 2024.
Identifiers: LCCN: 2023906202 | ISBN: 978-1-947305-75-5 (hardcover) | 978-1-947305-89-2 (paperback)
Subjects: LCSH Hospitals--Fiction. | Physicians--Fiction. | Hospital administrators--Fiction. | Medical fiction. | Humorous stories. | BISAC FICTION / Medical | FICTION / Psychological | FICTION / Small Town & Rural | FICTION / Humorous / General
Classification: LCC PS3606 .L88 M37 2023 | DDC 813.6--dc23

First Edition
Printed in the United States of America
10 9 8 7 6 5 4 3 2 1

*I dedicate this book to my mother,
Harlene White. Thank you for
instilling in me a love of reading.*

AUTHOR'S NOTE

This novel is a satirical fiction, but the problems outlined are real. Greed, corruption, and incompetence are rife in medicine (as is the bizarre!). It is the author's hope that by shining a light on healthcare as it is today, change will occur.

PREFACE

Where is Mars, Nebraska?

A Google search showed the town, population 50,000, in the northeast corner of Nebraska, near the South Dakota border and about 180 miles from Omaha. Basically, the middle of nowhere. As for the town itself, it was poor, with a median income far below the state average. And every other socioeconomic marker—education, health, unemployment rate, homelessness, et cetera—all lagged state and national benchmarks.

The search was prompted when a recruiter informed me that a one-year medical directorship was available. The two-hundred-bed hospital's medical director had died, and they needed an immediate replacement. No prior experience was required. In addition to the directorship, the position included seeing adult medical patients in a hospital-owned outpatient clinic adjacent to the main hospital. The recruiter thought the position perfect for my needs.

And what exactly were those needs? My goal was to obtain a similar position at a prestigious university or a large hospital system. In such a position, my medical skills could help far more people, but these types of positions were few and far between, and they all required prior experience—a thing missing from my résumé. I had graduated at the top of my medical class and had earned many awards in residency training, but I had just turned thirty, and in the three years since finishing training, I'd only filled a few minor administrative roles. If I didn't do something *right now*, my awards and honors would be ancient history and my chances of ever landing a medical directorship would evaporate.

Could I tolerate living in Mars, Nebraska?

Mars surely wasn't San Diego, my hometown. San Diego has mild winters, beautiful sunshine, and beaches. Mars has dreadful winters, gray skies, and corn. It's a good thing I was single, because convincing a spouse to move from the beach to a cornfield would have been difficult. But, realistically, places like Mars, Nebraska, are exactly the kinds of places medical director careers begin. You just aren't going to find a medical directorship in San Diego with "no experience required" in the job description. And this position was only a year. A year focused on medical directing/outpatient care would not be more difficult than a year of medical internship. It couldn't be. A year was doable. And as for any free time in Mars, Nebraska, instead of beaches and sun it would be Netflix movies and books. Yes, a year was doable.

My Skype interview went well. I was offered the job and accepted immediately.

Three days later, the adventure in Mars began.

1

OFFICE INTERLUDE

Having immediately received hospital privileges upon my arrival, I started patient care on day one. Being a doctor first, it was appropriate to begin caring for patients before meeting the CEO and doing administrative work.

The outpatient medicine clinic was across the street from the main hospital, near a canal that ran through town. On this same street were several medical buildings, a nursing home, a bar, a couple of restaurants, and a few old, broken-down, single-family homes. The clinic building that would be the home of my medical practice was small, with just a few exam rooms and one nurse who doubled as the front-desk clerk due to cost concerns. This office would be shared with a pediatrician.

Walking up to the clinic for the first time, I felt my heart sink. The sidewalk leading to the entrance was cracked and uneven, creating a serious risk for falls. As for landscaping, the front of the building was overgrown with weeds and bushes. Plus, for good measure, those bushes all had thorns poised to impale hapless patients. And there were spiders everywhere. The building itself was old, worn, and creepy. Was this a medical clinic or a haunted house?

The interior was also dilapidated. It had a waiting room filled with stained furniture from another era and shag carpet that emanated a musty smell and had probably last been cleaned sometime in the seventies. The interior was gloomy due to the thick plastic wrap that covered all the windows. Supposedly, it kept the clinic warm in the winter, but in truth, all it did was darken the space and obscure the street view. Some ceiling tiles were drooping and held up with string. All of them had water stains. And was that black mold growing in the corners?

What a dump.

There were already patients in the waiting room—both young children and elderly adults, all mixed together and sharing germs. This clinic wasn't just a dump; it was an infection control nightmare.

"Hello. You must be Dr. Wave." A twenty-something nurse with long, blonde hair and blue scrubs with purple flowers introduced herself. "I'm Sally, the nurse for you and Dr. Wurst." Dr. Wurst was the pediatrician sharing space in the clinic. His name was pronounced "worst," which I found amusing.

"Yes, I'm Dr. Wave. Nice to meet you, Sally."

"Nice to meet you." Sally wore a mischievous smile. "Are you ready for the Mars Clinic? Can anyone ever be?" She giggled and handed me a computer printout attached to a clipboard. "Here's the schedule. Our first patient is already here."

The patients were listed by time slot, name, and reason for their visit. The first patient's chief complaint was, "My ass smells like a sewer." I grimaced, and Sally giggled again.

"This first visit reason seems inappropriate."

"We are required to list the complaints exactly as the patients give them. That's the rule. We had a consultant come here a year or so ago, and they gave us that advice. If you ask me, it's nuts."

"I agree. Couldn't we use something medically specific?"

She wagged her index finger and said, "Around here, we never, ever, contradict the consultants."

The rest of the day's schedule was a mixed bag. There were typical-sounding visit reasons, such as "blood pressure follow-up" and "diabetes check," but not everything was normal. "I want a bionic dick," and "Why do I look like a pig?" were also listed.

Unbelievable.

"Oh, and a heads up. Your first patient is loaded. He's drunk as a skunk."

My watch, an old Timex with a worn strap, read 9 a.m.

"And he stinks. He does kind of smell like a sewer. Welcome to Mars!"

✦✦✦

Giggling from Exam Room One could be heard down the hallway. This was not a good sign. As I entered, the repugnant stench of beer, body odor, and stool hit me like a hammer.

"Hey, Doc. I bet you think I pissed myself." More tittering. The patient—a heavyset, balding, and clearly intoxicated forty-one-year-old gentleman—sat on the exam table in a large, wet circle of his own making. He wore denim work clothes, and his pants were soaking wet.

"Honestly, I don't know what to think. *Did* you?"

"Nah. I spilled my beer."

That must have been one hell of a giant beer.

"Don't you think it's a little early to be drinking?"

"Nah, I don't have to get to work until noon. I got a half-day off to come to see you." He had a good job at the state roads department driving a steamroller, according to his chart, but the thought of him driving anything, let alone a steamroller, was disconcerting.

"You shouldn't be driving today." *Or ever, for that matter.*

"Ah, lighten up, Doc."

"I think we should talk about your drinking."

"I don't want to talk about my drinking."

"What do you want to talk about?"

"My ass. It smells like a fucking sewer. It stinks like a septic tank. I am not joking. It smells like something crawled up there and died. It ain't right."

"Are you having excess gas?" A variety of conditions can cause this symptom. Gas was as good a place to start as any.

"No, it just fucking stinks."

"So, when you pass gas, is it excessively malodorous?"

"Mal-*what*orus?"

Clearly, he did not have an extensive vocabulary. "When you fart, does it smell unpleasant?"

"Doc, it just fucking stinks. It smells like a sewer."

"Are you practicing anal sex? Any trauma or injury to the region?" Sometimes infections are a source of odor.

"No! Christ, Doc, you think I take it up the ass? What's the matter with you?"

"This is a standard question."

"My standard answer is hell, no."

"Do you have any pain in the area, or does it hurt to go to the bathroom?"

"It sure don't."

"Are you incontinent of stool?" He gave a bewildered expression and remained silent. "Do you poop your pants?"

"What's wrong with you? I don't shit my pants!" He shook his head, then giggled.

"Do you have a history of cancer in your family?"

"Cancer. I knew it. Am I going to die?"

This was going nowhere. It's always hard to get information from an intoxicated patient. "I'm just asking if cancer runs in your family. It's also a standard question."

"My old man died at forty with ass cancer. Now I got it too. Fuck. Ass cancer." Tears rolled down his face. They left clear paths that looked like riverbeds. His face was filthy.

"A strange odor does not necessarily mean you have cancer. Calm down."

Next came the physical, and everything was normal until the rectal exam. There are many possible causes for the reported symptoms. Abscesses, for example, drain foul-smelling pus, but this was unlikely. Abscesses are painful, and he had reported no pain. Could it be a tumor? Could it be a passage between the intestines and the skin called a fistula? As his pants hit the floor, the disgusting odor intensified, and the cause became clear.

"See, Doc? I told you my ass was smelly."

My eyes burned, and tears rolled down my cheeks. *This does smell like a sewer.*

"I see the problem," I said. Feces caked his buttocks, some old and dry, some fresh and moist, and all of it smelling horrific. The examination itself, including for occult or hidden blood, a sign of possible cancer, was normal.

"Is it ass cancer?"

"You must wash your buttocks. Stool is causing the smell. Everything else seems normal. Do you clean yourself when you bathe or shower? Do you change your undershorts?"

"Huh? Yeah, I shower sometimes. I change my shorts after I shower."

"How often?"

"Well, it's been a few weeks. I've been busy."

You must be remarkably busy not to shower for weeks. And you must hate doing laundry.

"You need to do a better job of cleaning yourself. I'll run a few more tests, but I think the smell is related to hygiene." Ordering a battery of blood work, which this guy probably needed anyway, seemed a good idea. He also needed a colonoscopy given the family history of cancer and his father dying at a young age.

"That's it? Just wash my ass? Is that what you're saying?"

"For the smell, yes. But I do want to run some other tests."

"I took a half-day off work, and all you do is tell me to wash my ass?" His tone was highly annoyed.

"That's not all I am telling you. I want to run some other tests."

"What tests?"

"I want to check blood work. I will also refer you to a gastroenterologist for a colonoscopy."

"A what?"

"A colonoscopy. It's a fiber-optic tube used to examine the inside of your rear end."

"You mean you want to shove a hose up my ass? I told you, I don't take it up the ass."

"It's entirely painless and will rule out any cancers. You do have a family history, so we should check you out." Usually, colon cancer screening isn't necessary until age fifty, but this patient's circumstances called for it, though he was only forty-one.

"No fucking way. No one is sticking a hose up my ass."

"You are free to decline, but this is medically indicated."

"Fuck, no. I come here because my ass stinks, and all you do is tell me to wash it. Then you tell me you want to cornhole me." A hiccup that sounded like a frog's croak escaped his mouth.

"I also think we should talk about your drinking." All physicians know by heart the CAGE checklist, a standard screen for alcohol abuse frequently administered during patient evaluations. It asks the patient to report whether they've felt the need to "Cut down" on their drinking, if they've ever been "Annoyed" by someone criticizing their alcohol use, whether they've ever felt "Guilty" after drinking, and whether they've used alcohol first thing in the morning as an "Eye-opener." As the patient sat there drunk, hiccupping, and drenched in beer, without a doubt there would be at least two checks on the list, the medically significant number.

"My drinking? Why talk about that?"

"Because you're drunk at eight in the morning. You shouldn't report to work today and drive a steamroller." *Hello, Captain Obvious.* "Let's talk about treatment options."

The patient frowned. "I gotta work. I just had a few beers at the bar this morning, that's all. I work fine like this. I do it every day."

The CAGE checklist has its first check.

"You should not operate a steamroller while drunk." *Captain Obvious strikes again.*

"I came here to talk about my ass, not my drinking."

"I think it's important. We can talk about both."

"This is fucking nuts. I'm out of here." He stood up and stomped out of the office.

"What's going on, Dr. Wave?" Sally asked. She groaned when she heard the story. She had lived in Mars, Nebraska, her whole life and knew a lot of the patients, including this one.

"He's a drunk and a dirty bird. Doesn't even change his underwear. You pulled quite a first patient." She shook her head sadly and walked off to get the next.

A few minutes later, she returned.

"You're not going to believe this. I called out the patient's name, his wife stands up, looks around, and says, 'Oops, I forgot my husband. We're rescheduling.'"

"It's just as well," I said. "I need a little more time with this computer. The electronic record Mars uses is…interesting."

"The computer system sucks. If you want, I'll show you some of the workarounds we use in the electronic medical record."

"That would be great. No one has offered me training on anything."

"Good. The onboarding here is done by idiots. I'll train you before they get their hands on you."

The electronic record used by the outpatient clinics, which were owned and operated by Mars Hospital, was awful indeed. It was slow, inefficient, and very glitchy if it worked at all. But on her own, Sally had figured out how to make it work passably well, and in no time, she had taught me her tricks. When the trainers finally arrived weeks later, she shooed them away.

+ + +

This visit was routine, at least at the start. A young fellow came in for a checkup. The exam was normal. For preventive purposes, and given he had a family history of heart disease, I ordered blood work. Sally, who was the office phlebotomist in addition to the nurse, was drawing the blood when the patient started screaming, "I am a robot! I am a robot!"

The patient ran out to where I stood in the hallway. There, he held the palms of his hands against the side of his head and shook it, weeping. Seeing me, he directed his shouts in my direction. "Doctor! I am not human! I am a robot!"

"Sir, calm down. Go sit in the exam room."

He obeyed and returned to his seat, where he continued to cry.

"I am a robot. Oh, my God. What is happening?"

"Sir, you must calm down. Compose yourself. We'll get to the bottom of this. Sally, what *is* going on?"

"I was drawing his blood, and it came out white. I'm not kidding. I've never seen anything like it."

Hearing Sally, the patient groaned. He began shouting, "It's just like on TV. I don't have blood. I have white robot oil inside me. Robot oil! *Robot oil!*"

"Let me take a look." The tubes she collected were already layering out. *Bingo!* "Take these tubes and come with me to the patient room. I will explain everything." Together, Sally and I entered the exam room.

"Sir, you're not a robot. You have a hereditary form of high cholesterol, which is why the blood appears milky in color."

His eyes gazed at the tubes while he listened. "You mean I'm human?"

"Yes, you are human. And your blood is not robot oil. Look, the milky substance is already layering out." Holding the tubes right before his wide eyes, together we watched a thick, white layer separate above the normal red blood. "See? That's blood."

The patient's relief lasted only seconds. "Good God, how high is my cholesterol?"

"These are probably triglycerides, not cholesterol. That's not as bad, and it is treatable." While what I'd said was true, high triglycerides are still a problem. For his blood to have a milky appearance, his triglycerides must have been in the tens of thousands. The normal level is under 150. He was at risk for a heart attack and other life-threatening problems like pancreatitis.

"I'm going to die." He again burst into tears and started shaking his head. "I'm going to drop dead just like my old man."

"We'll start you on a treatment. We'll beat this." After repeating this a few times in a calm voice, he finally settled down.

The test results showed his triglycerides were more than a hundred times higher than normal. Medications were started at once, and his triglyceride levels returned to normal in a few weeks.

He will live a normal, human, non-robotic life.

+++

The next patient presented with the day's most unusual reason for visit: "I want a bionic dick."

"What's bionic?" Sally had never heard the term.

"It's from an old seventies TV show called *The Six Million Dollar Man*," I said. "Bionic means mechanical, with extraordinary power. The bionic man had a bionic arm, two bionic legs, and one bionic eye. The rest of his anatomy was of the normal, nonbionic, sort." *Including his penis, I guess. I don't think they ever mentioned it.*

"Good morning," I said cheerfully as I entered the exam room. The patient, an obese middle-aged gentleman, had unkempt red hair and a scruffy beard. His history included high blood pressure and borderline diabetes. This combination frequently sets the stage for erectile dysfunction. Making good eye contact, and following some small talk, it was time to cut to the chase. "I understand you're having some difficulty with your erections. What's the problem?"

"Doctor, my wing-wing got no zing-zing."

Wing-wing? Never heard that one heard before. "Could you explain the issue more precisely?"

"My pointer just hangs there like a useless ornament. My big number is not so big anymore. And I want a bionic dick."

Pointer? Big number?

"Well, I'm afraid there's no such thing as a bionic penis, but it sounds like you have erectile dysfunction. Perhaps we could consider

Viagra or some other medication after running some tests."

"Nah, I don't want no pills, Doc. I googled a thing about a guy who had a bionic dick. He would just hit a button and boom! His wing-wing blew up like a freaking balloon. It was amazing. It added inches to his size too. His big number was *really* big."

If it's on the internet, it must be true. Thanks, Bill Gates.

"There are penile prostheses and implants that can be placed surgically by a urologist. But typically, we try nonsurgical treatments first."

"No, I know what I want. I want to be in the foot-long club. Tell them to supersize me."

"They don't take orders on size like McDonald's. And I doubt you would qualify for an implant. Public aid does not typically cover them." The gentleman was on Nebraska Medicaid, the state insurance program with notoriously lousy coverage. It typically didn't include Viagra, either.

"Well, we got to try, Doc."

"I'll order some tests, and I guess I can make a surgical referral." Ordering the usual hormonal testing and other exams was fine, but making a referral to a urologist for a second opinion? They would hate this referral and certainly wouldn't be interested in doing surgery on this guy's penis. In spite of my misgivings, the patient left happy, referral card in hand.

"My wing-wing's gonna get some zing-zing," he sang repeatedly, hands on his sides and hips thrusting forward to the rhythm of the last two words.

Sally watched with an amused expression. "What's his story?"

She frowned as I told the story, then she said, "That's fucking great, our tax dollars going down the drain for some joker's 'wing-wing.' We sure have some winners coming into this clinic."

✦✦✦

"We got a last-minute call from someone wanting to come in, so I added him on," Sally informed me near the end of the morning as she handed me a revised schedule. The reason for the add-on visit was, "I have a splinter."

"Where? His finger?"

"He didn't say, and I didn't have time to ask any more questions."

No kidding. In addition to being the nurse for Dr. Wurst and myself, Sally was also answering phones, scheduling patients, and checking patients in at the front window. "Well, it should be an easy visit," I said.

"That's what I was thinking. Who goes to the doctor for a splinter?" Sally snickered.

"Why don't you put some tweezers in the exam room? I'll be in my office until the patient arrives."

A few minutes later, my thoughts were interrupted by the terrified screaming of patients in the waiting room.

"Doctor!" Sally shouted. "Get out here!"

As I arrived, a scene of chaos unfolded before my eyes. The patient with the splinter was an older man with short, white hair and bib overalls, and he lay on the waiting room floor, his abdomen impaled by a long piece of wood. Blood oozed from the edges of the wound, adding a new color to the already stained carpeting and a new reason to replace it. Sally, using her lab coat to apply pressure around the "splinter" to stop the bleeding, was working hard to save his life. He was pale, breathing fast, and close to bleeding to death. His bleeding had triggered general pandemonium in the waiting room. Children screamed. A mom was crying. Sally maintained pressure around the wound as my fingers punched 911 on the phone. After I'd ordered an ambulance, I then gloved up, grabbed a pressure dressing from an exam room, and relieved Sally. Blood stained her hands. Disregarding her personal safety, she hadn't even delayed applying pressure for the time it would have taken to retrieve and put on gloves. The ambulance arrived quickly, and the patient was wheeled away.

We learned his story later: At home, this sixty-year-old farmer had tripped and fallen into a wooden rocking chair, which shattered under his weight, a large piece of it spearing his abdomen. He had then called our office and made an appointment. He was lucky to have survived. Specialists from the university hospital handled his trauma surgery, as surgeons at Mars Hospital refused emergency room trauma call in the Mars Hospital ER because the pay wasn't high enough. That was probably just as well. Mars surgeons weren't board certified, a fact most troubling.

Fortunately for Sally, her HIV and hepatitis C testing later came back negative.

✦✦✦

Just as Splinter left on a gurney, Dr. Wurst arrived. Dr. Wurst was slender, short, and balding, with only a large tuft of red hair remaining on the top of his head. He was a board-certified pediatrician with impeccable credentials—part of the minority of qualified doctors at Mars Hospital. And he also had a good work ethic. In addition to clinic work, he ran the hospital nursery and took an enormous amount of emergency room on-call duty in Mars Hospital's understaffed ER.

"Welcome. I see your first day has been busy so far." Dr. Wurst extended his hand in greeting while looking around the waiting room. We shook hands.

"Yes, and it has certainly been interesting." I retold the splinter story as we walked to his office and sat down. "How do you like working for Mars Hospital, Dr. Wurst?"

"I hate it. This place is a mess. Want to hear some of the problems?"

"Sure."

"Contracts. Compensation. Computers. Billing irregularities. Pressure to bill falsely. Patient safety issues. Patient care issues. Quack doctors. Worse administrators. Wasted money. Greed. I could go on."

"Sounds like a lot of issues."

"There are. You'll see."

"I can't help but ask, why do you still work here if you hate it?"

"I'm from a local family of farmers, and we have deep ties to this part of Nebraska. In fact, I'm the first member of my family not to take up farming and instead go to college and medical school."

"That's quite an accomplishment."

"Thank you. There are few pediatricians in the area, so I decided to stay in spite of the problems. I am needed."

Sally entered Dr. Wurst's office as he spoke. "You're done for the day, Dr. Wave."

"What happened to the fellow who was coming in because he looked like a pig?" I asked her.

"He didn't show. We have a lot of no-shows here. I hope he reschedules. I want to see what he looks like."

Dr. Wurst smiled and shook his head after Sally's comment.

"I guess I'll head across the street to the main hospital," I said. "I just have a half day of clinic work today as I meet with our CEO this afternoon."

"Ground zero of incompetence. Good luck," Dr. Wurst stated as I walked from his office.

I hoped his comments were exaggerations, but in fact, they were understatements.

2

DOCTORS' LOUNGE

My first stop in the main hospital was the doctors' lounge. An attractive young lady in a fashionable outfit with a low-cut top manned a table outside the lounge entrance. She was a drug representative, a salesperson sent by a pharmaceutical company to woo doctors into prescribing their newest and most expensive drugs. They also show up with gifts—lots of them. Ethically, this is a problem. Doctors should not accept gifts, and they should prescribe the best drug, not the newest. Of course, to help make their pitch, drug reps always present studies sponsored by companies manufacturing the new drug. These questionable studies always "proved" the drug being hawked was the best.

Ignoring the drug rep and entering the lounge, I spotted three doctors chatting around a table. One of them, a large fellow sitting on a bench instead of a chair, spoke up the moment he saw me.

"Who the fuck are you?"

Your boss, the medical director, almost slipped my lips. But that was confrontational. Instead, I delivered a smooth, calm answer.

"I'm Dr. Wave. I was just hired by Skip as the new medical director." At Mars Hospital, it was the custom to call all administrators, including the Chief Executive Officer, by their first name. The CEO at Mars Hospital went by Skip. This informality made me uncomfortable. My personality tended toward the formal.

"So you're that guy? Good luck." Irony filled his voice. "This place is a shitshow, and there's nothing you, or anyone, can do to fix it."

The physician giving me this warm welcome was Dr. Slenderman, a general surgeon, known to me only through my careful review of the medical staff directory. He was a young surgeon in his late thirties, and he had been on staff for a few years. He was as bald as a cue ball, had a bushy, black ZZ Top-length beard, and was enormously fat, weighing *well* over 350 pounds. The old, blue scrubs he wore were covered with greasy stains and desperately needed laundering. How, given his size, could he even operate? It turns out, he operated sideways because his arms couldn't reach over his protuberant abdomen.

Surgeons, especially general surgeons, are notorious for their obnoxious personalities, and Slenderman was certainly living up to that reputation. As I nervously sat down at the table, Dr. Slenderman never even bothered to introduce himself or shake my hand. My heart raced. *First-day jitters*.

"I'm Beats." The doctor to my left introduced himself and shook my hand. Beats was young, thin, and blond, but the mop of hair on his head was much lighter than my own blond hair. He reminded me of surfer dudes back in California. He also wore blue scrubs, which, unlike Slenderman's, were clean. My medical staff review showed he wasn't board certified in medicine, cardiology, or interventional cardiology. But at least he shook my hand and was friendly, unlike

Slenderman, who also lacked board certification.

Mars Hospital was one of the few remaining hospitals in the nation that did not require board certification. Most hospitals had adopted a board certification requirement years before to ensure doctors on staff were competent. Less than half of Mars's full-time medical staff held board certification, and the percentage of uncertified doctors was increasing. Uncertified doctors from around the nation were drawn to Mars Hospital like moths to a flame in order to practice without the rigors of passing their boards. As medical director, adding a board-certification requirement was at the top of my list of things to change.

"I'm Rumpsmith." The doctor to my right introduced himself after Beats. Rumpsmith, a thin man in his seventies, looked like Albert Einstein, his white hair wild and uncombed. Rumpsmith was a gastroenterologist, and a good one. He held the rare board certification and was highly qualified. He wore shiny white scrubs. Scrubs seemed the uniform of choice at Mars Hospital. My attire was old school: a white, starched dress shirt and tie, with pressed black pants and a clean and pressed white lab coat. Proper attire projects professionalism. Scrubs don't. But my formal attire made me feel out of place.

"So are you a real doctor, or an administrator?" asked Dr. Slenderman. "You gonna see patients, or you just gonna sit on your ass in your office like our last medical director?" His deep chuckle reminded me of Jabba the Hutt from *Star Wars*.

"I work in the hospital outpatient clinic across the street. I saw patients this very morning."

"Great. Just don't send your surgeries to me."

"Why not?"

"That clinic is a wasteland. They either have public aid or no insurance. Neither pays."

Nice attitude.

"I am sure there are some patients with insurance," I said.

"Fine. Send them."

A pile of donuts sat before Slenderman on a plate. He gobbled down two in under a minute. "What are you doing here now, anyway? You only work half days?" he asked with a full mouth, white powder and crumbs erupting onto his ZZ Top beard as he spoke. Slenderman raised his right eyebrow. "What easy hours."

You're sitting here eating donuts and not working.

"I have my first meeting with the CEO directly. I'm on my way over to his office."

"Prancer. Ha! What an idiot," Slenderman replied.

"You call the hospital CEO Prancer?"

"Yeah. Watch him when he walks. He prances, like those horses that do the high-step. No wonder he's called Skip."

Beats took this as a cue from Slenderman. "He's short, so I call him Tiny Dancer." Beats started singing the Elton John song of the same name. "What do you call him, Rumpsmith?"

"I call him a tightwad." Rumpsmith explained that he'd been an employee of the hospital for more than twenty years. His contract called for a productivity bonus awarding him 15 percent of the amount of money the hospital had collected beyond his base salary, but when the time had come to pay the bonus, Skip, then a new CEO just appointed by the mayor, had balked. It was too much money, Skip had said. He'd told Rumpsmith to understand that doctors should not be overcompensated, so he wouldn't be receiving his bonus. Rumpsmith had quit on the spot, started his own practice as an independent contractor, and was currently earning triple what the hospital had paid him. Rumpsmith, as an independent contractor, could maintain his medical staff privileges and remain at Mars Hospital even though he was no longer an employee. Skip, hating this fact, had subsequently added restrictive covenants into contracts to prevent employed doctors from staying on staff if they quit or were fired. Beats and Slenderman had always been employed. Neither had ever run their own independent medical practices.

"It was so stupid," Rumpsmith continued. "I tried to explain that the hospital would make more money if they kept me employed and just paid my bonus. But he wouldn't listen. So, I quit. He even had the nerve to tell me I wouldn't make it as an independent practitioner. Now I keep all the money I collect, not just a cut of it. I'm making more now than I ever could as an employee."

"I told you Prancer was a fucking idiot. And he runs this hospital," Slenderman added.

Beats continued singing the chorus to "Tiny Dancer."

"Gentleman, on that note, I think I'll go to my meeting with our CEO."

✦ ✦ ✦

The recently expanded administrative wing was gorgeous. In the atrium accessible through two beautiful glass double doors, a magnificent fountain fed by a waterfall greeted visitors. The wing must have cost a fortune, even though Mars Hospital was incorporated as a not-for-profit charity.

Beyond that cavernous space, I came to the office section, where the CEO's voice cheerfully greeted my arrival. "Come on in, Dr. Wave." No one else was in the office section; the dozen vice presidents were nowhere to be seen. At about forty years old, Skip was slender and noticeably short with a height of no more than five feet. He was bald, had a black goatee, and wore a standard-issue black, corporate Armani suit. As he walked over to shake my hand, his odd gait was very noticeable—he raised his legs and bent his knees while walking. It did look a bit like a prance. "How was your first day in the clinic?"

"Interesting," I said. The landscaping crossed my mind. "You know, Skip, the front of the building is overgrown with weeds and thorn bushes and is infested with spiders. May I ask for new landscaping? And the sidewalk could also use refinishing. It's in serious disrepair and dangerous." Using his first name made my body tighten with discomfort, but this was the custom at Mars Hospital.

"Now… Dr. Wave, we're tight on money. But you know what? I'm going to approve your landscaping and your sidewalk. There isn't money to do every little thing the doctors are always requesting, but I'll make a special exception for my new medical director."

We sat down together at a small table in front of his large mahogany desk. Later, doctors would tell me the administrative wing was nicknamed Mahogany Row because of the fancy, expensive desks in the CEO's and vice presidents' offices. Skip's office was so luxurious, it looked like something from the television series Downton Abbey.

"Let's talk about your directorship duties." Skip sat as tall as he could in his plush leather chair. "There's not much to it. You run the quarterly physicians' meetings and report directly to me, like I told you in the interview. We will meet regularly. And I'll have you perform some other duties from time to time. You'll also deal with any physician issues that come up. But that doesn't happen very often, so don't worry too much about that. Any questions?"

"How often do you want to meet?"

"How about every Monday?"

"That's fine. There are going to be a lot of things to discuss. As medical director, I want to suggest changes to improve the hospital. I already have some ideas I'm working on."

"Like what?" Doubt clouded Skip's voice.

Where to begin? "I was surprised to find we don't require board certification for our physicians. That needs to change."

"Well, that's up to the doctors, and they would certainly vote down requiring board certification."

He was flat-out wrong. The requirements for staff privileges are up to the CEO, as leader and chief officer of the hospital. "Honestly, it's a national standard and not up to the doctors to decide," I said. "We should require certification. I'll draw up some proposals."

"Alright, but the doctors will never go for it. Anything else?"

"I saw a few drug reps in the hospital. I am concerned—"

Skip cut me off immediately. "They bring a lot of useful new information to the doctors."

"Skip, the information they bring is biased. And their giving out of gifts is unseemly and unethical at best, and illegal at worst."

"Now... Dr. Wave, that is simply not the case. Gifts are perfectly legal. We have always had drug reps come to Mars Hospital. And we always will. The doctors love the drug reps, and it's unthinkable to ban them. They stay."

The FBI had recently investigated several drug companies for enticing doctors with gifts. However, Skip's tone, both angry and determined, suggested now was not the time to fight this particular battle.

"I'd also like to mention something I saw today in the clinic. The visit reasons use the patient's exact words."

"That's our policy."

"But some of the visit reasons were worded offensively. One visit, and please pardon the profanity, was listed as 'my ass smells like a sewer.'" My face felt hot. *No doubt he will immediately change the policy.*

"If that's what the patient says, that's how we list it. We can't change it."

"Why not? Can we at least change the most offensive wording?" My face surely registered the shock I was feeling.

"No. I hired consultants to review our scheduling practices. They said this is how we must list visits. Unless some other consultants tell us differently, we can't change it."

"Who were these consultants?"

"They were from a nationally recognized medical think tank."

"Consultants only recommend changes. We can pick and choose from the recommendations and discard those that do not work well in our…"

"No!" Skip cut me off. "The hospital paid top dollar to this firm, and if I did not follow their recommendations *exactly*, it would make me look bad. We shall follow their scheduling guidelines to the letter."

Skip was unwilling to budge, and I did not want to argue with my new boss on the first day, so I dropped the matter. "Moving on, I was wondering if the hospital had a peer review committee to review physician medical cases." A peer review committee is the standard nationwide to monitor the quality of work performed by doctors. "I was also wondering if the hospital had a credentials committee to review physician qualifications when applying to the hospital medical staff." This is also standard practice. It appeared to me no physician had reviewed my own credentials before granting me medical privileges at the hospital, as my privileges were granted without submitting any documentation confirming my training, a fact that troubled me though I was happy to have the job.

"The individual departments do their own peer reviews," Skip answered dully. "The surgeons review surgical cases, the pediatricians review pediatric cases, and so on."

That sounds like the fox guarding the henhouse.

"And the chairs of the various departments review credentials, when they have time."

What if they don't have time? "I should be on these departmental committees," I suggested. "It would allow me to monitor peer review and physician credentialing."

"That would be up to the chairs of the committees, but they don't like outsiders at their meetings. I know for a fact Slenderman would never agree to allow you on his committee."

"I am the director, not an outsider. And Dr. Slenderman? He's not even the chair of the surgical department."

"Oh, he isn't the chair on paper. You'll learn the way things appear on paper around here isn't always the way they are in reality."

This statement made my stomach churn. "I met Dr. Slenderman today." *Best to leave out the details.*

"You did? Where?"

"In the doctors' lounge. He was there with Drs. Rumpsmith and Beats. I met the three of them."

"Did they bad-mouth me? Did they bad-mouth administration?" Skip's face showed concern as he asked this odd question. "If they bad-mouth me, I want you to tell me. I'll put it in their secret files."

"You keep secret files on doctors?"

"Of course! You never know when they'll come in handy." Skip pranced over to a large filing cabinet, opened it, and displayed a wall of files. "The file on you isn't that big yet, but I have a few others that are pretty substantial."

"What do you keep in these files?" There was an incredibly thick file under S.

"Oh, I keep lots of things. Reports on doctor behavior, and— Well, never mind." Skip grinned slyly, then winked. "Did they bad-mouth me today?"

"We didn't talk much." *Best not to mention Tiny Dancer and Prancer. It's bad-mouthing but would not be productive to mention.*

"I'd stay out of the doctors' lounge if I were you. Nothing good happens there. You are one of us, and they hate administrators. You won't be welcome."

One of us?

There is often friction between hospital administration and physicians. Physicians are an independent-minded bunch who don't take well to bureaucracy, rules, and regulations. But this comment, coming from the CEO, put this friction on a new level. This organization was extremely sick.

"Well, it seems like an excellent place to meet doctors," I said. "I won't spend much time there. I'll be busy with my clinic and my administrative duties."

Skip nodded then showed me the administrative tree, a schematic of all hospital administrators and how they report. For a modest 200-bed hospital, it was an amazingly complex diagram. One CEO, twelve vice presidents, and a spider's web of interconnecting lines showed how scores of middle managers reported. It turns out the total number of administrators at Mars Hospital exceeded the number of beds in the hospital.

There are more administrators than patients. Amazing.

Skip drifted off-topic and began discussing the new home he was building. "It's going to be the finest in Mars," he bragged.

After about an hour of this, he dismissed me.

Did I make the right choice coming here? Maybe the "no experience required" was a red flag. Well, it's only a year.

Days passed into weeks.

3
OFFICE INTERLUDE

One sunny spring morning, two kids were smoking in front of the office. Eight or nine years old at most, they had probably retrieved cigarette butts from the side of the road. Seeing me, they quickly took off on their bikes, the burning stubs still hanging from their lips. What a depressing start to the day. My mood was grim as I walked into the haunted house of a clinic. Sally, sitting in the nurse's station, worked at the computer. She was always busy doing something.

"Good morning, Sally."

"Morning, Dr. Wave. Hey, we should come up with a nickname for you. Dr. Wave is too formal. What do you think?"

"Well, I don't—"

"Wavesticks! That's what I'll call you. Wavesticks." She gave her trademark smile.

"How did you come up with that?"

"It just popped into my head because you're skinny like a stick. Hope you like it, Wavesticks."

Not really.

Sally knew the patients well and the clinic inside out. She was good at ordering tests, managing inventory, obtaining insurance approvals, and of course, hands-on nursing. She also ran the reception desk. She was worth her weight in gold, a rare talent at Mars Hospital. So without comment or complaint, Wavesticks it was.

"How is our schedule looking today?" I asked.

"Crazy. Here." She handed me the clipboard.

The schedule was full. Along with some valid medical reasons for visits, there were a few oddballs.

"Sally, what on earth is a flipper?"

"Oh, that's Rat Man. With him, who knows? He's a nutcase. It probably has something to do with his cock," Her tone was matter-of-fact.

Great, I can't wait.

✦✦✦

"He's ready," Sally said after she'd settled Rat Man in an exam room.

"So, what's the story? What did he mean by a broken flipper?"

"He didn't say. He wants to talk to you." She ambled back to the nurse's station as I entered the patient room.

"Hello. What can I do for you today?"

Rat Man sat on the exam table. He appeared slightly disheveled, with long, wild brown hair and old, torn clothing. *Maybe that's why they call him Rat Man. I'll have to ask Sally later.*

"Doc, my flipper's broke. There's something wrong with it. It don't look right."

"What exactly do you mean by a flipper?" *Here it comes.* My heart raced in anticipation.

"Flipper? Why, that's the little thing that hangs down in the back of your throat."

"That's the uvula," I said.

"Huh?" He scratched his head.

"Uvula. That's the medical term. What's the problem?"

"It's all swelled up."

Sometimes swelling of the uvula is caused by angioedema, a serious allergic condition. But clearly this wasn't the case. Angioedema has a variety of associated, severe allergic symptoms. There also are some infectious conditions, usually seen only in kids, which cause swelling of the uvula. But again, this seemed unlikely.

"Does it hurt? Do you have shortness of breath? Wheezing? Rash? Itching?" He answered no to everything as I rattled off an array of symptoms. The full physical exam was normal. As for the flipper itself, it was also perfectly normal. It was neither enlarged nor red, nor did it obstruct the airway in any way.

"Everything looks fine to me. Your exam is completely normal. I wouldn't worry about it." This man was one of the worried well, the polite term for a hypochondriac.

"Everything looks fine? My flipper is swelled up. That's not fine. I got a flipper problem, or an ooveedoobie problem, or whatever you call the damn thing. You gotta do something."

"There isn't anything to do. We can watch things, and if there are any changes, you can let me know."

"If things change, I might be dead. Aren't you going to give me an antibiotic?"

"No, an antibiotic is not indicated here."

A deep frown formed on the patient's face. "An injection?"

"You do not need an injection." Sometimes steroid injections are given for allergic reactions—clearly not the case here.

"I bet you'll give me a bill. You better do something. Can you send me to a flipper specialist?"

A "flipper specialist" would be an ear, nose, and throat doctor, but a referral here just wasn't indicated. "I'm sorry, but I will not refer at this time. You can call me if—"

Rat Man got up and marched out of the office. He slammed the door on his way out.

After he'd left, Sally said, "I told you he was nuts."

"Hey, why do they call him Rat Man?"

"He has a bunch of pet rats. People around town have called him that for years."

"That doesn't sound sanitary or safe." The seventies movie *Willard*, based on a book called *Ratman's Notebooks*, came to mind.

"No, it doesn't. He's a Mars dirty birdie." Sally began singing the Batman television series theme song with substitute words. "Rat Man is a dirty little birdie, Rat Man…"

Sally's gallows humor made me smile.

✦✦✦

Mars patients were different, but I didn't fully understand how much until I visited the local Walmart to buy soup one afternoon. I'd just finished retrieving a can of tomato soup for another customer—the curse of being tall—when a Mars clinic patient approached me.

"Hey, Dr. Wave. How are you?"

What is this guy's name? I am terrible with names.

"Hello. How are you?" Frozen pizzas and other junk food filled his cart. *We'll have to talk about diet at the next visit.*

"I'm fine. Doctor, I forgot to tell you the other day about a mole I have. Can I show you?"

"Perhaps it would be better to come by the office and show me." *I don't want to look at moles right now; I want to look at soup.*

"Oh, I don't mind showing it to you now."

He clearly did not get my hint.

"I'd be happy to see you tomorrow. What—?"

The patient dropped his pants to the floor, pulled down his drawers, bent over, and grabbed both knees. "The mole's on my ass, Dr. Wave."

The mole, located on the upper half of his right buttocks, did not appear cancerous.

"I can see that. The mole does not look dangerous. Please pull up your pants."

An elderly lady started pushing her shopping cart down the aisle. Seeing my patient's buttocks, she turned her shopping cart around. *I guess she isn't getting soup today either.*

"One more thing, Dr. Wave. I got some bug bites on my ass. See them?" Releasing his knees, he started scratching his buttocks vigorously with both hands while still bent over. "Is there some salve I could buy so my ass stops itching?" More people entered, then quickly exited the soup aisle.

"Yes, I can give you the name of a cream. Please pull up your pants." My voice squeaked with distress. *Soup sales today will plummet unless he makes himself decent.*

"Okay." He finally pulled up his drawers.

"Thank you." Sighing in relief, I pointed him in the direction of the pharmacy section after giving the name of a cream, and he left. Mission accomplished. Tomorrow, Sally would refer him to some lucky dermatologist.

I scurried out to my car with soup in-hand and my eyes aimed low to avoid eye contact with any other patients. That would be my last afternoon trip to the Walmart. All future trips would be done late at night or early in the morning.

+++

The hospital held an open house so patients could meet me, the new doctor in town. Signs were placed outside. An ad ran in the local paper. The open house was on a Saturday, and right at the noon start time, a guest arrived.

"Our first guest is here, Wavesticks," Sally announced with a chuckle. As I hurried to the waiting room, my heart leaped with excitement.

"Where are the goodies?" A visibly intoxicated man stood in the waiting room. He was slender, smelled like a brewery, and wore dirty, torn clothes. "You got some goodies?"

My mood crashed down to earth while I pointed to a tray of cookies. "Over there."

He grabbed a handful, then, to my dismay, sat down in one of the waiting room chairs, kicked off his muddy shoes, and started munching away. His stockinged feet produced a noticeable odor.

"We're off to a great start!" Sally quipped. For the next fifteen minutes, the patient sat there eating cookie after cookie, but no one else arrived.

"Sally, where is everyone?"

"No one wants to come to a doctor's office on a Saturday to meet you, even if they do get some free cookies. People have better things to do. We might get a few more drunks, but that'll be it."

Sally, however, was proven wrong. Ten minutes later, Skip and the mayor of Mars arrived. The mayor of Mars was an especially important person to Skip. As a nonprofit hospital, it was the mayor, along with the city council, who appointed the CEO of Mars Hospital. She was, therefore, Skip's boss. Skip introduced me.

"Doctor Wave, this is Ms. Elizabeth Dolos, the mayor of Mars, Nebraska."

"It's nice to meet you, Madam Mayor. I am honored you came to my open house." The mayor had long, blonde hair with spiral curls and wore a black blazer and pants set. She was about forty years old and looked very professional. She smiled and started to speak, but the drunk cut her off.

"*You're* the mayor?"

"Yes, sir. Nice to meet you." The mayor was about to shake the fellow's hand, but the drunk belched loudly. That stopped her cold.

"This town is shit. If you're the mayor, you must be shit too!" He guffawed and hit his thighs with his hands. The mayor looked as though cold water had been splashed in her face.

"Who are you?" Skip asked the drunk while nervously stroking his goatee.

"I am a citizen of Shitville, Nebraska. Hey, want a cookie?" His grubby hand extended a cookie toward Skip and the mayor. He blew a loud fart and snorted.

Skip made a horrified grimace. "I am sorry about this, Madam Mayor."

"Mayor McShit." The drunk cackled. "You want a cookie, Mayor McShit?" A cookie waved in the air while she silently looked on in disgust. He threw the cookie at her, but it fell short and landed on the stained carpet—which had yet to be removed despite my numerous requests—and broke apart.

Skip cut the visit short. "We will be going now, Dr. Wave."

"Thank you for coming." *I don't blame Skip for leaving so soon.*

"Yeah, thanks, Mayor McShit. See you around Shitville." A noisome fart again exploded as he blew the mayor kisses. My face warmed as I blushed. Sally groaned.

Skip and the mayor quickly exited. Skip gave not a backward glance, but the mayor shot the drunk a venomous look and started to say something, then she noticed me watching. She scowled deeply and left in silence.

No one else showed up at the open house the remainder of the afternoon, and the drunk was found beaten in an alleyway later that evening.

4

THE NURSING HOME

Treating nursing home patients was part of my clinical duties. Mars had only one nursing home in town, named as blandly as everything else—the Mars Nursing Home. It was located about two blocks from the hospital on the same street as my clinic and was reasonably large, with about 150 long-term residents. Although this nursing home sent patients who needed hospital care to Mars Hospital, it was a separate, independent entity with its own medical director.

Two patients, inherited from the previous doctor at the Mars Clinic, were assigned to me at this nursing home. Surprised more patients were not assigned, I believed this was an area I could build upon in my practice. Adult medical practices usually have large nursing home populations, but my list was a little short. My first patient, a lady named Ms. Geras, arrived at the nursing home after a hospitalization for pneumonia. The second, a gentleman named Mr. Algos, arrived at the nursing home after a prolonged hospital stay due to a hip fracture. Neither was a permanent resident of the facility. They were there only for rehabilitation and therapy.

Walking to the nursing home on a dazzling spring afternoon brightened my mood. But one glance at the building darkened it. The exterior of the facility was run down. The building desperately needed painting. It also had cracked windows, and the parking lot looked as though it had been bombed; there were countless potholes. In several areas the asphalt was not only covered with a spider's web of cracks but had also sunk. And cars were parked haphazardly among the faded lines.

Entering the locked front door required a security code, but a sign posted above it announced the code was 1-2-3-4.

Great security.

I punched in the numbers, a green light flashed, and the door popped open.

An orderly shouted a warning and I jumped in surprise, stopping my foot in the nick of time. "Watch your step, Doc. Pooper took a shit on the floor again. Don't step in it."

A pile of human excrement was just inches away from my shoe. It was fresh, moist, and smelly. This was an inauspicious start to my visit. It turned out one of the residents with Alzheimer's, whom the orderlies had cruelly nicknamed Pooper, would defecate anywhere— in other patients' rooms, in drawers, and once in a ventilation shaft. He was never adequately supervised, and it was a horrible situation both for the residents of the home and the patient.

As I walked by the nursing station, another orderly was yelling on the phone. "Call fucking housekeeping. I am not cleaning up that gomer's shit again." The rough-looking, heavily tattooed orderly looked like he'd just been released from prison. The degrading term *gomer* stands for "get out of my emergency room" and is sometimes applied to nursing home patients by ER doctors.

"Where is Ms. Geras's room?" I asked.

A nurse sitting in the station looked up from her phone. She was playing Candy Crush. "Are you her doctor?" Her voice sounded annoyed that I had interrupted her game.

"Yes."

"Down the hall, last room on the left." Her eyes immediately returned to her phone.

The trip down was unnerving. It was dim and dull, with chipped green paint on the walls and cracked green tiles on the floor that seemed to absorb light. Numerous patients, obviously sedated, sat in wheelchairs with blank looks on their faces. The only sounds in the hall were my footsteps followed by my knock on Ms. Geras's door.

"Hello, Ms. Geras. I'm Dr. Wave, your new physician." My voice sounded confident and cheerful despite my inner discomfort. Ms. Geras was sitting in a chair. She was short, somewhat plump, and wore a faded red hospital gown. Her hair was up in a bun, and she looked like the granny who took care of Tweety Bird in the *Looney Tunes* cartoons. But it was her bright eyes that captivated me.

"You are? Good. Get me out of here."

"What's wrong? Are you not being treated well?" It's not uncommon for patients in the nursing home to want to go home.

"This place is like the *Planet of the Apes*. They pull me out of bed at 2 a.m. They drag me naked down the hall and take me to a room. I'm strapped into a metal chair and hosed down with ice-cold water. And I mean, *ice*-cold. I scream, but they don't care. They do this to me every day. They hose me down like the apes hosed down Charlton Heston in the movie. They treat me like an animal."

"I have a hard time believing that, ma'am." *She must be exaggerating.*

"Go down the hall and see for yourself. The room is at the far end of the opposite hallway."

I figured I would humor her. "Okay. I'm going down there right now. I'll be back shortly." I passed again down the green, gloomy hallway. No one paid the least bit of attention to me until I reached the far end, where an old wooden door stood. It had a thick metal handle and an old-timey lock with a keyhole. It looked like something out of a Gothic horror movie. I pulled and twisted on the handle with all my might, but the door didn't budge.

A nurse took an interest as I tugged on the metal handle. "May I help you, Doctor?"

"I will see what's in this room."

"Why?"

"I had a patient complaint. I want to investigate to see if it's legitimate."

"Who complained?" The nurse snarled. "I bet it was Geras, that old b—." She caught herself before swearing. "Geras has dementia. She doesn't know what she's talking about."

"I think I'd like to take a look anyway."

"It's off-limits."

"Why is that?"

"Policy."

"Let me talk to the nursing director, please."

"I am the nursing director."

"Oh. In that case, there are two ways this is going to play out. One, you let me in to look. Two, I call and report the nursing home, and you, to the state. Which one will it be?" *Of course, I have already seen more than enough and will be reporting this nursing home anyway.*

Scowling, the nurse removed a large skeleton key from her pocket and unlocked the door. As she pulled it open, it issued a long, continuous squeak appropriate for the Gothic horror movie I seemed to have entered.

The room was dark, damp, and cold. Drip. Drip. Drip. Looking in the direction of the sound, I saw an old-fashioned fire hose hanging from the ceiling. The hose was made of cloth, and looked a hundred years old. A large metal nozzle at the end of the cloth hose was slowly dripping water.

But the center of the room really grabbed my attention. An old metal chair with a hole in the seat sat over an open drain. Thick leather restraining straps hung loosely from the arms and legs of the chair. The setup looked like something from an inquisitor's torture chamber and looking at it made me break into a cold sweat.

This does not belong in a nursing home.

Clearly, there was enough evidence here to believe Ms. Geras's report. The setup was arranged so that when the ice-cold water hit patients and they lost control of their bowels and bladder, urine and stool would fall directly into the open sewer via the hole in the seat of the chair. How efficient. And horrible.

"This is all up to standard and approved by the Inspection Commission," the head nurse volunteered through tightly pursed lips as she stood, stiff as a board, watching me. The Inspection Commission is one body that certifies hospitals and nursing homes. It is notoriously lax, but even the Inspection Commission would disapprove of this chamber of horrors.

"Sure, it is." *Nurse Ratched.* "Ms. Geras tells me she is taken from her bed at 2 a.m. and brought here."

"It is her morning bath."

"This is the morning bath?" *Unbelievable.*

"Yes."

"At 2 a.m.? Isn't that a little early for the morning bath?"

"We are understaffed. To finish all the baths before 6 a.m. medications are passed, the orderly must start early."

"Two in the morning?"

"Ms. Geras's room is the end where we start the baths. I could have the orderly start in another hall."

"And drag some other poor old person out of their bed at an ungodly hour instead?"

"We are understaffed. There is nothing we can do about it."

"She said the water was ice cold."

"It warms up eventually."

Grabbing the hose and seeing no temperature control, I pulled the iron bar to activate flow. A jet of freezing, high-pressure water shot out. The hose almost flew from my hand.

"You hose them down with this?" I asked. "Look at the pressure. And it is ice cold!" My heart pounded, and my face burned with anger.

"It warms up."

"Let's see." The water ran for a few minutes. The temperature did not change. Nurse Ratched stood watching the whole time. "I do not want my patients, or any patients for that matter, brought into this room."

"Fine. I will make a note of that. But this room is up to code. We were passed just last year."

"Did you show them this room?"

"Of course." She crossed her arms and frowned.

Liar. This nursing home is the worst I can imagine and must be reported.

My hearted continued to pound as I left Nurse Ratched and walked down the gloomy, green hall once again.

"Did you see the room?" Ms. Geras asked as I reentered her room.

"Yes."

"See? I told you. You have to get me out of here."

"I'll do it as soon as possible." I finished my exam and visit. There was no evidence of dementia. Ms. Geras had an excellent memory and was in good health.

My next and final nursing home patient, Mr. Algos, was in a room down a different, though equally green and gloomy, hallway.

The nursing home layout was three long hallways of rooms around a central dayroom and nursing station area.

I introduced myself to the thin, elderly man with stringy, white hair. He was weeping and very agitated. Still shaken from Ms. Geras's visit, my voice wavered. "What seems to be the trouble, sir? What's wrong?" *What could be the next horror in this nursing home?*

"It's the food. Look at this." His lunch was sitting in front of him. Nursing home food is rarely palatable. It looked like he had a TV dinner—Salisbury steak, mashed potatoes, and a vegetable were in a plastic tray on his bedside table.

"Does the food taste bad?"

"It's frozen!"

"Didn't they heat it enough?" *Perhaps food delivery was slow. The nurse did say they were understaffed.*

He took the TV dinner and started pounding the end that held the potatoes on his bedside table. It was frozen solid and made a hammering sound. "They do this to me every meal."

My face flushed. "That is unacceptable." *Starving patients is worse than the hose room.*

"They do this to punish me because I complained. The orderly said I was a troublemaker and needed to learn to keep my mouth shut."

"What did you complain about?"

"I complained about the bingo games."

"Tell me what happened."

"They took me to the dayroom. Everyone was just sitting there with their bingo cards in front of them, like a bunch of zombies. They just stared into space. After I played for a while, I got bingo and called it out. The orderly running the bingo game told me to shut the fuck up."

"Why did he tell you to shut up?"

"Doc, the orderly pulls the numbers out one at a time, until all the numbers are all gone. Then he says rec time is finished, and he takes everyone back to their rooms. This place is a crazy house. I made a fuss about it, and the orderly got mad."

"When did you complain?"

"Last week."

"They have been giving you frozen meals for a week?"

"Yes. I'm starving."

"I'm going to talk to the nurse and get you some food right now."

"No. Wait. If you complain, it will get worse." Mr. Algos's whole body began to shake.

"I am complaining. Your meals should not be served frozen."

"Please don't. They kill people around here if they make too much trouble. That's what another patient told me, and I believe her!"

"That's impossible." *But is it?*

"Please, Doctor."

"Very well. I won't talk to the nurse. But I am heating your dinner personally."

Nurse Ratched watched me intently while I heated his dinner in the break room. Neither of us said a word.

After that, he started getting heated meals again. And I started my war against the nursing home. The first thing I did was contact its director, Dr. Bacchus, to report the abuses I had witnessed. This doctor, who was also an independent practitioner on the Mars Hospital medical staff, only said, "I'll look into it." That wasn't good enough for me. I wrote letters to every state and federal agency involved in nursing home care as well as the Inspection Commission. I made sure my name, position, and address were prominently displayed in each letter reporting this dreadful care so they could contact me for follow-up. These letters were then followed with calls to the same agencies. Next, I wrote and called the local newspaper.

Alas, the nursing home director, state and federal agencies, and the Inspection Commission took no immediate action. The local newspaper was similarly disinterested. This especially surprised me. The story of the horrible care was a great scoop.

It turned out Skip was the reason for the disinterest. Skip had made his own set of phone calls after my visit and made every effort he could to block my reports. At a subsequent meeting, he angrily scolded me for reporting the nursing home.

"I heard about your report through the grapevine. Dr. Bacchus sends us a lot of patients from the nursing home. He was angry you reported the facility. I had to make numerous calls to fend off the trouble you caused. This is going into your secret file."

Sadness and anger washed over me as I sat quietly watching Skip tuck in his report.

What should I do next? I sent another round of letters.

Immediately after my nursing home visit, I discharged Mr. Algos. I was unable to discharge Ms. Geras, however, as her daughter fought discharge or transfer. Her daughter stated that things "were not ready for her to return home" and that it was "too much trouble" to move her mother. It was disheartening, to say the least. Over the coming weeks, I continued to report the nursing home in every way possible. I constantly worried about Ms. Geras and kept trying to get her discharged.

5

PHYSICIANS' MEETING

Every quarter, Mars Hospital held a meeting for all employed physicians. There once was a time, years ago, when most doctors on staff at Mars Hospital were independent practitioners. After finishing their medical training, doctors would open a private office, hire staff, do billing, collect money, and run every aspect of their medical practice. Often these doctors were solo practitioners of the type pictured in a Norman Rockwell artwork. Occasionally, a few doctors would band together and form loosely knit groups, sharing office space, staff, and equipment to save on overhead. But even though some expenses were shared, each doctor ran the show for their own practice.

Those days were gone. Now most doctors on the medical staff were employees of the hospital. At Mars Hospital, there were still a handful of independent practitioners—older doctors, for the most part, those like Rumpsmith, who refused to sell out to the hospital or could not tolerate being employed by one. These were usually specialists who did lucrative procedures and could afford to be independent.

But no new doctors had come on staff at Mars Hospital as independent practitioners in years, and none would. It was just too expensive. Most young doctors had six figures worth of medical school debt, and the expenses of setting up a practice were astronomical. Some physicians paid more than $100,000 a year for malpractice insurance alone. Then there are computers to buy, office space to rent, staff to hire, medical equipment to purchase, and many more expenses, large and small. And the time when a doctor could walk into a local bank and get an open-ended signature loan to pay for all these start-up costs was also long past.

So most doctors at Mars Hospital were now employees. Thus, the quarterly meetings were an important way Skip and I could communicate with the employed doctors. There were about 200 in total. The medical staff of Mars Hospital was much larger, numbering nearly 1,000, but a minority of these doctors were full-time. Many were specialists from the University of Nebraska on staff for consultation purposes only. And some, like Dr. Bacchus, the nursing home medical director, were independent practitioners who worked at other facilities but maintained Mars Hospital medical staff membership for referral of new patients as well as consultation purposes. As a result, the 200 employed doctors made up more than 80 percent of the full-time medical staff at Mars Hospital. As I watched the doctors enter the meeting room, remembering their names was difficult.

"You're Dr. Wave?" A young female physician with wild, uncombed, blonde hair stood before me.

"Yes, and you must be Dr. Lyssa. Nice to meet you." Relief washed over me as I remembered her name. It must have been the crazy hair. It stood out in the photos of the physician directory.

"You'll help me buy a car." She walked away.

What was that all about? Does she want a salary advance?

Dr. Wurst smiled broadly. "I see you met Dr. Lyssa." He had

overheard her comment. "Don't pay any attention. She's a little different."

"Thanks for the warning." The meeting was supposed to start at 9 a.m., but by then only about a dozen doctors had arrived. Also, Skip was conspicuously absent. Being unable to start on time was discouraging, as was the low turnout.

About ten minutes after nine, Slenderman waddled in. He grabbed as many donuts as he could carry from the nearby refreshment table, then took a seat on the sofa at the back of the room, which groaned under his weight. It must have been placed there specifically for him as his enormous size precluded a regular seat. It was time to start, despite no sign of Skip.

"Good morning, everyone. Let's go ahead and get started. I'm Dr. Wave, the new medical director. I have not yet had the chance to meet all of you, but be assured I will make every effort to meet everyone as soon as possible. As medical director, I feel it's important to know each physician I'm working with." The room quieted down.

"The agenda today has a few items that Skip will present when he arrives." Skip had given me a list of informational discussion points, such as upcoming parties and events. "I'll start first, however, by talking about staff certification requirements. As you know, Mars Hospital does not currently require board certification. I think this should change, and—"

"I'm not certified," Slenderman interrupted immediately, shouting from his couch. "Hell, half the doctors at this hospital aren't. Certification is stupid, and it doesn't mean anything,"

"Certification is important. It is a sign of excellence that—"

"Are you certified?" Slenderman interrupted again.

"Yes."

"Well, good for you. Did you pass your first try?"

"That is not relevant."

"Ha! How many times did it take you to pass, smarty-pants?" A gotcha grin spread across his face. He should have let me finish.

"As I said, the number of attempts is not relevant, but for the record, since you asked, I passed the first time. I was in the top one percent." Crushing the board certification exam on the first attempt was rare and something to be proud of.

"Well, that doesn't mean you're smart."

"It doesn't mean he's stupid, either," Wurst said on my behalf to scattered chuckles. This comment was my chance to get the discussion back on track.

"Almost all hospitals in the US require board certification. We are an outlier. While currently the Inspection Commission that accredits hospitals does not, for some reason, have a rule requiring board certification, it is only a matter of time."

"You don't know that," Slenderman challenged.

"It is only a matter of time until it is universally required." My eyes focused sternly on Slenderman. "Also, because we do not require certification, we are a magnet for doctors who cannot pass their boards. This is not where we want to be."

"Like it attracted you? What brought you here, Mr. Board-certified?"

"As I was saying, this is not where we should be as an organization. I propose we recommend to the CEO the adoption of a requirement, for new members of the medical staff, to obtain and maintain board certification."

"No way. You're trying to run me out," Slenderman shouted angrily. "Me and the other doctors without that stupid certification."

"As I was saying, Dr. Slenderman, I recommend this apply to new members. All current members would be grandfathered in, including you. This is how most hospitals implement the board certification requirement." *Allowing even the grossly incompetent doctors to be grandfathered in.*

"I am still against it."

"Why?"

"It's stupid."

"That's it, Dr. Slenderman? It's stupid? Is that all you have to say? I again point out this is a universal standard. I would also point out that years ago, hospitals did not require physicians to complete residency programs. Now they do. Standards for education and training have increased over time."

"Mars Hospital didn't require doctors to complete a residency until the 1990s, and it was a big fight," Slenderman noted.

"That's about thirty years after residency training for doctors became a national standard in the 1960s. Let's try for Mars Hospital not to be that far behind once again in our credentialing requirements." Irreverent laughter erupted in the room.

"Let's vote on recommending this change," I said. Although a vote would not be binding on Skip, it would show the support of the physicians. "Does anyone else have anything to say on this matter?" Silence. "Dr. Wurst?"

"I'm just enjoying the show. Of course we should require certification."

More doctors spoke up in favor of the idea. Of the few doctors in attendance, all of them were certified, except Slenderman and Lyssa. The many other uncertified doctors who were hospital employees were not present. Lyssa said nothing, staring blankly into space. Maybe she was thinking about cars. After a few minutes of discussion, it was time to vote.

"Let's see a show of hands. Who's in favor of this recommendation?" A half-dozen hands went up. "Against?" Slenderman raised his hand. No one else joined him. Unfortunately, several doctors did not cast a vote. Maybe they feared upsetting Slenderman. Perhaps they were busy enjoying their telephones or thinking about other things. Nonetheless, the recommendation did pass.

"You can bet this isn't going to happen, vote or not," Slenderman barked.

No doubt Slenderman would do what he could to stop this "controversial" proposal. But I did not see how anyone could seriously object to this basic standard. Then Skip walked in. Or, more precisely, he pranced in. Doctors quietly snickered as he high-stepped across the room and took his seat.

"Hello, everyone. I see you all have met Dr. Wave."

"We sure have. He's making trouble, Skip. He wants to require board certification," Slenderman breathlessly reported. "He even took a vote when you weren't here. A *vote*! He wants to make board certification a requirement. He's trying to run me out, and I'll probably have to take my surgeries to another hospital."

Skip looked horrified. He grabbed his goatee as though he were grabbing a life preserver. He started talking before I could point out that Slenderman wouldn't be taking his surgeries anywhere. No other hospital near Mars would allow him to join their medical staff uncertified, so his threat was hollow. "Dr. Wave is just trying to make a good first impression. We won't worry about board certification any further."

"Skip, the physicians voted in support of this by a wide margin. And I specifically recommended grandfathering in uncertified doctors already on-staff, such as Dr. Slenderman. So it will not affect him or them in any way."

"It's not our way. We won't talk about it any further." And just like that, Skip cut my legs out from under me. All my credibility evaporated. Slenderman leaned back on his sofa and crossed his arms with a smug look on his face.

"Let's talk about something fun." Skip announced an upcoming

sale at the hospital gift shop and then gave updates on a new advertising campaign. None of this was of particular interest to the doctors.
We then moved to open discussion. During open discussion, doctors
could voice concerns, and they had several.

"The computer system in my office is so slow I can barely see
patients," one physician reported.

"We will send someone out to take a look," Skip replied.

"You said that last meeting, but no one came."

"This time, someone will come."

A young female physician, practicing in a small town outside of
Mars, asked, "I'm anxious about security. When I leave the office at
night, it's pitch black. The walk to the parking lot is scary. Could we
get some lights?" Lighting in the parking lot seemed a very reasonable request.

Skip shot down any immediate action. "Lights are expensive.
We'll look at putting it in the budget for next year."

Another doctor then spoke up. "The electronic medical record
we started using three years ago is crap." A few others murmured in
agreement. "When we used paper charts, we could get work done
much faster. Now it takes me a dozen clicks to order a simple test.
There has got to be some way to speed things up. May I use written
orders?"

"No. You must use the computer. We are looking at getting a new
computer system in a few years. The new system will work better."

Several doctors groaned. "A few years? I'll go insane by then."

"No one else has trouble entering orders."

Chatter filled the room as doctors disagreed with Skip's statement and attested to their troubles.

"Fine," Skip said. "I will have our computer specialist take a
look at your issues."

Dr. Wurst spoke up. "We only have one computer specialist, and she's already overwhelmed. We need more support." The room quieted down. Clearly other doctors respected him.

"Now... Dr. Wurst, you and everyone else are just going to have to get used to using the computer."

"It's not about getting used to using the computer. We're not idiots. This is about a system that does not work properly now and has never since the day it was installed."

"Well, I'll look into the matter and get back to you. I'm afraid I must go. I have another meeting." With that, Skip got up and pranced right out of the room. As he left, some doctors sighed and shook their heads in frustration, while others quietly giggled.

"I think it's time to wrap things up," I said. Indeed, the meeting had run over time due to our late start. "Doctors, before you go, please set up a time to meet with me or take one of my cards and call me later. I will meet with each of you individually over the coming weeks." As doctors filed out of the room, Dr. Wurst approached.

"Looks like Skip put the kibosh on board certification. It's a good idea, but it will never fly around here. There are just too many quacks. Dr. Coeus took his board-certification exam seven times and flunked every time before finally giving up."

"Eighth time is the charm?"

"Not for him. Eight hundredth maybe. But he thinks he's the smartest doctor on the medical staff. Good luck trying to get certification passed."

And with that, Dr. Wurst left, but not a single doctor scheduled a meeting or took one of my cards.

6
OFFICE INTERLUDE

After weeks of waiting, the clinic had a new sidewalk. And a landscaping crew had torn out all the old weeds and thorn bushes and replaced them with several nice shrubberies that spread their green branches toward the sun and rows of flowers. Red, blue, purple, and pink petals of varied shapes waved in the breeze. And best of all, the spiders were gone. My heart soared as I had given up hope the landscaping work would ever be completed.

Inside, however, little had changed. Improvements had been done strictly outdoors. *Why hadn't I asked for interior renovations as well?* Sally and I had removed the gloom-wrap from the windows, but the clinic still relied on decrepit furniture, ceiling tiles held up by string, and old, stinky carpeting everywhere but the waiting room. That carpeting had finally been ripped out after my numerous complaints about the bloody stains left by the patient with the splinter, but had not been replaced. Its removal revealed hideous linoleum flooring patterned with cracked squares and rectangles of various shades of orange.

And now there were ants everywhere. The clinic had become heavily infested with ants and various other insects over the past couple of weeks. When questioning Sally about this, she said, "It's spring. We get ants and bugs every year, but don't worry, they'll leave by winter."

"We have new landscaping and a new sidewalk." I grinned at this small victory.

"Yes, I saw it. It looks nice. Good job getting it done, Wavesticks. You must have had to kiss some real ass. People have complained about the landscaping and sidewalk around here for years." She handed me the day's schedule, my review of which never failed to amuse and amaze. Sally always enjoyed my reactions. The first patient of the day had a visit reason listed as "I need Dick Tea."

"What the hell is Dick Tea?"

"No idea, but we're going to find out. He's right here." Sally showed him to the exam room, and in a few minutes, she returned.

"He's ready, Wavesticks. He wants you to write him a prescription for Dick Tea, LOL." She actually said the acronym.

"Any idea what Dick Tea is?"

"You're the doctor. I'm sure you'll figure it out."

The patient was a middle-aged gentleman, dressed all in green like a leprechaun, and he was in a boisterously good mood.

"Hey, Doc! How you doing? Nice to meet you."

"I am well, and it's nice to meet you. What may I do for you?"

"Doc, I want to know what kind of tea is Dick Tea?"

"Dick Tea?"

"Yep, that's the ticket. I need some of that tea."

"I have never heard that term. What exactly are you looking for in this tea?"

"It makes your dick big, Doc. I want to know what kind of tea to drink that will make my cock grow and grow. But I don't want the tea too strong. Just add a few inches. I don't want to end up with a three-footer."

"I'm afraid there's no tea like that. There are medicines like Viagra, which help with erectile dysfunction, if that's what you mean."

"No, I don't need Viagra. I need Dick Tea. I get hard just fine, I just want to add three or four inches so the ladies go crazy."

"There is really no such tea. Where did you hear about this?"

"My buddy at Sal's, the bar down the street, told me. He said you could buy it. I think it's from some town in China."

Perhaps he meant some sort of Chinese herbal supplement. Whatever he meant, it was nonsense. No medically approved tea adds inches to penis size, despite what his bar buddy had told him. "I suppose there might be some unlicensed and untested herbal product that makes such a claim, but those sorts of products are nothing but snake oil, and you must be careful. Many of them have toxic side effects, and they don't work."

"I'll take some snake oil if that will make my dick grow. Do you just rub it in?"

"Snake oil is a term for a fraudulent product."

"Oh, just the tea then. Where do you go to buy it? Chinatown? I asked the pharmacist, and he said go ask your doctor."

Gee, thanks, pharmacist.

"There is no such thing. Are you having any problems with your penis? Pain, discharge, anything?"

"Nope. Just the size. Does the tea make your nuts bigger too?"

"As I said, nothing will grow your penis or increase the size of your testicles."

"I guess you need Nut Tea for those, huh?" He grinned. "Can I order the tea on the internet?"

"No doubt you could find some sort of rip-off product making such claims." *Maybe check your spam inbox.*

"For a doctor, you sure don't seem to know much. Are you going to give me a prescription for Dick Tea or not? How expensive is it?"

"I can't give you a prescription for something that doesn't exist. I've been trying to tell you this, but you simply aren't listening."

"I bet the old doc here would have given me some. He might have had samples. He used to give out free samples of medications. Do you have any tea samples in the back?"

"There are no samples in the back," I said. After Sally had brought her concerns to me about giving out free samples, we removed all sample medications from the office. Storing medications on-site and acting as a pharmacy is not a recommended medical practice.

"How do you know, Doc? You didn't even look."

"I know because no such tea exists, and we no longer give out any kind of medication samples."

"Could your nurse go back there and take a peek to see if there isn't a box? I don't need much—just a few inches worth. I'm at seven now, and ten or eleven would be just about right. I don't want anything more than a foot long."

He is just not listening to me.

"I am telling you, there is no such tea!"

"Well, is there a vitamin or something I can take to get a big dick? Got any dick vitamins?"

"Do you have any other issues you want to discuss today?"

"My dick is my issue."

"You have not had a general checkup in quite some time. Let's proceed with some blood work as well as a general exam."

"No thanks. I'm going to find a new doctor. I need someone who'll give me Dick Tea."

With that, the patient stormed out of the office, demanding

samples as he left. Sally watched him with incredible patience, then turned to me. "He won't be the only patient upset that we no longer give out drug samples. I bet he ends up with Dr. Lyssa. She's a known quack and will probably give him some sort of crazy concoction she brews up at home."

"When I first met Lyssa, she came up and out of the blue told me I must help her buy a car."

"She's a nut. Watch out. I bet she wants to sleep with you."

I sure hope not. "That will not happen. In fact, it's impossible. As medical director, I can't get involved with subordinates."

"Well, you'll be the only doctor who isn't fucking subordinates." Noticing my blush, she continued, "Wavesticks, you're so innocent."

"Which doctors are doing that?"

"Let's see. You know Beats. His first wife divorced him when he was caught fucking a radiology tech in a broom closet. Then he married the broom closet babe. He's also very handsy, always grabbing and touching nurses. Then there's Dr. Pan."

"The chair of the surgery department?"

"Yep. His wife caught him fucking his nurse in their marital bed, but she didn't divorce him. She did burn the marital bed, though."

I couldn't keep my jaw from dropping. Dr. Pan's wife was a famous author known nationwide.

"Shall I go on?"

"What about Dr. Wurst?"

"Not him. He's a Sally. He'd never sleep around. It's not in his nature. Besides, his wife would cut off his balls if he did."

"A Sally like you?"

"My name is Sally. He is a Sally."

"Oh." My voice sounded weak. *What is a Sally?* "Well, I guess then it's not all the doctors."

"Most of them. You'll see."

Hopefully not.

✦✦✦

"You should talk to this guy about insurance," Sally announced. The patient was here for the unremarkable reason that he had been sick for three weeks.

"Why is that?"

"He's probably going to need tests, and he doesn't have insurance. He's dirt poor, so I'm sure he would qualify for Medicaid or Obamacare." Sally signed up as many poor patients as she could for insurance. She was single-handedly responsible for scores of those in need getting the medical insurance available to them.

"I'll talk to him." The patient—a thin, forty-two-year-old man with brown, wavy hair and dressed in clean jeans and a t-shirt—reported he had been sick with the flu for three weeks. He had a fever, a cough, and chills. As Sally suspected, he needed some medical tests.

"Doc, I don't have insurance. I can't afford testing." Even a few simple tests and an X-ray would cost thousands of dollars.

"I understand your income is low. You might qualify for Obamacare with subsidies or even Medicaid. Sally can help you sign up."

"Obama-what?"

"Obamacare, officially called the Affordable Care Act."

"What's that?"

"You've never heard of Obamacare?"

"I heard of Obama. He was president, right?" His tone was doubtful.

How could someone not have heard of Obamacare? It had been in the news for years. Love it or hate it, I figured everyone must have at least heard of it. But not in Mars.

"Yes, he was our president. He passed a significant expansion of health care insurance in the US."

"Well ain't that a kick in the teeth? I never heard of it."

After explaining the program, Sally took a laptop computer and got to work. The patient ended up qualifying for Medicaid, the state insurance program for the poor. There would be no cost for his testing and only a modest co-pay for the office visit.

The patient was quite happy. He obtained his testing, and nothing serious was found.

He had a full recovery, and medical insurance for any future problems.

+ + +

One spring day, a patient presented for "hemorrhoid medication fail." This patient, a fifty-year-old gentleman, had been in the office a couple of weeks earlier. He reported, "My mother discovered a hemorrhoid when checking my ass." He never elaborated as to why his mother was the investigator of this issue.

This didn't seem a particularly strange visit reason. Hemorrhoids are a common problem, and sometimes the first treatment—a hydrocortisone suppository—fails. It was probably time to try a different treatment.

"I understand you are having trouble with your hemorrhoids, and the medication is not working."

"Yeah, it isn't working at all."

"Have you noticed any improvement at all using the suppository?" He had been suffering from typical symptoms of discomfort, bleeding, and swelling.

"No, Dr. Wave."

"Have you been using them twice a day?"

"I try, but it's really hard. I have a hell of a time swallowing those pills. They're so big. I almost choked to death one time when I swallowed the damned thing."

My heart sank. The rectal suppository, which looks like a rocket, would indeed have been exceedingly difficult to swallow. "Just to make sure I get this right, you were *swallowing* the suppositories?"

"I've been trying, but sometimes I have to cut them in half to get them down. I hope it's alright to do that."

"Sir, you're not supposed to swallow them."

"I'm not?" A confused look formed on his face. "Then what do you do with them?"

"Have you ever heard the term 'suppository'?"

"I think so."

"They are placed inside your rectum, where they dissolve, delivering the medication."

"You mean they go up my ass?" He sounded stunned.

"Yes."

"*What?* You want me to stick the pills up my ass? Are you serious?"

"They are not pills. They are suppositories. That's how the treatment works. It's not an uncommon method."

"Not uncommon? People don't stick pills up their ass. That's crazy! I have never heard of anything like that. No way I am sticking anything up my ass. It is an exit only. Exit *only*!"

"If medications fail or you refuse to use them, you might have to see a specialist."

"A proctologist?"

Surprisingly, he knew this term.

"Basically. They have a scope they insert and can use to remove the hemorrhoids. Usually, we try medications first before doing this procedure."

"You mean they put a telescope up your ass and start cutting?"

"I wouldn't put it like that. A scope is inserted in the rectum, and banding is performed on—"

"Jesus, no. That sounds painful."

"There is only mild discomfort."

"I bet. I don't want a telescope shoved up my ass."

"Perhaps you could give the medication a try?"

"I don't know. Is there another way?"

"You should be taking fiber as we discussed on the last visit. But the suppositories are the most important initial treatment."

"Alright, alright. How do you use these things again?"

While I explained in detail how to use the suppositories correctly, he looked as though he might vomit.

The patient left clutching a prescription for additional suppositories. It was beginning to dawn on me that Mars patients were generally uneducated and that detailed explanations for even the simplest things were clearly required. Who on Earth would try to swallow a suppository? Lesson learned.

Once the patient began taking the suppositories properly, his symptoms cleared right up. His mother was undoubtedly pleased.

7

SKIP MEETING

My meetings with Skip fell into a routine. In theory, we would meet every Monday, but Skip frequently canceled meetings to attend conferences at luxury resorts around the world. He was away at these conferences about half of the time.

That suited me fine. Meetings with Skip were unproductive. He would talk about ideas, but nothing was ever implemented. Skip only acted if a hired consultant had made a recommendation. Any ideas or suggestions I made, he dismissed.

Arriving for a meeting one Monday in late spring, I found a man in an Armani suit sitting in Skip's office. He was clearly a consultant. Skip's next idea had arrived.

"Hello, Dr. Wave. This is our new advisor Mr. Koalemos." A rumor in the doctors' lounge was that consultants had been slinking around the hospital for a few days. It was a rumor no more.

"You must be one of the new consultants I have heard about." We shook hands.

"No, no, Dr. Wave. Mr. Koalemos is not a consultant." Skip stated excitedly. "He is an advisor. We are not to call him or his associates consultants. We don't use that word anymore. It's too negative."

A rose by any other name is still a rose. "I stand corrected… advisor." Consultants, advisors, or whatever they were called, were uniformly despised by doctors across the country. From think tanks and other oddly named associations, these individuals were always coming up with wacky new ideas to sell, and they were always out of touch with reality.

"How should we start?" Skip asked the consultant (or advisor, I should say).

"I think we should start with a seminar to build trust among our doctors."

My heart sank. *Trust seminar?* These were notorious, the most famous example being a trust seminar held by some Fortune 500 company where employees had to walk barefoot across hot coals. The employees who did this trust walk were taken away in an ambulance with severe burns. Clearly, they didn't have enough trust.

Skip's face glowed. "I think that is an excellent idea. We can have a trust seminar at our next physicians' meeting."

The consultant explained his plan. Doctors would engage in a variety of trust-building activities including the use of coloring books and the singing of group songs. The seminar would also have individual doctors take turns being blindfolded and led through a trust maze by another doctor. At the end of the trust maze, a trust fall would occur where the blindfolded doctor would lean backward and be caught by the doctor leading them through the maze.

"What do you think of that, Dr. Wave?" Skip asked with breathless excitement.

"I doubt our physicians will go for this."

Skip frowned and gently caressed his goatee. His disappointment was obvious.

"We have done this successfully at other hospitals," the consultant sharply interjected.

"That may be so," I said. "But this is Mars. And the Mars medical staff, in my opinion, will have no interest in participating."

Slenderman, trust falling? Never. And who could possibly catch him without being squashed like a bug?

"Well, you'll just have to make it mandatory." Mr. Koalemos sounded irate. He was full of fine ideas today.

"A mandatory trust maze? That seems like a contradiction. And just how exactly do we make it mandatory? Do we tell doctors they will be suspended or fired if they don't participate?"

"Now... Dr. Wave, you don't seem very supportive," Skip said.

"You asked me what I thought, and I'm giving you my honest opinion."

"Well, we'll see. Put it on the agenda. Tell Dr. Wave about Get Crabby, our new program," Skip told the consultant.

Get Crabby? Just when I thought it couldn't get any worse.

The consultant walked over to a box full of books in the corner of the room. He pulled out a book titled *Get Crabby!* and handed it to me. "Here's your copy."

The book had a dancing cartoon crab on the cover. I thumbed through the pages as the consultant spoke.

"This book is based on things done in a crab market in Boston. It's an amazing business where employees are passionate about their work, bring a positive attitude, and provide great customer service. By learning the lessons these crab sellers teach, we can elevate the medical staff's enthusiasm, passion, and customer service. We need Mars Hospital doctors to get crabby!"

Having pushed back against the trust maze and the trust fall, I kept my mouth shut. You must choose your battles.

"Skip, if there are enough copies to distribute to the medical staff, I'll hand out the books at the next physicians' meeting in a few weeks," I said.

"That's what I was thinking. I've ordered hundreds of copies. There'll be more than enough books."

The consultants are going to make a fortune.

What remained unspoken was the fact that not a single doctor would read this book. The title alone was a turnoff. And the cartoon crab on the cover was ridiculous. This method of presenting customer service lessons to physicians wouldn't be effective. Physicians are extraordinarily busy with multiple demands on their time, and they hate wasting time on silly things, and they would learn nothing about how to better care for patients from crab sellers.

"The books can be handed out at the start of the trust seminar," Skip continued. He had his stubborn heart set on the idea. This was not a good sign.

The consultant gave a long discourse on the program. He had a *Get Crabby!* movie that could be shown in physicians' offices as well as a variety of branded activities. And he had a lengthy implementation timeline. It sounded like this guy was planning to drag this out for months. I resigned myself to dealing with "crabbiness" for the foreseeable future.

8

OFFICE INTERLUDE

It took me a second to notice what was wrong when I arrived at the office. Then it dawned on me: The shrubberies were gone. *Where are they?* The flowers were gone too. *What happened?* Sally would know. You could always count on her to know what was going on at the clinic.

"What happened to our shrubberies out front?"

"Someone stole them last night."

"Someone stole our shrubberies and flowers? Seriously?"

"Yeah, probably a doper. The shrubberies were probably sold for dope money." She explained the plants used in landscaping were expensive and therefore a good payday for fiends.

"Did you report it?"

"I did, but don't expect the FBI to be breaking down any doors." Sally smiled slyly. "Your first patient is ready," she said, handing me the schedule.

The visit reason at the top of the list was "death follow-up." "So what's the deal, here?" I asked. *This should be interesting.*

"He says he was dead, but now he needs to go back to work."

"He's not a zombie, is he?" Dr. Wurst came to mind. Sally had told me he was absolutely terrified of anything related to zombies. Watching movies, especially zombie movies, was a hobby of mine, which suddenly seemed well-suited to this strange town.

"He sure smells like one," Sally said. "He could use a shower."

Body odor certainly was a common problem in Mars.

Reviewing the patient's file, the reason for his death follow-up visit became apparent. He *had* been dead, clinically speaking! The patient had been in the emergency room just a few days prior. He'd collapsed in the front yard of his neighbor's house. Fortunately, the neighbor had seen him and called 911. When the paramedics arrived, he was not breathing and had no pulse. He was young, just twenty-eight, and the cause of the respiratory arrest had been a heroin over-dose. A single dose of Narcan, the antidote, had revived him. It had been close. Had there been a delay of any sort, even for a few more minutes, this fellow would certainly have been dead—another statistic in the opioid epidemic that has engulfed our nation.

"Hello, there," I said upon entering the exam room. "I looked over your file before coming in. You are lucky to be alive." The young man was thin and appeared somewhat nervous. He had wild, brown hair that needed combing. His white t-shirt and jeans were dirty, and as Sally had pointed out, he needed to bathe. A musty scent permeated the room.

"Yeah, it was really stupid of me. I made a dumb mistake."

"I think it's important not to look at drug addiction as a moral failing but as an illness. Treatment is available and important. And though it's difficult, it is effective."

"I don't need rehab. I'm fine now. I just need a note to go back to work."

"I think it's fairly safe to say that you need rehab. You were literally dead on your neighbor's front lawn earlier this week."

"It was a dumb mistake on my part. Here's what happened. I went to a different dealer who had a new supply. Instead of testing it out first like I should have, I just shot up my usual amount like an idiot. It turns out the dope was pretty good, and I OD'd. I know better than that. I won't make that mistake again."

The way he casually explained his testing error with no acknowledgment of his addiction was troubling. Dealers, one should note, will often sell potent product when trying to gain a market share. Indeed, drug addicts often seek out dealers with customers who overdose because this indicates "good" dope. A few overdoses are good for business.

"It wasn't just a dumb mistake. Heroin is very addictive. There are a few treatment programs I can recommend. Also, Narcotics Anonymous is a good program, and it's free. There is a meeting, in fact—"

"I'm not going to any meetings. I don't need a meeting. I can quit any time I want to."

The oldest cliché in the book.

"It's not impossible, but it isn't easy to quit outside of treatment programs. That's your best bet."

"I'm not quitting is what I mean. But I will be more careful from now on. I promise. I'm going back to my old dealer."

"You are incredibly lucky to be alive right now. You understand that, don't you?"

"Yeah, I had a hot batch."

"Next time, you might not be so lucky."

"There won't be a next time. I know what I'm doing, I'll be more careful, and I'll be fine. Can I get a note to go back to work?"

Everything checked out fine in the complete physical examination that followed. I inquired as to what kind of work he performed, hoping he didn't operate a steamroller. He reported he worked at a local pizzeria, and I figured he was medically fit for making pizza. He smiled when I gave him his back-to-work note.

"If you change your mind and wish to enter treatment, let me know."

"Not a chance. I'll be fine."

As he left, a thought flashed across my mind.

Was he the one who had stolen my shrubberies?

+++

Holding his left hand, I helped a nice, elderly gentleman walk slowly out of the exam room as he grasped a three-pronged cane in his right hand. We navigated into the waiting room where his granddaughter took his hand.

Sally called out the name of the next patient. A woman got up and walked toward Sally, passing my elderly patient along the way. She turned and gave him a sharp, nasty look.

A short time later, Sally informed me the next patient was ready.

"What's her story?" I asked.

"She's here to adjust her blood pressure medication."

"Got it. But what is her *story*?"

"She's the town gossip and lives down the road. She watches our comings and goings from her bedroom window, with binoculars."

"So much for patient confidentiality."

The woman was in her late fifties, with short, sandy brown hair, and dressed in a black jumpsuit. She wore thick glasses with black frames that made her eyes appear larger.

"Hello, Dr. Wave. How are you today?" We exchanged pleasantries. She then proved Sally right about her being the town gossip.

"Dr. Wave, do you know what that man you just walked out did?"

"No, I do not."

"Well, I just have to tell you. He drove to Omaha." This surprised me. Omaha is a long way from Mars, and he didn't have a driver's license. "And do you know what he was doing in Omaha?" A wicked grin crossed her face. "He was seeing a prostitute."

My eyes widened in surprise. "I find that hard to believe."

"It's true! And everyone in town knows it. He was caught in a sex sting operation and was arrested and taken to jail," she breathlessly continued. "It was just like those shows you see on television where they bust perverts doing the nasty with hookers."

"Really? I just don't believe it. He's a genuinely nice man."

"Well, you better believe it. He's certainly not nice. He's a filthy old pervert. He was arrested, spent the night in jail, and his wife had to come and bail him out the next morning. Shame, shame." As she chanted "shame," it was clear she was mixing up my patient with someone else. It absolutely could not have been him.

"He couldn't be the man you're talking about," I said. "His wife passed on twenty years ago."

"Oh, this was in 1962."

My jaw dropped. *1962?* He was a young man in 1962. Assuming any of what she said was true, it sounded like that young man had made a mistake.

"And let me tell you about his wife. She was the town slut in high school. She did the nasty with the entire Mars football team. No wonder that old pervert ended up marrying her. He sure likes slutty women."

"We should not speak ill of the dead," I said. His wife would have been in high school in the 1950s, before the town gossip had even been born.

"Sorry, Doctor, but she was nothing but a tramp, and he is

nothing but a dirty old pervert."

After she left, Sally listened to my retelling of the story.

"That old bitch. I told you she was the town gossip. She'll be telling people those stories at the poor guy's wake."

9

AT THE HOSPITAL

"We have someone coming for a job interview." Skip called me at my clinic one afternoon in late spring. He was extremely excited.

"What's the position?"

"It's for the office just outside of town. The old one."

The office to which Skip was referring was known to everyone in the hospital as "the old office." Built in 1915, it was in a dreadful state of disrepair. It had no central heating, and holes had been drilled in the walls to slip extension cords through to power space heaters in the winter. However, the space heaters were insufficient and the rooms still froze. In the summer, due to lack of air conditioning, the rooms boiled. The list of code violations was a mile long and included my personal favorite, an infestation of squirrels living inside the walls. And I thought having ants was bad.

But one doctor still practiced there. Dr. Essex, who was in his eighties, had been in the office his entire career. I had just heard a rumor that he was getting forgetful, and this required immediate investigation. He had wisely sold the decrepit old building and his practice to the hospital several years earlier for seven figures, with the caveat that he continued to practice until we recruited a replacement. Given the shape of the building, which Skip had refused to demolish or repair citing "cost concerns," he might be practicing until age ninety-nine. Finding someone interested in this practice would be a lucky break.

"May I review the résumé?" I asked. "And when will the applicant be coming for the interview?" It was standard practice to have the medical director look over the credentials of any potential new hire before offering an interview, but Skip had skipped that step.

"Today."

"That seems quick." Typically, you do checks before applicants come out for a visit. But this didn't surprise me; my own recruitment had been done with equal haste.

"Mars needs doctors!" Skip replied.

That sounds like the title to a bad movie. And I'm in it.

"She's going to be here in an hour. Can you be here?"

There goes my afternoon clinic. I sighed. "I'll be there."

When I arrived, only Skip was in the conference room. He had invited no one else to assist in the interview.

"Oh, you actually came!" He sounded surprised.

"I said I would be here. Do you have the applicant's résumé?" Skip handed me a single sheet of paper. After a brief review, it became clear why the physician to be interviewed would be happy taking the job, though it was in a hundred-year-old office. In addition to not being board certified, there were other significant problems.

"Skip, this doctor doesn't have a DEA license for controlled substances. It's suspended." For doctors to prescribe narcotics, a special license from the federal Drug Enforcement Administration is required. This license was also a requirement for membership on the hospital medical staff, even at Mars Hospital. That fact alone precluded her from the job.

"Well, she told me about that. She is going to get her license back in a couple of months. We can overlook the suspension."

We can? "Why was it suspended in the first place?"

"She said it was a misunderstanding."

"I'm skeptical. License suspensions are a big deal and not to be taken lightly." It was more likely she'd been suspended due to a felony conviction, improper prescribing, or her own substance abuse issue. Or maybe she even had the trifecta.

"Whatever it is, I'm sure we can work around it. We need someone in the old office."

"There are some other issues here, too." This doctor had held six jobs in two years. And her references were interesting. Instead of listing other physicians, directors of her training program, or employers, she'd listed her mother.

Skip didn't appear bothered by any of this. His phone buzzed. "She's here." The applicant arrived in the conference room a short time later.

"Hello, Dr. Do," Skip said, making introductions. We engaged in small talk, then started the interview. Skip began the questioning. "So why are you interested in Mars Hospital?"

"I need a job. I'm unemployed."

"How long have you been out of work?"

"About a month."

"What happened?"

"The CEO at my last job was an idiot. He didn't have a clue how to run things. He wouldn't let me write for narcotics, which was stupid. One day, he fired me for no reason. I should sue."

"Well, don't worry. I'm a good CEO." Skip brushed off her troubling answer.

"Really? That's a first." Dr. Do's face and tone were full of doubt. She was giving a great demonstration of how not to answer interview questions. Skip, however, didn't seem to care.

"Do you have any particular patient care interests?" he asked.

"No. I hate hospitals. I hate nursing homes. I just want to stay in the office."

This answer rubbed me the wrong way. Many doctors choose to practice only in the office. But her response was so negative. She was projecting a bad vibe.

"Okay, that's all I've got for you. Dr. Wave, do you have any questions?"

You had better believe it. "I do. I see that the Drug Enforcement Administration has suspended your controlled substance license. What happened?"

"I'm going to get it back in a few months. It was a mix-up."

"Has the DEA informed you of a reinstatement date?"

"No."

"Then how do you know you will get your license back in a couple of months?"

"My lawyer told me he was going to get it back for me."

"Why was it suspended in the first place?"

"Here's what happened. My husband needed surgery. After surgery, the surgeon cut off his supply of pain pills after just a few months. He needed pain pills. So I started writing him a prescription."

"I can understand that," Skip interjected.

What? That behavior is completely unethical! "Skip, with all due respect, I cannot. Was your husband even your patient?" Treating immediate family members is against the guidelines of the American Medical Association.

"No, but he is my husband. He needed the pills, so I gave him the pills. Every doctor does this. The DEA was very wrong to make a big deal out of it. The stupid pharmacist in town reported me, and the DEA came to my office and treated me like a criminal. They even took my charts."

Lucky they didn't haul you off to jail. And no, every doctor does not do this. "Has your state medical license ever been disciplined, and have you ever had any malpractice cases?"

"I don't like these questions. That sort of thing is personal."

"I understand, but you are applying for a job, and these questions are relevant to the application."

"Skip said when I spoke with him on the phone that none of that would matter."

He sat in silence, confirming he'd told her precisely that.

"Well this is my question, so please answer it. Has your license ever been disciplined, and have you had any malpractice cases?" I asked.

"I've had six malpractice cases, but they're all settled. And my license got suspended once, but it was reinstated."

"What happened?"

"To the license?"

"Yes."

"They said I wasn't examining patients and was just treating them over the phone and giving them narcotics, but every doctor does this, so I don't know why they picked on me."

Are you kidding me with this? All disciplinary hearing transcripts are public and available for review online. Those transcripts would require immediate review.

"And what about the malpractice cases?" She'd only been out of training for a couple of years. To have six cases in such a short time was extraordinary, especially for an office-based doctor not performing higher-risk inpatient hospital work.

"I don't feel good." Dr. Do stood up and ran out the door.

A retching sound then echoed from the hallway. This was followed by a loud splat. Skip pranced out after her with me right behind.

The main hospital conference room was located just across from the double door entrance to the administrative atrium. Those glass doors now needed cleaning. Our applicant had vomited all over them. She must have eaten pea soup for lunch; green goo was everywhere. She continued retching right in front of the doors. A green pool of large chunks expanded rapidly before her feet.

Skip grimaced in horror. "We'd better call housekeeping."

"I think we should call the ER."

The applicant continued loudly retching, and a stream of green slime flowed from her mouth like a waterfall. Then, suddenly, it stopped. "I'm fine. Don't call the ER." Green vomit dripped from her lips as she spoke.

"Are you sure?" My own stomach started churning.

"Yes." One more retch followed, for good measure. My own bile rose as a few final globs of green flew from her mouth and an overpowering stench filled the hallway. What had she eaten today?

"Skip, I think I'm going to go now. I need to rest."

"That's fine." Skip didn't make eye contact but stared at the green-slime-covered doors. "We will get back to you about the job."

A crowd of vice presidents, gathered on the other side of the doors, watched us intently. Two housekeepers suddenly appeared. They were running behind their housekeeping carts. Without a doubt, this was the fastest housekeeping had ever moved in the history of Mars Hospital.

"Do you need some water?" My voice was filled with concern.

"No, I'm fine."

"Can you drive? I could call someone for you."

"I told you, I'm fine. You just got me upset with all your stupid questions. You made me throw up."

"I am sorry you became sick. They were standard questions, and you can provide full answers when you're feeling better. Do you need help getting to your car?"

"No. Go away. Leave me alone." With that, she left.

After she left, Skip spoke up. "So what do you think? We can probably give her the job, right?"

"Are you serious?"

"Just because she got upset and vomited doesn't mean we can't employ her."

"True, but the fact that her DEA license is suspended, her medical license disciplined, and she has a history of six malpractice cases means she shouldn't get the job."

"Well, maybe. Please investigate and put together a report. Let's not be hasty. We aren't getting much interest in the old office, so we shouldn't just reject her out of hand."

This lady was clearly unqualified and, as a bonus, had a disturbing attitude. She was bad news. But diplomacy seemed appropriate.

"Certainly. I will review everything in detail and get back to you."

"Excellent. Let's see if we can make this work. I'm counting on you." Skip pranced away with a smile as housekeeping got busy scrubbing.

As the interview had ended early, it was off to the doctors' lounge.

In the doctors' lounge, physicians were already boisterously laughing about the applicant puking on the administrative suite's doors. Gossip travels fast at Mars Hospital.

"Hey, Wave, did her head spin around after she barfed?" Beats asked. Rumpsmith and Slenderman were there with him.

When do these guys work? They were fixtures in the doctors' lounge. An anesthesiologist and an ER doctor were also present.

"How'd you learn about that so quickly? That happened just a few minutes ago," I answered.

"Someone called from admin and told me the story," Beats stated.

"Don't tell him that. You'll end up getting *someone* fired. He's one of them!" Slenderman warned. He had three quarter pounders in front of him, and he was shoveling a burger into his mouth while he spoke. Mustard and ketchup stained his beard. There were even red and yellow splotches on his hairless head.

"Don't worry. Even though I am one of them, I won't say anything or get anyone fired," I said in a spooky voice, wiggling my fingers like the legs of a spider, which made Slenderman frown. "And, no, her head did not spin. She just got sick during the interview."

Rumpsmith chimed in. "I know this chick." He ran his fingers through his Einstein hair as he talked. "Dr. Do. They should call her Dr. Doo-Doo because she is shit. She got tossed off the medical staff at her last hospital. Apparently, she's a pill-pusher and a totally incompetent doctor. I also heard she's hooked on drugs. But Skip will probably hire her anyway. He'd hire anyone with a pulse."

"Yeah, like he hired our new medical director," Slenderman said.

"Well played, Dr. Slenderman. You sunk my battleship." My comment clearly annoyed him. *Don't let him get under your skin.*

"Hey, Beats, tell Wave about the Stercus Steamer," Rumpsmith continued. "It would be appropriate after interviewing Dr. Doo-Doo. Barfing on the administration door is nothing compared to him."

"You ever hear of Dr. Stercus?" Beats asked me.

"Nope."

"Well, let me tell you a story. Dr. Stercus was an employed pediatrician at Mars Hospital. He was hired to care for pediatric patients—inpatient and outpatient. From the start, things did not go well. He couldn't handle being on call."

On-call duties at Mars Hospital are burdensome. And this is especially true in pediatrics. Unlike most hospitals, Mars Hospital delivers neonatal care to infants using general pediatricians. This situation is not ideal. The care of newborns, especially high-risk premature ones, is usually provided by neonatal specialists. These doctors, who obtain years of additional training beyond that of a general pediatrician, can manage these often critically ill premature infants. It has become the accepted standard of care nationwide to provide neonatal specialty care to newborns.

But not at Mars Hospital. To save money, general pediatricians performed all neonatal care duties. And the pediatricians were in over their heads. General pediatricians were also required to attend every C-section, which meant they were always on call, an incredibly stressful situation. And while a highly skilled and competent general pediatrician like Dr. Wurst can handle this setup, many general pediatricians are neither trained nor capable of doing this job—like Dr. Stercus.

"And Stercus complained nonstop," Beats continued. "He complained he was lied to by Skip and told he would only be on call one day in twelve. Actually, he was on call every day. He complained he was exhausted and never got more than a couple of hours of sleep at a time. And he complained he didn't have the critical care training he needed to provide proper care to infants."

Stercus had every right to complain. Some of these infants are so small they can fit into the palm of your hand. Caring for them requires special expertise. Doctors should not practice beyond their level of training and competence.

"None of this sat well with Skip. Skip told him doctors should suck it up, take care of their patients, and not complain about being on call."

Knowing Skip, the fact that Dr. Stercus was sleep deprived and in over his head wouldn't matter.

"And all the old-time doctors on staff supported Skip's position. They told Stercus that back in the day they took calls every night for years on end."

Back in the day, hospitalized patients were nowhere near as sick as they are now, and doctors would not be called nearly as often.

"So, annoyed by Dr. Stercus's endless complaining, Skip decided to punish him. He sent Dr. Stercus a new contract with a twenty percent pay cut. I'm sure in his mind, Stercus would have no choice but to agree to this and sign the new contract. Skip, after all, is the boss." Beats's voice dripped with contempt.

"Stercus responded the very same evening he received the new contract. He went to the administrative suite shortly after five in the afternoon, so of course no one was there. The administration office doors were locked, so he slid his resignation letter under those closed doors and was never seen or heard from again. It's rumored he moved to Las Vegas. As for the contract itself, he set it on the floor in front of the administration doors, dropped his pants, and shit on it. When Skip arrived the next morning, he saw the contract sitting there under a large pile of still-steaming turds, according to the legend. The Stercus Steamer was thus born and will live on forever in the hospital staff's memory." Beats burst into laughter when he'd concluded his story.

"I never did like Stercus," Slenderman commented. "But I will be the first to say that shitting on that contract was brilliant."

"Now... Dr. Slenderman," Beats said, imitating Skip's voice, "shitting on contracts is not appropriate." Beats stroked an invisible goatee to mock another one of Skip's mannerisms.

10
THE END OF SPRING

My visit to Dr. Essex's office occurred on a damp spring morning the day after Dr. Do's interview. As I entered the office, the strong odor of mildew immediately hit me. There were noticeable water stains on the ceiling and a few speckles of black mold on the wall. The place looked unfit for human habitation. It was far worse than my own office.

After I introduced myself, the receptionist went back to fetch Dr. Essex and returned with him a few minutes later.

"Welcome. My nurse tells me you're new."

It was his receptionist—small error, no big deal.

"Dr. Wave," I said. "Nice to meet you. I'm the new medical director."

"Since when? We already have a medical director."

His actual nurse emerged from a side room. "He died, remember?" she told Dr. Essex.

"Oh, yeah," he said. "So you're the new guy?"

That is a more significant lapse of memory.

"I am, and I also work in the Mars Hospital general medicine clinic."

"Terrific. You can send me all your surgeries. I do every kind of surgery there is—obstetrics, gynecology, orthopedics, lung surgery, heart surgery, abdominal surgery…" He then went off on a tangent about how he'd been a trauma surgeon during the Vietnam War.

"You're doing general surgery now, right?" I asked. General surgeons did things like remove gallbladders and other organs in the abdominal cavity, procedures only allowed with his credentials.

"Oh. That's right. I just do general surgery these days. But I know how to do everything. Let me show you around." My follow-up review of surgery schedules confirmed he was only doing general surgery.

His clinic was small, with just four exam rooms, a physician's office, a lab, a medical supply room, and a tiny bathroom with no disabled access. Extension cords crisscrossed the office, some passing through holes drilled in the walls. And there were strange noises emanating from within them, probably due to the nesting squirrels. A small door near the bathroom caught my eye; it was marked "Stretching Closet."

Interesting.

"What is a stretching closet?" I asked.

He turned to face the door. "That's where I stretch people's necks for pain, headaches, and back issues. It cures them."

I gave him a dubious look and he continued explaining himself.

"I also practice general medicine. Back when I started, doctors didn't specialize as they do now. If you couldn't take care of everything, you were not a doctor. I also take care of farm animals." Before I'd fully digested that fact, he continued. "Here, look." He opened the door to the stretching closet. It was appropriately named.

The room was, in fact, a small closet. In it, a patient hung in some sort of traction. He dangled in the air, his head in something that looked like a birdcage.

"What on earth are you doing?"

"I am stretching this fellow's neck. How are you doing? Feeling better?" Dr. Essex shut the door before the patient could reply. My stomach knotted up. We couldn't just leave that poor fellow hanging in the closet.

"Dr. Essex, I think your patient's stretching is finished."

"What?" He appeared confused.

"Your patient in the stretching closet."

"Oh, you're right." He opened the closet and unlocked the birdcage. The patient quickly exited the clinic. This concluded the tour and we sat down in Dr. Essex's office.

"So what kind of doctor are you?" he asked.

"General internal medicine."

"Where are you practicing?"

"At the Mars Clinic." *We covered this ground earlier.* "I am also the new medical director."

"What happened to the old director? Did Jacob get rid of him?"

Jacob? Could he mean an administrator at the hospital decades ago?

"The medical director died a couple of months ago."

"Oh. Nobody tells me anything around here." His face turned red. His hands trembled. He then began furiously digging through papers on his desk. Almost yelling, he proclaimed, "I built this hospital. When I first came here, there were only three doctors on staff, myself included."

He proceeded to tell me a long story of how he came to work in Mars, Nebraska. According to the story, he'd been driving with his wife to a new job in Texas, but their car had broken down outside of town. While he was waiting for car repairs, having nothing better to do to kill a few hours, he visited Mars Hospital. He was offered a job on the spot and started practicing that day. No one had even checked out his credentials. Some things, it seems, never change.

"Who are you?" he asked after finishing his story. I told him again.

And again.

And again.

As I left the old office, my conclusion was clear. Dr. Essex was not fit to be practicing medicine. It would have to be brought to Skip's attention that the old doctor needed to be retired immediately. Fortunately, I had already scheduled a meeting with Skip for the very next morning, and, checking the schedule, Dr. Essex had no surgeries scheduled.

+++

Before the meeting, I had also completed Dr. Do's background investigation. The results were eye-popping. Dr. Do had a half-dozen malpractice settlements listed in the National Practitioner Data Bank, the nationwide collection of all malpractice settlements in the US. And her Nebraska license had been previously suspended for inappropriate prescription of narcotics. Of note, she had not been disciplined for malpractice. In Nebraska, as in other states, doctors are seldom held accountable for malpractice by the licensing boards.

But that was not all. Dr. Do had also been convicted of felony theft in medical school and had been given probation. The medical school and licensing board had either ignored or missed this.

In addition, as Rumpsmith had mentioned, Dr. Do had been kicked off the medical staff at her previous hospital for reasons unknown. Her employee file was sealed, and no one at that hospital would say much about her. This is a common problem in medicine.

Fearing lawsuits, former employers clam up and bad apples move on to the next hospital. Finally, her federal DEA license had been suspended with no indication of any reinstatement date. This was an easy hiring decision: run from this applicant as fast as possible.

"Did you do the review for the new hire?" Skip asked as the meeting started. It was surprising and worrisome that he'd said "new hire" and not "applicant."

"I did." Skip's face flashed surprise when I pulled out documents from a folder. "I have looked at all of the available information, and it does not look good. Not only does she have licensure and malpractice issues, but Dr. Rumpsmith reports she was also kicked off the medical staff of her last hospital. It's hard to confirm this as her prior hospital has sealed her files. And even worse, she is a convicted felon. This, I could confirm. It's amazing she still has a medical license at all." Skip gave the documents a cursory glance, then gathered them up and pranced to his file cabinet. He already had a secret file for Dr. Do, and he placed the documents into it.

"So you don't think we should hire her?"

"Correct. We absolutely should not hire this applicant."

"Did you call her references?"

"No."

"Why not?" Skip's voice was filled with concern.

"She listed her mother as a reference!"

"Oh, that's right. Should we ask Dr. Do to give us some doctors as references?"

"Honestly, I don't think it matters at this point. There's nothing any doctor could say that would change the documented evidence we already have, and certainly nothing that would change my mind. She is not suitable for employment."

"Well, no one is perfect. People deserve second chances."

"Skip, that may be true in a general sense. But not in this case.

We can't go forward with this applicant."

"Let me think about it." Skip gathered up random papers on his desk, signaling the meeting was at its end.

"Skip, there's one more thing."

"What's that?" He made no eye contact and sounded irate.

"I met Dr. Essex yesterday."

"Yes, I heard. Isn't he great? He's the longest-serving doctor on our medical staff. Almost fifty years running."

"I have grave concerns." Skip listened intently, with an ever-deepening scowl, to my summation of my previous meeting.

"I believe Dr. Essex has Alzheimer's disease," I said. "We must require a formal neuropsychiatric evaluation to confirm my suspicions. This formal testing clearly and objectively determines whether a patient is suffering from significant cognitive impairment. And we must, for patient safety, immediately suspend him from the medical staff pending this formal evaluation."

"Now...Dr. Wave, we can't do that. He's been on staff for fifty years." He started petting his goatee like a kitten.

"That's exactly why we have to do it. He's almost ninety years old! The incidence of cognitive impairment in that age group is high. And he's acting as a general surgeon, something that requires a doctor to be at the highest level of mental acuity. In fact, in his confusion, he told me he was doing 'all kinds of different surgeries' beyond just general surgery. I checked and this is not the case, thank goodness. But I witnessed his decline first-hand. He even told me he was treating farm animals. His confusion is profound. We must suspend him immediately."

"If we hire someone for his practice, he's going to retire. That's why we need a replacement." Skip sounded as though he'd put anyone in the old office. Perhaps he already knew of the impairment. Indeed, anyone who'd spent any time with Dr. Essex would know his memory was gone. But you couldn't put an unqualified doctor in the office just to ease out the old one. That would merely replace one problem with another.

"It's a patient care issue," I said. "We need to have him evaluated to prevent possible patient injury, and as I've already said, immediately suspend him. I've found an excellent neuropsychiatrist at the University of Nebraska who can evaluate—"

"I am not on board with this at all. Dr. Essex would be insulted. How about this? I'll go ahead and tell Dr. Do we aren't going to hire her. And you drop this whole Essex matter. It will be a good compromise, a fifty-fifty split." Skip's voice sounded desperate.

"No. This is not something we can negotiate. In my capacity as medical director, I am filing an emergency suspension after this meeting."

"I am the CEO, and I am *your* boss. It is within my authority to override this emergency suspension. And I just did." Skip put an exclamation point on his statement by yanking his goatee with a clenched fist.

"Dr. Essex has advanced Alzheimer's!" I argued. "He is a clear and present danger to patients!"

"He is not being suspended. Period. He's a great surgeon, and the hospital would lose a fortune if we suspended him."

Unacceptable. My stomach churned and my face felt warm.

"Skip, understand that I must report this immediately. While it is true you are my boss and you can override any decision I make, this is morally wrong. I am ethically bound to report Dr. Essex."

"Fine. Report it to Slenderman." Skip's voice was full of fury.

Mars Hospital had no physician impairment committee. Aware of the response Slenderman would give, my heart sank. "Alright, I will. But I will also report this to other appropriate parties."

Skip said nothing, but his eyes narrowed. With this gesture, the meeting ended, and I left angry, saddened, and discouraged.

My options at this point were limited. In the US, the CEO of a hospital has enormous latitude regarding medical staffing issues. Most CEOs delegate authority regarding physician impairment to a committee with special expertise in handling such matters. But at Mars Hospital, Skip retained this authority. Oversight in reporting to state and federal regulatory agencies was minimal at Mars Hospital, a common problem nationwide, and peer reviews were controlled by the department chairs. This arrangement ensured conflict of interest and made it highly unlikely that an unbiased review would occur. Nonetheless, I filed a formal incident report with the surgery department. That was the protocol.

Slenderman, although not actually the chair, was assigned this incident report. When I tried to discuss it with him, he refused to listen, literally placing his hands over his ears and shouting "la, la, la" as I spoke. Of course, he did nothing with the report.

I next reported my concerns to numerous other senior medical staff members. They also did nothing. But at least they didn't cover their ears and shout.

Then I called the Inspection Commission and several other federal and state agencies and verbally reported my concerns. I followed up each call up with a detailed letter. But no immediate action was taken.

Finally, I called Ms. Dolus, the mayor. She was Skip's boss. Mars Hospital was first chartered as a nonprofit hospital in 1868, shortly after Nebraska was admitted to the union. The charter called for the mayor of Mars to "assign or replace, with the advice and consent of the city council, the leader of the hospital."

The call did not go well. As I started explaining the situation, the mayor hung up the phone. Skip called me not five minutes later.

"Dr. Wave, I just got off the phone with the mayor. She says you were complaining about me."

"Yes. I called to complain and report your refusal to suspend Dr. Essex."

"You are not to go behind my back like this again." Skip's voice trembled with anger.

"Skip, I told you I was going to report this to other appropriate parties. I will not apologize for what I did. It was the right thing to do." *I am not backing down.*

"Now... Dr. Wave, I understand you're angry." Perhaps I'd intimidated him a little. His voice held a tone of reconciliation. "But I am not suspending Dr. Essex. Period. This matter is closed."

"Understood." I hung up the phone. To add insult to injury, Skip hired Dr. Do the next day. It almost made me regret not taking the fifty-fifty split Skip had offered. At least then Dr. Do would not have been hired. But that would be unethical and would have made me complicit.

After learning of her hiring, I reported Dr. Do's criminal conviction and other issues both to the medicine department chair via an incident report as well as to the Nebraska Department of Health and Human services, the agency in Nebraska charged with licensing physicians.

No action was taken after any of my reports.

And after Dr. Do was hired, Dr. Essex decided he would continue to practice "just a little longer." He wasn't "quite ready to retire just yet." This was yet another slap in the face.

Should I quit on the spot? Resigning was an appropriate move for a medical director in such serious disagreement with his boss. But that would be surrender. And with both Do hired and Essex staying in practice, who would look out for their patients if I quit?

I decided to stay. But this was a major defeat the likes of which must never happen again.

SUMMER

11
OFFICE INTERLUDE

"Ms. Geras is here, and she brought a coconut cream pie," Sally announced, smiling with delight as she held it in the air.

It was Monday, the first day of summer. Ms. Geras was in the office waiting that morning, though she was supposed to be in the nursing home. Sally took her to a room, and a short time later announced the patient was ready to be seen.

"Don't stay in there too long, Wavesticks. I might eat the whole pie before you come out." Hopefully, Sally was joking.

"Good afternoon, Ms. Geras. Thank you for the pie. It looks delicious."

"You're welcome. I've been making pies my whole life." Ms. Geras told me she had started baking pies at age eight. As an adult, she'd worked at a local restaurant for thirty years baking pies. The restaurant owner, of course, had deducted Social Security taxes from every paycheck, but when she turned sixty-five and filed for her benefits, she'd had no earnings history. The restaurant owner had pocketed the money. He'd never turned in a dime of it to the Social Security Administration. Ms. Geras had no Social Security credits at all and was denied Social Security and SSI benefits.

Ms. Geras had complained to the Social Security Administration and filed a police report, but nothing had happened. By that time, the restaurant had gone out of business and the owner had died. She ended up with a widow's pension from her late husband, which paid her only $300 a month. She lived on this money and a few other benefits she was poor enough to qualify for, such as food stamps and heating assistance.

"Ms. Geras, what are you doing here?"

"I flew the coop. I was sick of the nursing home, and I couldn't stand it one minute longer. I wanted out."

"I was trying to get you discharged." Guilt swept over me. *I should have tried harder.*

"Doctor, I know you tried. But things were going nowhere. My daughter didn't want me to leave, and I had had enough of that place. So I left."

"What exactly happened?"

Ms. Geras explained her escape. The patient dayroom is located just off the nurse's station, she said. The dayroom has a large cage full of birds and, "if you behave," the staff allows you to sit and watch the birds for a few hours as a reward. The room also has a large picture window that faces the parking lot.

To get to the dayroom, Ms. Geras had stayed on her best behavior. She didn't complain. She caused no trouble for the nurses or orderlies. She'd even kept quiet when getting hosed down with ice-cold water, which, Ms. Geras informed me, still happened despite my orders to the contrary. On Sunday, after a week of good behavior, she asked if she could sit in the dayroom. The head nurse agreed and told her she could go after lunch.

"I changed into street clothes and covered them as best I could with my red hospital gown. I then called a taxi and gave instructions to come to the nursing home for a pick-up. I took my house key and pocketbook, which, along with my cell phone, I had kept hidden so they wouldn't be stolen or confiscated, and wrapped them all in a blanket. When the orderly came with the wheelchair, I sat down and placed the blanket on my lap. The orderly paid no attention at all; his eyes were glued to his telephone. Once rolled out to the dayroom, I started looking at the birds but also watched the parking lot through the window. After about an hour, a cab pulled into the parking lot."

Ms. Geras had correctly surmised that the chronically under-staffed nursing home would be especially short-staffed on a Sunday. The nurse's station sat empty that afternoon. The one nurse and two orderlies on duty—for a home of 150 residents—were nowhere to be seen. Maybe they were taking care of patients. Or perhaps they were hanging out in the break room. Either way, the coast was clear.

"I got up from the wheelchair and shed my hospital gown. With keys and pocketbook in hand, I strolled past the empty nursing station to the exit. My heart was pounding. I felt like a teenager trying to sneak out of a bedroom window! I didn't know if I would be caught. But there was no staff around at all.

"I rushed to the door, but it was locked. My heart sank, and I thought my plan was going to fail. Then I saw the large sign, 'Enter 1-2-3-4 to unlock the door.' I punched in the code, a green light flashed, the door clicked open, and I walked out into the parking lot. Freedom was at hand. I slowly walked to the waiting cab to avoid drawing attention to myself. My pulse was racing, and it took all my self-control to walk instead of run. It felt like it was a thousand miles to that cab. But I made it and was driven away from my prison. It was one of the happiest moments in my life. I told the driver I was there to visit a relative. He bought it hook, line, and sinker. He also told me the nursing home was crap, and that I should get my relative out of there. No kidding."

"Sounds like you had an amazing escape plan. I'm sorry it came to that." *I knew the nursing home was terrible, and I will continue to report them.*

"Doctor, I'm not going back there. My daughter wants me to. She was furious I escaped, but I refuse. She wants to sell my house and keep the money."

Sadly, this sort of thing happens to a lot of folks in nursing homes. They get robbed by greedy family members, often their own children.

"I'm going to make a note of your refusal. As your doctor, I follow your instructions." *She's not going back there if I have anything to say about it.* Ms. Geras, despite her advanced age, was sharp. She passed a detailed mental status exam. She was fully competent and able to make her own decisions.

The visit ended. What a delightful lady. And how sharp she was compared to Dr. Essex, who was of a similar age. She was, indeed, fortunate.

"I saved you some pie," Sally reported after I exited the exam room.

"Thank you, Sally," I replied.

"That pie was fabulous," she said to Ms. Geras. "Thank you."

Ms. Geras squealed with delight at Sally's compliment. "Next time, I'll bake you two some cookies."

"Terrific!" Sally said as she enthusiastically scheduled a follow-up visit.

"There's no need to bring cookies. It's too much trouble," I countered, but Sally shot me the evil eye.

Ms. Geras smiled broadly. "It's no bother. I love making cookies." It was good to see her happy.

In the nurse's station, plenty of pie remained, and it was absolutely delicious.

✦ ✦ ✦

A patient arrived for the mundane reason, to "fill out forms." Doctors are often asked to fill out all manner of forms. It's never fun. "'Mr. Big' is ready to be seen," Sally jokingly announced. "He topped out the scale with just one foot on it." That was doubtful, and Sally had that mischievous look in her eyes. "And just wait until you see how he's carrying his forms." She sighed and shook her head. "Oh, and watch out. His kid is with him, and he's one of the children of the corn."

Great, another bratty kid.

Although not encouraged, parents often brought their children along to medical visits. Childcare was yet another of the many issues poor Mars residents faced.

"Hello, Mr. Maya. How are you doing today?" My voice was warm, but surely my face showed surprise. Sally wasn't kidding. This guy was huge. He was not as fat as Dr. Slenderman, but he was close. And he was round. Because he was so short, he was almost shaped like a sphere.

"Hello, Dr. Wave. I need some forms filled out."

A smacking sound drew my attention. His child, who had sandy brown hair and looked to be about ten, was sitting on a chair staring at a phone. And he was chewing gum—loudly. It had to be intentional as the *smack, smack, smack* was too loud and annoying not to be.

"What sort of forms do you have for me?"

Smack. Smack. Smack.

"I need a walker. I don't get around so good."

Smack. Smack. Smack.

What you need is a walk. I must help this fellow lose weight with a diet and exercise program before obesity kills him. Obesity is a serious problem nationwide but is much more common in poor regions of the nation.

Smack. Smack. Smack.

"Let me see the forms," I said. Sally's earlier comment then became clear, as he was holding the forms in his abdominal fat folds, some of which pinched together tightly.

The forms were straightforward. They authorized the use of a walker. My chart review confirmed his knees and hips were shot, undoubtedly due to his weight. And given his reported difficulty with walking, he would probably benefit from a walker.

Smack. Smack. Smack.

"Tick! Stop chewing that goddamn gum. I am sick of hearing it."

I jumped at the sound and the forms slipped from my hands, falling to the floor. Mr. Maya bellowed loudly at his son, while I picked up the papers and quickly filled them out.

Tick made no response. He continued to look at his phone and continued to smack away at the gum. In fact, it seemed even louder.

Smack. Smack. Smack.

"Goddamn it, Tick, you listen to me. Throw out that gum."

Smack. Smack. Smack.

"Don't make me get off this table. Throw it out. Now."

Smack. Smack. Smack.

"Tick!"

My mouth opened to speak. But before saying a word, Tick looked up and gave his dad a wicked grin. On the wall hung a painting depicting a wooden dock extending out into the ocean as the sun set beyond it. He took out his gum and threw it at the painting where it briefly stuck on the setting sun before falling to the floor.

"Goddamn it. I am going to smack you in the face, boy." He

started to rise from the table.

"Please don't hit your child. I understand your frustration, but I won't allow that in my exam room." As I spoke, Tick stood up and ran to his father. With a tightly balled fist, Tick hit him as hard as he could right in the testicles.

"Ooh. My nuts," Mr. Maya groaned and bent over.

Tick started screaming at the top of his lungs. "I hate you! I hate you! I hate you!" He then ran from the room.

Sally came in to see what was going on. She saw Mr. Maya doubled over and groaning and quickly assessed the situation.

"I'll follow the kid while you tend to the patient." Sally rushed down the hall after Tick.

"You alright?" I asked. "I should examine you to see if you were injured. And we also need to talk about diet and exercise. Blood work and other testing are in order."

"No, I'm fine. I just need those forms. We can talk about that stuff some other time." He sucked in a loud gasp of air. "And I better go get Tick before he burns down the building. Are you done filling them out?"

"Just about." I finished the forms and handed them to Mr. Maya as he walked out of the room.

I followed him to the waiting room, where we found his son. There, Tick was throwing toys from the pediatrics play area in every direction. Luckily, there were no other children in the room and just one adult patient who was quietly waiting. Sally positioned herself in front of the patient protecting him with her body from any stray projectiles. Wisely, she did not try to physically restrain the child as this might have escalated the situation.

"I hate you. I hate you. I hate you!" A small toy car went flying. "I hate you. I hate you. I hate you!" Tick threw a doll to the floor and stomped on her face. "I hate you. I hate you. I hate you!"

"Tick, let's go. We're done here. Let's go to McDonald's."

"McDonald's!" Tick screamed his new word and stopped throwing toys.

"Sir, we have a pediatrician here named Dr. Wurst," I said. "I think you should bring your son in for an evaluation."

"Oh, my boy already sees Dr. Wurst. He's a great doctor. He's got him on a bunch of pills. You should see how Tick acts when he doesn't take them. This is nothing."

Yikes.

Once the door had clicked shut behind Mr. Maya, Sally sighed deeply. "I told you he was a little monster."

"Nebraska is the Cornhusker State, after all," I quipped, invoking her earlier movie reference, but she didn't catch it.

"Huh?"

"*Children of the Corn!*"

She smiled. "Good one, Wavesticks!"

12
PHYSICIANS' MEETING

Doctors giggled as they filed into the conference room. A large tarp covered the floor. On it, boxes of various sizes were linked with tape—the trust maze for the team-building exercise. After Skip's introduction of the consultant, Mr. Koalemos, dressed in a crisp, black Gucci suit with a red tie, explained the procedure. It worked like this: A doctor would be blindfolded, then another doctor would guide them through the maze. At the end of the trust maze, the blindfolded doctor would fall backward to be caught by the other doctor. After the fall, coloring books would be passed out, followed by a trust-building sing-along.

The fourteen doctors who had bothered to show up for the meeting were not impressed. Dr. Slenderman spoke up promptly. "Seriously? How is this nonsense supposed to help me better care for patients?"

"It will build trust with your care team, allowing you to provide better, more integrated care."

"So walking through this maze blindfolded is going to make us all work better together? Is that what you're saying?" Slenderman's face was a picture of disbelief.

"Exactly."

"Bullshit. Do you have any data to support that this helps in the care of patients?"

"Well, it has been studied." The consultant stammered and broke out in a sweat. He had been warned Mars physicians would not be receptive.

"Doctors," Skip interjected. "This will be a fun exercise. Give it a try. Clearly, we all could use a little trust-building in this room."

Slenderman wasn't backing down. "Why? Because we won't play along with this shyster? How much are you paying for this consultant's crap?"

"He is an advisor, not a consultant," Skip stated flatly.

"Is that what we're calling them now? How much? I bet he's earning a fortune to waste our time." Slenderman frowned as the consultant squirmed. He was probably used to dealing with corporate types who would play along, kiss their CEO's ass, and walk over hot coals as ordered.

"That is not relevant."

"Right. I am not spending another second on this. I'm going to see patients." Slenderman stood up from his sofa and waddled out of the room. For Slenderman, going to see patients probably translated to eating donuts in the doctors' lounge. Three other doctors also left without comment. Only ten remained, either sitting back and enjoying the show or flicking their phone screens. This meeting was going downhill fast.

Trying to regain control, the consultant asked, "Will anyone volunteer for the trust maze?" His question was met with dead silence.

"Dr. Wurst, how about you?" Skip called out. This was an understandable selection. Dr. Wurst was agreeable for the most part.

"Skip, with all due respect, I decline to be blindfolded."

"It really will be okay, Dr. Wurst. You have to trust your fellow doctors." Although the consultant was trying to sound enthusiastic, the distress in his voice was obvious.

"Again, I decline."

"But Doctor, why? This will help us all build trust and teamwork," the consultant whined.

"I am a professional. I find it not only humiliating and demeaning to be blindfolded, but I also take issue with the very premise that this juvenile activity will somehow allow us to provide better care." With that, the wind went out of the consultant's sails. He looked glum and stopped talking.

Are those tears in his eyes?

Skip asked a couple of other doctors to participate. Dr. Lyssa stared into space after he asked her, saying nothing at first. Then she whispered the word "trust." It was creepy. The other doctors then spoke up.

"I concur with Dr. Wurst."

"I also decline."

"No way."

"I think I'll pass on Fifty Shades of Trust," someone said, send the group into whooping laughter. But neither Skip nor the horrified consultant so much as cracked a smile. It was time to throw Skip a lifeline.

"Skip, perhaps we should move on to *Get Crabby!*" I suggested. He and the consultant agreed. We skipped the trust maze, coloring books, and trust-building sing-along. The consultant took a deep breath and started talking.

"We are going to move on to the next topic. This topic is related to a book Skip would like every doctor to read. This book aims to help increase both your satisfaction on the job and patient satisfaction."

Doctors rolled their eyes as the consultant handed out the books. When the doctors saw the book cover, with its cartoon picture of a dancing crab, groans filled the room. It looked downright childish, and following the trust maze fiasco, this was going to be a hard sell.

The consultant, getting his second wind, continued. "This book is based on the experiences of crab sellers in Boston."

Doctors shook their heads, and there were a few facepalms.

"Wait a second. You are telling us that guys who sell crabs know how to run a medical practice, take care of patients, and somehow do a better job at that than all of us who have been doing this for years?" Dr. Wurst said, anger rising in his voice.

"Well, I wouldn't put it like that, Doctor. You see, these crab sellers have learned many valuable lessons in customer service and work satisfaction that can be transferred to other industries."

"So we're an industry now? I don't have customers, sir. I have patients."

"I have patients. I have patients. I have patients." Dr. Lyssa echoed a few times before returning to silence. She had placed her *Get Crabby!* book on her chair and was sitting on it like a hen on an egg.

What's wrong with her?

"It's better to call them customers or clients," the consultant quietly stated while sending a worried glance in Lyssa's direction.

"Clients? Like a lawyer?" Dr. Wurst's tone became sharp, and his face reddened. Dr. Lyssa started bouncing up and down on the book. She, too, was clearly agitated.

"Well, yes, our job is to satisfy our clients, after all."

"That might be *your* job, but it isn't my job. My job is to provide excellent, evidence-based care to my patients. My job is to do what's right, even if it doesn't satisfy the patient."

"I have patients," echoed Dr. Lyssa.

"Well, excellent care and patient satisfaction go together," the consultant said. "If you do one, you do both. The Get Crabby program will help you accomplish this."

Another doctor joined the fray. "What if a drug addict comes in demanding a narcotics prescription that isn't appropriate? He isn't going to leave satisfied." This doctor had a large primary care practice in town, and, like all primary care doctors, had to deal with drug-seeking individuals.

"Wrong. With proper explanation and discussion, you can take that difficult situation and turn it around. The patient will leave satisfied. This is exactly what the crab sellers from Boston teach us in the book."

"What planet do you come from? That is ridiculous and would never happen."

"I don't think we should look at specific cases," Skip said, chiming in. "Generally, the Get Crabby program can be immensely helpful in building client satisfaction and office morale."

"Yes, it can be immensely helpful indeed," the consultant parroted. "Doctors, have some of these." Reaching down into a bag on the floor, he pulled out crab dolls and tossed them about the room to doctors. Wurst caught the first. Several more flew to every corner of the room.

"It is a Crabby the Crab doll. I will now sing the 'Get Crabby' theme song."

The consultant began singing. It was painful to watch.

Hey! Ho! Here we go. This is how the crab song goes.
Sing it high! Sing it low! Do the crabby do-si-do.

He began dancing in a circle, snapping fingers like crab pincers.

Every crab must be the best. We will settle for nothing less.
Every crab must be a king. For this we will dance and sing.

He held his hands overhead and hit an operatic high note while dancing in place.

Whenever a crab is sold, this is what customers are told.
Best crabs only for the kettle. Second best, we will not settle.

He put one arm in a circle, signifying the top of a kettle. He tossed a toy crab into the imaginary kettle.

When we eat, we must have fun. In a circle, we will run.
Singing songs, spirits high. Getting crabby you must try.

He walked in a circle, clapping hands and singing a high note.

"Come on, doctors, join in the song and dance," the consultant called out as he sang, clapped, and walked in a circle. "Come, join me in the crab dance."

Most sat in disbelief, mortified looks on their faces.

"This is ridiculous." Dr. Wurst stood up and began gathering his things. "I never thought I would say it, but I agree with Dr. Slenderman. I'm going to see patients. Anyone want a crab doll?" He handed his doll to Dr. Lyssa. She took it and sat on it too. Dr. Wurst walked out the door. Two more doctors filed out behind him.

The consultant stopped dancing and began to speak, his voice cracking. "Who would like me to come out to their offices and do a Get Crabby presentation? Of course, be ready to do the crab dance."

Dead silence.

Skip eventually spoke up. "I think it would be a good idea to do the program in all of the offices."

"Excellent idea. Who wants to go first?"

"I nominate Dr. Slenderman," a doctor in the corner of the room suggested. More doctors spoke up volunteering Dr. Slenderman. Skip frowned and continued to hold onto his goatee, as though it were for dear life.

"I can go to his office first. Is Dr. Slenderman here?" The consultant looked around helplessly. When it was pointed out Slenderman was the first doctor to leave, his face dropped like a stone.

"You can come out to my office first," I volunteered.

Time to take one for the team. I am the medical director and as such I need to step up and lead, whether I like this program or not. And things will certainly go better in my office than Slenderman's.

"Excellent. Dr. Wave will go first," Skip quickly confirmed as the consultant gave a noticeable sign of relief. Skip smiled for the first time and released his goatee. His tired hand fell to the table.

"Skip, I suggest we do a general sign up, and then we can schedule Get Crabby program training based on that."

"Excellent idea, Dr. Wave."

The consultant was dismissed. It was time to try to cram the meeting's real business into the remaining time. There were a lot of real issues to deal with: electronic medical record problems, new rules and regulations, insurance company issues related to testing approvals…The list went on and on. Of course, there were also issues still outstanding from the last meeting.

I only had time to touch on these issues briefly, and the few remaining doctors made the same complaints as in the previous meeting. Skip assured them their concerns would be investigated, but no one believed him. After only a few minutes of discussion, the meeting was adjourned. Skip quickly pranced out the door.

"Now that's a crab dance," a doctor said to a mix of chuckling and agreement.

Doctors filed out of the room, leaving a couple of dolls and many Get Crabby! books behind. Dr. Lyssa stuffed the dolls in her pants pockets and gathered up as many of the leftover books as she could carry.

What is she going to do with all those? Is she mentally fit to practice medicine?

13
THE DOCTORS' LOUNGE

Dr. Slenderman sat eating donuts in the doctors' lounge. The usual crew of Beats and Rumpsmith sat with him around a table, and I took a seat beside them.

"That consultant is full of shit. I don't have time for his crap." Slenderman looked at me sharply. His words were almost unintelligible through his mouthful of red jelly, powder, and some sort of goo that might be cream.

"I have volunteered my office. Let's see how it goes." Turning from Slenderman, I focused on Beats. "Hey, what's up with Dr. Lyssa?"

"She's a nut," Beats replied. "The cheese has definitely slipped off the cracker."

"It slipped off the cracker a long time ago," Rumpsmith interjected. "She's crazier than House."

"You mean the doctor from the TV show?"

"We had a doctor here a couple years back who thought he was House," Slenderman said. "He dressed like House, acted like House, and he even had a fake House limp." Slenderman laughed and a puff of white powder appeared before his face.

"What did Skip do about it?"

"Nothing." Beats answered as Slenderman chewed. "He couldn't care less so long as you were billing and bringing in money to the hospital. Eventually, House had a mental breakdown, was hospitalized, and never returned. Mark my words, Lyssa is next for the loony farm."

"I'm going to meet with her in her office immediately."

Slenderman laughed again. "Your meetings are worthless."

My one-on-one meeting a few weeks earlier with Dr. Slenderman had been worthless. Refusing to sit down with me in his office, he met with me on the other side of a closed office door. A meeting with Lyssa couldn't possibly be worse.

"Best of luck, but watch out, she's a loon," warned Beats.

"Yeah, watch your step," Rumpsmith seconded.

Their comments made me nervous.

✦✦✦

Dr. Lyssa's office was not in Mars but located far from town in an adjacent county. This remoteness was one reason I had yet to visit her clinic. In hindsight, I should have made the trip sooner. Her odd comments in the spring physicians' meeting should have raised an alarm. And Sally saying she was a "known quack" also should have prompted me to visit.

But there were many offices I needed to visit. I had set a goal to visit all 200 employed physicians in their offices. But this goal, given my other administrative and patient care duties, was hard to meet. Of course, I could do chart reviews online—my review of Lyssa's charts was shocking—but nothing took the place of an on-site clinic review and one-on-one meeting with the doctor.

Dr. Lyssa was the only physician in her county. Like many rural areas in the US, there was a desperate shortage of physicians, qualified or otherwise. This led to Dr. Lyssa having a booming practice despite the fact she had no board certification and was peculiar. Patients simply had no other choice if they wanted a doctor nearby.

Lyssa's parking lot was jammed, and her waiting room was crowded. As I entered her office, Dr. Lyssa called out a patient's name. The patient stood up as Dr. Lyssa's eyes locked on me.

She pointed at the patient. "No. You wait." He sat back down. "Dr. Wave. Come! Come. Come." As I walked toward her, she kept repeating the word. When I reached her location near the waiting room door, she pulled me out of the waiting room and into the adjacent hallway, slammed the door shut, and wrapped both arms around me, squeezing me in a tight embrace.

Awkward.

"Dr. Wave, come into my office so we can be together in private." Her voice brimmed with enthusiasm.

Alone with her in the office? No way.

Warnings echoed through my mind and sweat beaded on my forehead. "I would like your nurse to accompany us."

"I don't have a nurse. I do everything myself, except reception."

No nurse? How can you see all these patients with no nurse to assist?

"Then we can talk here in the hallway."

Dr. Lyssa grabbed my hand and pulled me toward her office. Hard. "Come on, baby," she mewed.

Baby?

"Dr. Lyssa, this behavior is inappropriate. I came here today to talk about your charting, billing, and behavior in our physicians' meetings. And now this? You need an immediate psychological evaluation." *And if she's behaving like this toward me, her medical director, how is she behaving toward patients?*

"Behavior?" Dr. Lyssa seemed confused. She repeated the word a few times, then lunged forward and seized my crotch with a surprisingly strong hand.

"Hey!" My back slammed against the waiting room door. Panic swept over me. Turning, I ripped open the door and fled back into the crowded waiting room. With an aching groin and a pounding heart, I waited for my composure to slowly return. Patients looked on with baffled expressions.

After a few minutes, the door opened again. Dr. Lyssa nonchalantly called out a patient name and once again the named patient stood up. She then looked toward me and winked.

Leaving Dr. Lyssa's office, my mind raced.

Report the assault to Skip? Waste of time and counterproductive. But she needed a psychological evaluation and should not be seeing patients unsupervised. Without Skip's approval, I could not take any significant action. And I also needed to report the charting irregularities.

Report her to the police? What exactly would I say? It was a clear-cut assault, but would they believe me? My stomach knotted up.

No police report was filed. But with mixed feelings, I scheduled an emergency meeting with Skip for the next morning.

+++

"Why are we here?" Skip sounded annoyed as I arrived early the next morning, so I started with the charts.

"I have concerns about Dr. Lyssa's charting and billing. I have reviewed her charts. She has completed only ten percent of her notes from all visits in the last six months. Ten percent! And of the ten percent she did complete, the notes are often either incomplete or contain little information. And yet she billed at the highest level for almost all these visits, even the ones with no office note. There's no way her documentation supports this level of billing."

"Now... Dr. Wave." A deep frown creased Skip's face. "She is very productive. She sees more than sixty patients a day. I'm sure she will get to the notes."

"Policy states—"

"For a doctor generating her level of billing, we make exceptions."

The policy stated all notes had to be completed the same day as the visit, without exception. "If we are ever audited—"

"We will deal with that in the unlikely event it happens. But don't worry. Auditors never travel to backwoods Nebraska." Skip irritably picked at his goatee with one hand. The other hand nervously picked at his bald head.

Doesn't he know that audits these days are done electronically? The days of paper charts and on-site reviews are over. Does he care?

"And you had no business looking at her charts. None."

"As the medical director—"

"Let me be very clear here. You are not to look at charts again. I'm sick of it. Are we done here, Dr. Wave?"

"You've heard her comments in physicians' meetings," I said. After the words "physicians' meeting," an even darker look flashed across Skip's face.

I went on. "Her comments are bizarre. I insist on a psychological evaluation. I am concerned about her mental well-being. And we should monitor her interaction with patients. Given her strange behavior, she should not be seeing patients unsupervised."

"Out of the question. She's a top biller. She bills a lot more than you, that's for sure. This meeting is over."

"There is one more thing."

"This meeting is over." Skip got up and pranced out of the office.

So much for telling him about the assault. Why bother even reporting it? Skip will do nothing. No point in reporting anything. I give up.

+ + +

I proceeded to my office after the failed meeting, and Sally noted my dejection immediately.

"What's wrong, Wavesticks? You don't look so good."

"Well, I had a meeting with Skip…" Sally listened to the full story of the irregularities in billing, the visit to Dr. Lyssa's office, and the crotch grab.

Sally looked horrified. "Dr. Wave, that's terrible! You are going to take action, right now." Calling me Dr. Wave instead of Wavesticks was a sure sign she was dead serious. She picked up the phone. "I'm calling the police."

"Sally—"

"You are reporting that nutcase to the cops. You have to. What if she's assaulted other people? Did you think of that?"

I felt ashamed. I had thought of that but lacked the courage to act immediately. Sally was correct. Lyssa's conduct had to be reported. And Sally didn't stop with a phone call. While waiting for the police to arrive from the neighboring county, she printed out a form and handed it to me.

"What's this?"

"It's a reporting form for the Office of the Inspector General. You're going to report her irregular billing too. You're the medical director, and you need to do what's right. If you don't, who will?"

I nodded and got started. By the time the police had arrived, I was signing my name to the form. Sally mailed it to the Office of the Inspector General that afternoon.

The police took my statement, and they took it seriously. Unlike the Mars Police Department, which had an unsavory reputation, the department in the next county was highly respected. One of their officers, in fact, had recently received a national award from the US Marshals as the nation's law enforcement officer of the year.

An arrest warrant was issued a few days later. Dr. Lyssa was allowed to turn herself in. Fortunately, the detailed investigation that followed found no evidence of previous patient assaults. I was the only one she'd grabbed. To avoid prosecution, Dr. Lyssa agreed to a psychological evaluation and treatment. The details of her arrest and plea agreement were public and they were also reported to both the state licensing board and Mars Hospital. My identity as a victim, however, was kept confidential.

The medical licensing board did nothing. The Office of the Inspector General did nothing. And Skip, of course, did nothing. He refused to take any action that might impede her "level of billing," and steadfastly refused my recommendation that she only be allowed to practice under supervision. Dr. Lyssa continued seeing sixty-plus patients a day in the office. But at least she was getting psychological evaluation and treatment.

I sent several more letters to the Nebraska medical licensing board and the Office of the Inspector General.

None were answered.

14
OFFICE INTERLUDE

Sally and I both were excited this patient had finally showed up for his visit. He had missed several prior appointments. The mystery, at last, would be solved. Why, oh why, does he look like a pig?

Sally tried to hide her smile. "He's ready."

"What's so funny?"

"He does." A little snort escaped from her, and she covered her mouth. "He does look like a pig. And he smells like one too. This guy stinks. He's filthy. Be careful. He probably has cooties. Good luck, Wavesticks."

Hopefully, cooties are the worst of his problems.

"Good afternoon. What can I do for you?"

A chubby fellow, wearing denim bib overalls, was sitting on the exam table. He had a round face and a flat, squished-in nose that looked like a snout. He was bald, except for a small tuft of white hair on the top of his head. And boy, did he stink. His overalls were filthy, and he even had dust bunnies on his shoulders.

"Doc, why do I look like a pig?"

"What, exactly, do you mean?"

"Don't lie to me, man. Look at me. Look at this face. Just look at my pig nose."

"You are overweight. Perhaps a diet—"

"A diet isn't going to fix my nose."

"Has it ever been broken?"

"A few times, in bar fights."

"Well, that might be the explanation. A surgeon could fix your nose."

"And why do I stink? Everyone tells me I stink like a pig."

"When did you last shower or bathe?"

"I don't know. It's been a while."

"How often do you change your clothes?" A thick crust of filth covered his overalls.

"Every few weeks, I guess."

"Daily showers and daily changing of clothes will help greatly with the odor."

An incredulous look appeared on his face. "You want me to shower and change clothes every single day?"

"Yes." *Some people in this town really hate showers and laundry.*

"So you think showers, changing clothes, a diet, and a nose job will do the trick? Then I won't look like a pig?"

"It would be a good start."

"Let me ask you something, Dr. Wave. Am I turning into a pig? Like from a curse or something?"

"What do you mean?"

"I mean like a voodoo hex or curse or witch's spell or something like that. Am I really turning into a pig?"

Oh, my goodness. I tried to hide a smile. "No, sir. Neither voodoo nor witchcraft are responsible for your problem."

"Are you sure?"

"I guarantee it."

He sighed deeply in relief. "Thanks, Dr. Wave. As long as you're sure."

He declined a surgical referral for his nose. All he really wanted was reassurance he wasn't changing into a pig. Sally found that hilarious.

"I don't know, Wavesticks," she said after he left. "Maybe the Wicked Witch of Mars has him in her crosshairs. Or maybe he pissed off a Martian voodoo queen. I've heard stranger things. Isn't this town something?"

"Yes, it is something."

+++

A patient presented with the visit reason of "I have a cold." This was not unusual, except for the location of said cold—his ass. "I have a cold in my ass" were the patient's exact words when making his appointment. Despite me bringing the matter up several times, Skip had steadfastly refused changing the policy regarding how patient visits were listed. The policy was still to obey the consultants and dictate reasons for visits in patients' exact words.

Sally's report did nothing to shed light on the mysterious cold. "He won't tell me a thing; he only wants to talk about it with you."

I entered the room with trepidation. The patient, a slim, middle-aged gentleman dressed in faded blue jeans and a grubby white tank top, looked visibly uncomfortable. As he fidgeted, he twiddled his long, brown hair.

"Good morning," I said. "What can I do for you today?"

"I don't want to talk about it."

"I'm sorry, but we have to talk about it for me to help you. What seems to be the trouble?"

"I have a cold."

"Tell me about your cold."

"It's in my ass."

"I'm not sure what you mean. What, exactly, are your symptoms?"

"You know how, when you catch a cold, you get a sore throat?"

"Yes."

"My ass has a sore throat."

"You mean you have pain in your anal area?"

"My what?"

"Your butthole." After I switched to Mars vernacular, the patient's face lit up with understanding.

"Yeah, it's sore all the time. When I take a dump, it kills me."

"Are you passing blood?" Anal pain has many causes. The most serious among them is cancer. Anal cancers usually also have bleeding.

"I don't look."

"Have you seen any blood? Perhaps on the toilet paper?"

"No."

Standard questions continued. Then it was time for the next step. "I need to do an examination."

"Can't you just give me an antibiotic?"

"I need to see what the problem is before I can prescribe anything."

"My last doctor never had to examine me."

That's disturbing. The patient reluctantly agreed to an exam, during which the cause of his discomfort became immediately apparent. A thick forest of venereal warts surrounded his anus. They were classic in appearance. He must have had them for a long time and had been suffering for quite a while.

"Alright. Here's what I see. You have venereal warts. These are causing your pain. The good news is they can be removed. I will make a referral for this procedure. You won't have to keep suffering." Immediate laser or surgical treatment was needed. His case of anal warts was so awful, it could be in a textbook.

"Venereal warts? You mean like VD?"

"Yes."

"Well, how did I get them?"

"In order to understand this, we need to discuss sexual matters. The most likely way warts such as these are contracted is unprotected anal sex with men."

"What are you saying? You calling me queer?" His face turned a deep shade of red. This clearly was sensitive ground for him.

"I'm not calling you anything. I'm asking, are you having unprotected sex with men?"

Silence.

"It would be wise to test you for other STDs," I added.

"You mean like AIDS? You think I'm queer and have AIDS? I'm married!"

Marriage proved nothing, especially in a religiously conservative and homophobic town like Mars. And he still had not answered my question about sex with men. "I am not saying you have AIDS. I *am* saying we must test you for sexually transmitted diseases."

"There has to be some other way I could have got this. Could it have been from sitting on a toilet? I sat on a toilet at a highway rest stop. Everyone knows queers sit on those all the time. Maybe I got it from that?"

"This is not spread from toilet seats at the rest stop." *But having unprotected sex at a highway rest stop might be a bingo.*

"There has got to be some other way I got this. What the hell am I going to tell my wife?"

"You don't have to tell her anything. Your medical visit is confidential."

"She already knows I'm seeing you for a cold in my ass. What can I tell her?"

"Tell her it's an infection. Warts are, in fact, a form of viral infection."

He shook his head. "Telling her I have an ass infection sounds bad."

"We will do some blood tests and a urine test to check you out for other infections." He agreed to additional testing. The visit ended with a detailed discussion on safer sex, a referral for laser surgery to remove the warts, and a recommendation to avoid sexual relations until the test results were in.

The next day, when the test results arrived, Sally called him back to the office. He came in immediately and was very distressed. Every patient knows you are not called back in for test results the next day if the results are good.

"What's the bad news, Dr. Wave?" He paced back and forth in the exam room. "It's AIDS, isn't it? I got AIDS." He looked near to tears.

"No. That's the really, really, good news. You are HIV negative."

He heaved a sigh of relief and grinned, then his brows knitted again. "Wait. I got something else, don't I?"

I nodded. "Yes. You have a few different infections."

The color drained from his face. "A few? How many?"

"All of them can be treated."

"How many?"

I took a breath. "You have hepatitis C. You also have syphilis, gonorrhea, and chlamydia." He was relieved to learn all of these were curable with antiviral and antibacterial treatment.

"At least I don't have AIDS."

"Yes. And it is imperative that all your sexual contacts receive testing, including your wife, who must receive testing immediately. The lab has automatically notified the public health department in accordance with Nebraska health regulations and contact tracing will begin."

"Doctor! You can't tell my wife. You gonna tell her I take it in the ass? She will lose her mind. It's not even true! I don't do it with dudes. You know that, right?"

Right. "It's required that all your sexual contacts be notified. Details on specific behaviors are not included in the notification, nor is your identity."

"I don't sleep with no one but my wife." He folded his arms and looked down at his tapping foot.

He is lying.

"It is essential you give a list of contacts. The Department of Public Health will also be contacting you. You must give names."

He stuck with his story. "I only sleep with my wife."

Antibiotics to treat his gonorrhea, syphilis, and chlamydia were started that day. And Sally made a referral to a specialist for treatment of his hepatitis C. A few weeks later, the Department of Public Health contacted me. The patient, with reluctance, had finally given the department information on his contacts. In addition to his wife, he listed eight men and six women as sexual contacts. He was a veritable venereal disease super-spreader. All these people, many of whom were my patients, were tested and treated.

+++

A few days after receiving the follow-up from the Department of Public Health, a ruckus occurred at the front desk. Sally ran breathlessly to my office to report.

"A lady is yelling in the waiting room. She's demanding to see you."

"Is she a patient?"

"Nope. She's the ass guy's wife."

"Who?"

"The guy with the warts on his ass. The STD guy." Medical personnel, unfortunately, often refer to patients by their diseases and often use coarse terminology. It's not proper, but it's a hard habit to change.

"Great." My stomach tightened on the walk to the front desk. *What does she want?* "Hello, ma'am. I would be happy to speak with you."

Sally led her to an exam room and accompanied me on the visit. In delicate scenarios, it's wise to have a chaperone act as witness whenever there is the slightest chance of misunderstanding or false accusations regarding exams or discussions.

Once we'd closed the exam room door, I asked, "What may I do for you?"

"I want to know the names of my husband's concubines."

That's what she called them—not mistresses, girlfriends, or lovers—concubines. The choice of words was both interesting and unexpected.

"I'm afraid I don't have anything to give you. And even if I did have names, I wouldn't be able to release them due to patient confidentiality."

"You're lying! I want the names of those concubines, and I want them now. Every time I see a lady in this town, I wonder if she's one of them. It's driving me crazy. I have to know. I'm going to kill them!"

Her comments weren't making me more inclined to release names. "I understand you're upset. But you shouldn't talk about killing anyone."

"Those little sluts gave me the clap. They gave me chlamydia." She explained how she tested positive for gonorrhea and chlamydia. She was, fortunately, negative for syphilis and hepatitis C. It was interesting she said "the concubines" had given her gonorrhea and chlamydia and not her husband. The blame was his.

"Ma'am, what is important is that you're getting treatment. You should expect a full recovery."

"What's important is that I break the necks of those slutty little whores. Now who were they?" She began rattling off unfamiliar names. Sally's eyes glowed with humor at her colorful language.

"I don't know any of those people, ma'am." They were all female names. Her husband probably hadn't told her he was bisexual.

"Those are the town sluts." The Mars town gossip I'd met weeks ago came to mind. She probably knew the name of every "town slut" of her generation. As did Sally, from the look in her eyes.

"As I said, I don't know any names. You should be having this conversation with your husband."

"My husband is a dog in heat. He humps anything that moves. And he won't tell me names. He says he doesn't want to cause any trouble."

That is probably wise.

"I think you should stop trying to find out who you should blame and consider marriage counseling."

"Marriage counseling my ass. I want to counsel those little home-wreckers with my fists."

"I understand you are terribly upset. But as I said, I will give you no names. Do you understand this?"

"Yeah, I understand. I understand you're useless." At that, she got up and left the office. Relief swept over me.

"Boy, was she pissed," Sally said after the wife had exited the building.

"That's the understatement of the day. Did you know any of the names she rattled off?"

"Yes."

"Who are they?"

Sally smiled slyly. "Let's just say the woman knows her gossip."

The visit was documented with great care and Sally recorded as witness. Fortunately, this lady neither murdered nor beat up any town sluts or concubines—at least, we didn't hear about it or read it in the news.

✦✦✦

Sally held a plate of cookies in her hands as she walked by my office. "Ms. Geras is pretty upset, but she still brought treats."

"What is she upset about?"

"The hospital sent her a great big bill. She brought it along."

Why a big bill? She's on Medicare. My mind raced as I walked to the exam room.

"Hello, Ms. Geras. How are you today?" My voice was cheerful. Ms. Geras's was not.

"Not very well at all, Dr. Wave. Look at this." She handed me a thick envelope containing a bill from Mars Hospital, pages and pages long. "They want to take all my money."

The envelope contained an itemized bill from her recent hospital stay. Before my arrival in Mars, she had been in the hospital for three days with pneumonia. Medicare pays for nursing home treatment if a patient stays in the hospital for three days or more. Like many Medicare patients hospitalized, she stayed precisely three days and was then discharged to the nursing home. This suspicious pattern often suggests criminal billing fraud.

The hospital bill listed a vast array of charges. She was billed for several thousand dollars out of pocket, making the total much larger. Her out-of-pocket costs included her co-pay amount and various uncovered services such as a television, phone, and a private room.

"Look at that bill. They charged me fifteen dollars for a Tylenol.

Fifteen dollars!" There it was, on page seven, a fifteen-dollar charge. "And they didn't even give me one! And they also charged me six dollars and twenty-five cents for the nurse to give me the pill. Which she never did. And they charged me eight dollars for a tissue, which I never received." *Eight bucks for a tissue?* Ms. Geras went on and on. She had reviewed her bill in detail, and many crazy charges were very questionable.

"And they are charging me for a private room. Doctor, another lady shared my room. It was not private. How can they charge me for all these things I never got?" The private room charge was a big part of her out-of-pocket costs.

"They certainly can't," I said. "But they appear to have done so. This must be an error."

"That's what I thought, but when I called the hospital, the lady on the phone said I was wrong and had been in a private room. How do I prove I wasn't?"

"There must be a record somewhere. Do you have secondary insurance?" Secondary insurance is what Medicare patients can purchase to cover extra charges. But it isn't cheap.

"I can't afford it. I barely have enough money to eat."

Feeling a pang of guilt about the cookies, I was saddened that she was so poor despite working hard her whole life.

"And take a look at this." She handed me another stack of bills in a variety of differently sized envelopes. "These are bills from other doctors. I never saw any of them!"

There were bills from a variety of specialists—including doctors of lungs, kidneys, and infectious diseases—and a surgeon. At Mars Hospital, like at most hospitals, doctors billed separately from the hospital, adding to billing confusion and complexity. But in this case, the surgeon was Dr. Slenderman. That especially struck me as odd.

Why would a general surgeon see her when she was in the

hospital for pneumonia?

"Are you sure you didn't see any of these doctors?"

"I swear it. My old doctor came in every morning, and we would talk a little bit, and then he would go. He is the only doctor I saw, and he didn't even send me a bill." Her prior doctor was the previous medical director. He must have died before he'd sent out a bill.

"Do you recall seeing a heavyset doctor who performs surgery?" I asked.

"Who, Slenderman? No, he never came to see me. I would remember that fat slob."

"You know him?"

"Yes, he practically killed my daughter. I would have thrown him out of the room if he came in." She explained Slenderman had performed a colonoscopy, a minor outpatient procedure in which a fiber-optic scope inspects the colon. But it had gone horribly wrong. He'd ruptured the patient's colon. Her daughter had almost died from this usually safe and straightforward procedure.

"Well, it certainly seems like there were some billing errors made. Did you call these doctors?"

"I called everyone. The hospital gave me the runaround. They told me they don't make mistakes, and that I had to pay the bill. They said they would send me to a collection agency if I didn't pay up."

That's a bit heavy-handed.

"And none of the doctors would even talk to me when I called. I talked only to whoever answers the phones. And they all said I must be mistaken."

"I tell you what, Ms. Geras, I will make a few calls and investigate the matter for you." *It's the least I can do for the pies and cookies.*

"Thank you, Dr. Wave. My daughter says I'll have to sell the house to pay the bill."

"I cannot imagine we can't work out some way for the hospital to waive the bill, especially given all the errors," I said, trying to reassure her. Mars Hospital was a not-for-profit charity, which means it was tax-exempt. In return for this considerable tax savings, the hospital was required to provide free or reduced-price care for the poor. And Ms. Geras was undoubtedly poor.

When the office visit was finished, Sally listened intently to the story while munching on a cookie. "They are real ball-breakers here," she said. "Mars Hospital is all about the money. They do this kind of shit all the time. It's a disgrace. It's time you did something about it."

"You're right. I will."

"Go Wavesticks!" Sally cheered, lifting a half-eaten cookie in the air.

15

AT THE HOSPITAL

The next day, my investigation into Ms. Geras's bill began. First stop—the billing department. Finding the office was difficult. It was located in the sub-basement of the hospital, through a maze of unmarked hallways. To make things more difficult, these hallways were blocked with wheelchairs, beds, boxes, and medical equipment. This clutter was certainly unsafe, likely a code violation, and could lead to a citation from the Inspection Commission, one of the many quasi-governmental bodies that certifies hospitals.

If, that is, Mars Hospital was ever caught. Sally had told me that whenever the Inspection Commission or any other certifying body arrived, advanced warning was always given. An alarm would go out before the inspectors arrived, and the staff would clear hallways and hide as many other violations as possible. Mars Hospital almost always achieved high scores on these inspections and therefore earned the Inspection Commission's rubber stamp, valid for two years. Of course, as soon as the certifying body left, things would immediately revert to normal, and the violations would return. The whole Inspection Commission certification process was theater and a big joke.

A variety of odd looks were cast at me while I navigated the clutter. Doctors rarely came this way, and the workers must have wondered what was up. Finally, at the end of one' long, messy hallway, there was a windowless closed door concisely labeled BILLS. *This must be it.* Inside, the room was dimly lit and dreary. One small counter stood empty a few steps from the door. Behind it, a few ladies were sitting at desks. They didn't even look at me when I entered.

"One of my patients has complained to me about her bill," I announced. "I was wondering if I could speak to someone here and get them to look at her charges?"

Silence. I walked to the counter. After repeating the same question twice, one lady stood up and slowly walked over. She had short white hair, horn-rimmed glasses, and a deep frown.

"Who complained?"

"Her name is Ms. Geras."

"Oh, her. She has called several times complaining. I told her the bill is fine."

"She claims she was charged for some things she didn't receive, like a private room."

The lady crossed her arms and frowned even deeper. "She's wrong. I looked at her bill. It's fine. She had a private room."

"She says she was in with another patient."

"She's wrong. She probably has Alzheimer's and hallucinated."

"That is not the case, I assure you." My tone turned angry. "There are other errors in the bill as well. Many of them, in fact."

"I told you, the bill is fine."

"If you looked at the bill, you would see on page seven a Tylenol was charged. How do you know it was given? Did anyone look at the chart?" The patient chart would have a log of all medications given. This could be cross-referenced with the bill.

"We don't have time to look at charts. We're busy." The office was quiet, and no one seemed particularly well-occupied. One lady was filing her nails.

"Well, maybe I should take a look."

"For a Tylenol? It's just one charge." Her face made it clear she thought a madman stood before her.

"It's a fifteen-dollar charge, which is high for one Tylenol tablet, by the way. And she had other billing concerns. There were a variety of errors, large and small."

"The bill is fine. We don't make errors."

Nonsense. Hospital bills were notorious for being riddled with errors. One study found 80 percent of all hospital bills contained errors. Of course, this study must be wrong because that would mean 20 percent of hospital bills were actually correct.

"She is being billed for thousands of dollars, despite being on Medicare," I said. "If that bill stands, it will destroy her financially. We should at least make sure the bill is correct."

"She should have Medicare supplemental insurance. Then she wouldn't have to worry about the bill. It's not my fault she doesn't have proper insurance."

"I didn't say it was your fault. But this bill is going to be impossible to pay."

"She can get on a payment plan."

"She only gets three hundred dollars a month from a widow's pension."

"That can't be right. No one can live on that."

"She does. It's all she has."

"Well, she has to pay up. Either she pays, gets on a payment plan, or we send her bill to collections."

"She could lose her house."

"She has a house? If she has assets, she certainly can pay."

This was going nowhere; this biller had no sympathy whatsoever. Time to change my approach.

"Do we have a charity care program?"

"Yes. As a nonprofit, we are required to have a charity care program," she replied.

Like many nonprofits, Mars Hospital kept the program as quiet and infrequently used as possible.

"I think Ms. Geras would qualify. Is there any way she can be enrolled?"

"She owns a house. She would not qualify as you cannot have assets of more than six hundred dollars."

"The asset limit is only six hundred dollars? That seems rather harsh."

"That's the policy."

"Are there any ways around this? Any exceptions?"

"No. She has to pay, or it's off to collections." The lady started walking back to her desk. This conversation was clearly over.

Discouraged, my next stop was medical records, where Ms. Geras's chart from her hospital visit could be accessed. The chart review was stunning.

It was a short hospital stay. She had pneumonia. But her vitals were stable, and her hospital course unremarkable. It was perplexing that she stayed three days. Even an overnight stay was unjustified. Clearly, she had stayed precisely three days to qualify her for Medicare coverage and for a nursing home transfer. Although illegal, doctors and hospitals do this sort of thing all the time.

It was also odd that although numerous consults were ordered, there were no actual consult notes in the chart. The consultations were ordered, including a surgery consult from Dr. Slenderman. But nowhere in the chart was any documentation showing the consultants had seen the patient. Nor was any specialty treatment ordered or received.

And the medication log proved Ms. Geras right—she had received no Tylenol. The fifteen-dollar charge was flat-out incorrect. Many other things showing up in the bill were not in the medical record. All she had received was three days of IV antibiotics, three visits from her primary care doctor, and meal delivery. There were no therapy notes, no x-rays ordered, and no blood work drawn. But there were charges for all these things in her bill. And no order was written for a private room. Again, Ms. Geras was right. She was being squeezed.

My next stop was the doctors' lounge to track down Slenderman and perhaps some of the other mystery consultants who'd charged Ms. Geras for visits never performed. These charges ran into thousands of dollars, and Ms. Geras was responsible for 20 percent of the total. *What will Slenderman and the other doctors say?*

✚✚✚

Slenderman announced my entrance. "Here comes trouble." He was talking to Beats, and there were several other physicians in the lounge. Everyone became quiet. It was disconcerting. Every doctor in the unusually crowded lounge, except me, held a goody bag. Drug reps, despite my almost weekly protests to Skip at our regular meetings, had continued to visit the hospital. Today, just outside the doctors' lounge, they were giving away gift certificates for local restaurants, free car washes, free oil changes, and many other things. The goody bags included pens, magnets, and candy. According to the American Medical Association code of ethics, gifts from drug reps that are primarily of benefit to patients and have no substantial value, such as pens and notepads, are acceptable. But the gift certificates clearly had value and were of no benefit to patients whatsoever. These were solely to influence physicians' prescribing habits and, in addition to being clearly unethical, the gifts violated federal anti-kickback laws. The drug reps today were pushing some new blood pressure pill that cost several hundred dollars a month more than the inexpensive generic drug they would have it replace. This was appalling to me, but I had more important business.

"Did you come here to talk to me about that dumbass crab program? I don't want them coming to my office." Slenderman, who was collecting unwanted candy from other doctors' goody bags, must have been told he had been volunteered for a Get Crabby visit.

"Actually, I'm coming here to talk to you about Ms. Geras."

"Who?" Slenderman's lips narrowed as I explained the case. He was clearly annoyed. "Look, this is the way it works around here. Her previous doctor was old school. Whenever he admitted a patient, he would consult everyone. That's just how he did it. He gave us all business and supported our practices and income. He cared. Unlike you."

"Did you actually see the patient?"

"I don't remember. Maybe. I might have stuck my head in and saw she didn't need surgery."

"But you sent her a bill. A rather large one."

"Look, don't start causing trouble. Why are you digging around in charts anyway?"

"She's my patient."

"Maybe we should start digging around in your charts to see how you practice. Watch out. What goes around, comes around."

This is not going well. Clearly, he bills fraudulently. And this seems a widespread problem.

"I am trying to get to the bottom of this. This poor old lady got slammed with a bunch of bills for services she didn't receive. I think you should drop the bill." Doctors started quickly filing out of the lounge.

"Fine. I will. What's her name?"

"Geras."

He wrote it down. "Anything else?"

"Thanks for taking care of the bill." *And let's hope there isn't anything else.* Later, I confronted the other consultants who had fraudulently billed Ms. Geras, and they all canceled their bills too.

False billing gets doctors thrown in jail and hospitals closed. So for this reason and the sake of protocol, I filed an incident report and copied it to Skip. But more importantly, I immediately reported this clear case of Medicare fraud to the Office of the Inspector General.

It made Sally proud.

16
OFFICE INTERLUDE

Sally handed me a stack of papers. "Your next patient wants you to fill out these forms so he can get Social Security disability. I wonder what other free stuff he'll want." We had patients coming in all the time with forms for disability or free stuff.

"What's his disability?"

"You'll love this one. He says he has high blood pressure." His medical history showed it only slightly elevated at 140/90—insufficient for Social Security. And he was a young guy, aged twenty-eight, with an obvious cause of the elevation. When Sally weighed him, she found him medically obese.

"Looks like he needs a diet, not disability."

"Yep, he's a fatty. He's also a human chimney. Good luck."

Entering the exam room, I was hit by the overpowering stench of cigarette smoke. The patient was sitting on the exam table. He had curly red hair, was short and fat, and had an angry scowl twisted his face.

I made my voice as cheerful as I could. "Good morning."

"You got my papers?"

"Right here." I held up the forms.

"You fill them out yet?"

"First, let's talk. What kind of issues are you facing at work?"

He heaved a big sigh. "Well, it's like this. I have high blood pressure. When I go to work, it goes up because my boss is an ass."

"A couple of things could remedy that situation. You could stop smoking and start a diet to lose some weight. If you stopped smoking and we were able to get your weight down, this would likely control your blood pressure."

"But my boss would still be an ass. He makes me so angry."

"I understand. If necessary, we could control your blood pressure with medications. That's good news for the short term. While it is mildly elevated, it should be easy to get under control, giving you time and energy to stop smoking and lose weight so that in the long term, your blood pressure could be controlled without medications."

His deepening scowl suggested he didn't think this was good news.

"What about the forms? I need that disability cash."

"Sir, Social Security disability is for people who are unable to work any job. I understand you don't get along with your boss. But that fact and mildly elevated blood pressure are not, in my opinion, qualifiers for disability."

"What are you saying? I gotta work?"

"I don't think disability is appropriate here. You have a condition that millions of people have, and we're just starting treatment. I'm confident we can control your high blood pressure."

"But I told you it's my boss! My blood pressure goes through the roof when I see him. I can't work there."

"Then you might want to consider finding a different job. But not getting along with your boss doesn't qualify you for Social Security disability."

"Can't you just fill out those papers? I just came here for my disability."

This wasn't going well. The Get Crabby consultant came to mind. He would want me to satisfy this "client." It was clear this guy wanted Uncle Sam to send him a check so he didn't have to work. And nothing short of certifying a nonexistent disability would satisfy him. But ethically, certifying his claim was out of the question. This fellow simply did not qualify, and it would be wrong to pretend otherwise. Perhaps explaining things in accordance with the Get Crabby program would help.

"I am sorry, but in my opinion, you do not have a disabling condition. We can treat, manage, and even cure this problem. You're a young man. We'll do interventions now before you permanently damage your body from smoking, excess weight, and high blood pressure. Interventions now will be lifesaving." My voice brimmed with optimism.

"You've got to fill out the forms, man." He wasn't listening.

"I'm sorry, sir. I just don't think it's appropriate."

"You're not gonna do it?" His voice rose.

"What I can do is start some medications for your blood pressure—"

He began to shout. "Fill out my forms *right now*, or I'll..." As he shouted, his face turned beet red. No doubt, his blood pressure was also skyrocketing.

"Please calm down, sir. Relax a moment. I need to listen to your heart and lungs and perform an exam. Then we can talk more about treatment."

He continued to shout. "I don't need *treatment*! I need those *forms*!"

If he doesn't calm down, I'm going to ask him to leave.

"Sir, you must calm down. This is not helpful."

"*You* aren't helpful, you ass. You are a fucking piss-poor worthless sack of S-H-I-T, shit!"

Remain calm. My teeth were clenched.

Since he'd cursed at me, there could be no physician-patient relationship. Physician-patient relationships are founded on mutual trust. "I'm very sorry you feel that way. Given your lack of confidence in my abilities, I think it best you find a different doctor to care for you. I'm going to have to ask you to leave." So much for getting crabby.

"I am *not* leaving until you fill out those forms." He folded his arms across his chest and sat there scowling.

Time to step out into the hall and let him cool off. "Alright. You sit tight, and I'll be right back."

Sally met me in the hallway. "You alright? I heard yelling."

"The patient is unhappy I won't fill out his disability forms. He is refusing to leave until I fill out the forms."

"Guess we'll have to call the cops on him."

"I hope it doesn't come to that. Let's give him a little time to cool off."

"It's up to you, but we are going to have to call the cops. He won't leave. Trust me."

Time passed. Other patients came and went. And he remained holed up in the exam room, which I needed. Space was tight. It was time to talk to him again.

"Hello?" My voice was cautious as I snuck back in. "I gave you some time to collect yourself. We can talk a little more if you like."

"You going to fill out those forms?"

After another lengthy explanation, his only response was, "I am not leaving without the forms."

"Sir, this is inappropriate. I offered to start treatment, and you declined. I already told you I will not certify a disability, so this visit is over. I request that you leave right now."

"You want me to go? Easy. Fill out the forms."

"I am asking you for the last time, please leave voluntarily."

"Not without those forms."

"I'll call the police."

"The police? You're going to call the *cops* on me? I should call them on you, you A-S-S, ass." His face turned red again. I opened the exam room door and gave Sally the order.

"You can go ahead and call them," I said, as calmly as I could.

"Good," the patient said. "I'm glad. I'm going to report you for not filling out these damned forms."

"They said they're on the way," Sally replied.

Then the patient really started yelling. "Fuck! You ass!"

"There's still time to leave." I checked my watch. "The police will take about five minutes."

"Fuck you! Fill out the forms."

I must admit, he is persistent.

He waited it out, and soon the sound of sirens filled the air. Two Mars police officers entered the waiting room, and Sally told them the story. One of the officers ran the fellow's name and, sure enough, he had an outstanding arrest warrant. Apparently, he had not shown up to court for a minor traffic ticket, and the judge had issued a bench warrant for his arrest. This was a common way folks in Mars ended up in the hoosegow.

"Don't worry, Dr. Wave," one of the officers told me as they approached the exam room. "This guy's going to jail."

The officers entered, and the patient shouted, "Officers, arrest the doctor! He won't fill out my forms. Arrest him!" The cops laughed, cuffed him, and took him away without incident. He continued demanding I fill out the forms as they walked him to their squad car.

He was subsequently charged with trespassing in addition to the outstanding warrant from the unpaid traffic ticket. When he was booked at the police station, a small quantity of cocaine was found in his pocket. This discovery added a drug charge. No wonder his blood pressure was high.

The patient ended up being held in jail as he could not make bail. He lost his job as a result of his jail stay. While this didn't make me happy, it did at least solve the friction he'd been having with his boss, and I felt lucky. As distressing as it was, the situation could have been a lot worse.

What if the patient had brandished a weapon? What if he had assaulted Sally or me?

After stewing on this for a few minutes, I said "Sally, we should have panic buttons installed in the clinic."

"Good idea," she said. "Someday one of these crazies is going to flip out and hurt someone. And that someone will be you."

"I'll ask Skip about it at our next meeting."

Sally gave me a doubtful look.

+ + +

"Saloon Sally is ready," Sally said a few hours later while eyeing the chart she held.

"Any relation?"

"Very funny. That's what everyone calls her. She runs Sal's, the saloon down by the canal. You ever go there for a nightcap?"

"No." Sal's Saloon had a reputation. Every weekend an array of bar fights occurred, followed by several arrests. We always made sure to check the crime blotter on Mondays, looking for patients in jail and thus unlikely to show for medical appointments.

"It doesn't seem like your kind of place anyway," Sally said, "and she runs a tattoo parlor in the back. She does them herself. You got any tats, Wavesticks?" She winked.

"I'm afraid of needles," I confessed, a revelation that seemed to surprise Sally.

In the exam room, Saloon Sally sat quietly. She wore a tank top and shorts and looked to be more than her sixty years of age, with long, stringy, gray hair and dry, wrinkled skin. She was well-muscled, clearly physically active, and covered in tattoos.

A tattoo for a band called the Insane Clown Posse was on one arm. A tattoo of a large, erect penis was on the other. One leg bore a tattoo of Satan torturing a man, whom Saloon Sally later told me was her ex-husband. On the other, ghostly faces were inked from foot to thigh. And her forehead had tattoos of a couple of pistols bracketing the words "Born Crazy."

Yikes. But her eyes were glowing, her smile was contagious, and her voice was friendly.

"Hey, Doc. I hurt my shoulder busting up a fight."

"What happened?"

To break up barroom brawls, Saloon Sally explained she pulls out a baseball bat kept hidden under the counter. Over the years, she'd learned how to jab customers in the chest with the bat just hard enough to knock the wind out of them but not so hard as to do serious harm.

"It works like a charm, Doc. When you knock the wind out, they stop fighting. But I didn't get close enough last time, stretched too far, and hurt my shoulder. I guess I'm getting too old for this shit." Even her voice sounded tired.

"How long have you been running this bar?" I asked while examining her.

She said she'd taken over operations forty years ago when her father "keeled over," and she ran the business well. Cheap draft beer was the key, she said, and she claimed to have the last dollar drafts in the state.

She explained her first challenge running the business occurred a few years after her father died, when the box factory closed. The factory sits behind her bar on the other side of a canal. A bridge connects the box factory parking lot to hers, and after every shift, workers would march across the bridge into her bar, but they stopped coming in after the closure.

In response to the loss of customers, she started opening the bar earlier. And business boomed. "When the box factory was open, the guys would only drop by after work, but after it closed, they would come all day." Saloon Sally was a smart businesswoman.

Another challenge was a major storm the prior year, when the canal behind her bar had swollen and flooded the entire neighborhood. "As soon as the water went down, I opened the doors, turned on some fans, and started serving." Sal's was serving days before any of her competition. She was resourceful.

"I had to cover up the windows of the bar when I started opening early." She was getting complaints. Several ladies from a nearby trailer park, babies in tow, started drinking as soon as she unlocked her doors each morning. Her bar had several bay windows with large sills. The ladies would set their baby carriers on the windowsills so the little ones could get some sun while their moms guzzled down dollar drafts.

Saloon Sally laughed. "How much is that baby in the window, right? People started complaining when they saw them." So she put up thick black drapes. The babies no longer got any sun, but the complaints stopped.

The tattoo business was merely a side endeavor. "It generates extra cash. When the bar ain't busy, I go in the back and do tattoos. I did your girl, Doc, you know that?"

"My girl?"

"Sally. I inked a chariot pulled by a couple dolphins, but I won't tell you where they are."

She winked, and I turned my head to hide my blushing face.

During the detailed examination, while she talked, I discovered Saloon Sally had a small tear in her rotator cuff caused by hyperextension during her latest baseball bat maneuver. I referred her to a university surgeon for outpatient surgery and sent her on her way.

"What did you think of Saloon Sally?" Sally asked after the visit ended.

"I like her. And she can sure tell a good story."

"She sure can. And she does *great* tattoo work." Sally smiled, with a sparkle in her eyes.

I blushed again.

Saloon Sally went back to the bar with her arm in a sling the day after her operation. This wasn't advised, but one couldn't fault her for her work ethic. During the weeks of therapy that followed, I heard she wielded the bat with her other arm with satisfactory results.

✦✦✦

"Sally, I just want to know one thing about this patient." The schedule declared the visit reason for the last patient of the day as "my ugly stinks."

"What's that?"

"What is an ugly?"

"No idea, and I didn't ask. That's why they pay you the big bucks. But he has a rash. And so does his wife and kids who are in there with him."

As I entered the room, their rashes were immediately obvious. He was a slim man with brown hair, and the red, blotted rash stretched over his face and arms. His bare feet were also inflamed. He wore long pants, but certainly the rash covered his entire body. And as Sally had observed, his wife and three kids' symptoms looked pretty much identical.

"Look at us, Doc. Ain't we a pretty picture?" The patient grinned. He had no teeth.

"Hello! It looks like all of you have a pretty bad rash."

"Yep. And on top of that, my ugly has a nasty stank." His wife grimaced at the comment and his children giggled.

"And what do you mean by that?"

He pointed to his groin. "You know, my wiener. You better take a look at it. And take a sniff."

How lovely.

"I think we should have your wife and children go into a different room."

"Nah, they see my ugly all the time."

That's disturbing.

"Well, be that as it may, we should assess you each individually. Our pediatrician should look at the children. And I should examine your wife when I finish here. I don't want them to go to the waiting room in the event they have something contagious." Scabies came to mind although the rash didn't look like a perfect match, and he hadn't complained, at least yet, of itching.

"All right, Doc."

Sally led his rash-covered family members to another room. Then I began my examination.

The problem with his "ugly" was straightforward. He was uncircumcised, had poor hygiene, and had subsequently developed a problem in his foreskin.

"You have a yeast infection, sir. I'll prescribe an antifungal cream. And you need to clean your foreskin and penis regularly."

"The wife always tells me I should take better care of my ugly."
She's right.

"And my ugly sure does stank, don't it?"

"Yes." The hot aroma made my eyes water. *Repulsive.* "Now, on to the matter of the rash." The rash was generalized, did not appear infectious, and it did not itch. Sometimes new medications or foods can cause such a rash, but he denied both.

"Do you have any new pets?" I asked.

"No. We have the same two old flea-bitten hound dogs. Had 'em for a long time."

"Any new sorts of chemicals or products, such as a new soap or shampoo?"

"No, Doc. We use the same old stuff."

"Can you think of anything out of the ordinary that might have happened recently?"

"Well, the hound dogs got a extra bad case of the fleas. That's all."

"These don't look like flea bites."

"Oh, they ain't biting us. I've been putting powder on everyone to keep them fleas away."

Bingo. Upon further questioning, he confessed to dousing the entire family head to toe with flea powder he'd bought for his hounds.

"Did the rash start about the same time as you applied flea powder to your family?"

"Now that you mention it, yes. That's when it started. You think it's the flea powder?"

"I'm certain. You should not be applying doggy flea powder to humans." *Captain Obvious returns.* "You may, however, keep using the powder on your flea-ridden hound dogs."

The patient left happy, and Dr. Wurst concurred that stopping the powder was the order of the day for the children as well. After examining the wife, that was also my plan for her rash. In a couple of weeks, the entire family's rash cleared up.

I'm not sure how things went for the hound dogs.

17
SKIP MEETING

The moment Skip saw me walk into his office, he pounced. "We have a lot to talk about today, Dr. Wave. I've heard a lot of complaints about you. We need to talk."

"What kind of complaints?"

"Dr. Slenderman complained and so did the billing department."

Surprise, surprise.

"Dr. Wave, you can't just go down to the billing department and demand a bill be dropped."

"I demanded no such thing. I did, however, point out that the bill was in error."

"That's impossible. We don't make billing mistakes."

My ears burned. "On the contrary, Skip. I reviewed the chart and I found several billing errors. The bill was riddled with them!"

"That's another thing, Dr. Wave. You had no business going through her chart. I told you before, stop looking through charts."

"She is my patient."

A smug look crossed his face. "No, Dr. Wave. During the hospital stay you reviewed, she was not yet your patient."

"That is irrelevant. She is my patient now, and as such, I have full authorization to look at all of her medical records."

"Now... Dr. Wave, that's just a technicality. You know you had no business going through that chart."

"Skip, she asked me for help. She is an elderly lady on a fixed income who will lose what little she has to a hospital bill. That would be appalling under any circumstance, but in this case, the bill isn't even correct. She was charged for all kinds of things that were never provided."

"That's not true. The bill is correct. And you had no business suggesting that Slenderman didn't see the patient. He was offended."

"But he didn't! He as much as admitted that. And he sent her a huge bill anyway."

"He says that's not true. He complained and said he wants you fired."

Ugh. Getting fired would end any chance at another medical directorship, as Slenderman undoubtably knew. Sally's voice echoed in my mind.

Time to fight back!

"The patient attests that she never saw him. And there is not a single note in the chart documenting he ever saw the patient. And when I spoke to him, he admitted he might have just 'stuck his head in the room' and not formally examined her. There were numerous witnesses present as well when he made that statement. Shall we get statements from them? Perhaps under oath?"

Clearly, Skip did not like me standing my ground and directly confronting him. Beads of sweat appeared on his smooth head. It looked like he had applied some sort of oil to his scalp. It glistened. "I'm sure he did nothing wrong."

Will he grab his goatee?

"He committed Medicare billing fraud," I said, "a federal crime."

"Now... Dr. Wave, don't say things like that." Skip's face creased with worry. He wiped the sweat from his bald head with his right palm, then dried it on his goatee. His hand lingered, gently teasing it, before gripping it tightly.

"And as for our billing department," I continued, sensing he was on his heels, "we should rethink our charitable care policy. They are aggressively going after patients with little or no ability to pay. Our charity program should be more accessible to the poor."

"Our charity program is fine. Last year we gave away millions of dollars in free care."

I don't believe that for a second.

Skip scowled, let go of his goatee, and crossed his arms. "The billing department has looked at your patient's bill, and they say it's fine, so that's the end of it. Either she pays her bill, or she goes to collections like everyone else. End of discussion." He clearly would not drop or even correct the problem. "The next matter I want to discuss with you is your calling the police on a patient. I received a report from the sheriff. We can't have you calling the cops!"

Does he know it was I who reported Dr. Lyssa to the police as well?

"Did you even read *Get Crabby!*? What kind of a customer review do you think the patient will give you now?"

Probably not a very good one, but at least he won't write it until he gets out of jail.

"I did read the book. However, in this situation, the patient absolutely refused to leave the clinic unless I filled out disability forms."

"Why didn't you fill out his forms? That seems like an easy answer."

"Because he wanted me to fill out disability forms when, in fact, he was not disabled."

"In your opinion."

"In my *medical* opinion, he did not qualify for disability. I am a doctor, after all. And as you know, it is both unethical and illegal to fill out forms claiming disability when a disability is not present."

"Yes, I know that. But it sounds like you're too strict. The sheriff said he had high blood pressure."

"Maybe it was the cocaine he was on. In any case, a large percent of the population has high blood pressure. That is insufficient, in and of itself, for disability. I should not have to explain this to you. The patient became incredibly angry and belligerent. He refused to leave. Fearing for the safety of myself and the staff, the police were called. He had outstanding warrants and cocaine in his possession. If he were high, that would not only explain his high blood pressure, but it would also mean he was at an even greater risk of becoming violent. In fact, panic buttons are appropriate for the clinic—any clinic. We should look at installing panic buttons in all the offices in case a patient gets out of hand."

"I think you're overreacting," Skip said. "There's no need for all that. The patients aren't the enemy here. What we need to do is get the Get Crabby program implemented as quickly as possible."

He then gave a long thesis on getting crabby. It was going to increase patient satisfaction. It was going to increase volumes and revenue. It was going to end physician burnout and staff stress. "The lessons of the crab sellers are going to save this hospital."

That's less believable than the hospital giving away millions in free care.

"As I said, I am happy to volunteer the clinic for the program. In fact, the advisor is coming to my clinic Monday as we have no meeting since you will be out of town at a seminar." I tried my best to hide my disgust while mentioning his upcoming junket at the hospital's expense.

"Good. Dr. Wave, consider yourself warned on the trouble you stirred up regarding patient billing. You are to drop the matter. And consider yourself warned that you are not to call the police on your patients anymore. We can't have that."

"Is this an official verbal warning that will go in my employee file?"

"No. But I will make a note of it in your secret file." He pranced over to the locked cabinet, opened it, and pulled out my secret file. It had grown considerably over the past few months. He added some papers and then put the file back.

"Okay. I take note."

"Good. I'm going to tell Dr. Slenderman I gave you a talking-to. Especially regarding this billing nonsense. That patient needs to pay her bill like everyone else. Do you understand me?"

"I understand what you're saying." *If Skip thinks I'm dropping this, he is sorely mistaken.*

"Very good. As we have an understanding, I will overlook this incident. Furthermore, I will approve panic buttons for only your office. Just don't expect anything expensive."

"Thank you."

Clearly, he's trying to buy me off. Don't make waves with billing, and here are your panic buttons.

I wrote a long letter again outlining the Medicare billing fraud as well as my discussion with Skip and mailed it before sundown to the Office of the Inspector General. This letter was also copied to the Health Care Fraud Unit at the Department of Justice. All letters included my name, office address, and phone number in bold print as anonymous complaints were more likely to be ignored. Hopefully, continuing to complain would lead to some sort of action.

As for Ms. Geras's bill, a new approach was needed. Ms. Geras came into the office that afternoon. We filled out a payment plan form together that Sally had downloaded from the hospital website. The payment plan form specified, given Ms. Geras's income level, the minimum payment would be one hundred dollars per month. But this minimum still represented a third of her monthly income and was impossible to pay. Ms. Geras signed the form, and I donated a money order making the first six months' payments, including a detailed protest letter disputing the fraudulent charges and noting the fraud had been reported to the government.

This payment made my bank account lighter, but my heart was lighter still.

18

OFFICE INTERLUDE

The consultant arrived bright and early in my office Monday morning for our Get Crabby training. He wore a crisp, new Brooks Brothers single-breasted pinstripe suit. *Must be his outfit for working in the trenches. They don't even cost a thousand dollars.*

The entire morning schedule was blocked off so that patients wouldn't distract us from this vital training. Dr. Wurst wasn't present, so it was just Sally and me in the nurse's station, listening to his presentation. The consultant brimmed with enthusiasm.

"Is everyone ready to Get Crabby?" The consultant spoke much too loudly. "I'm going to introduce you today to the Crab program."

"The Crap program?" Sally quipped.

I groaned. *We're off to a great start.*

The consultant's lips pursed in annoyance. "The Crab program. We're all going to Get Crabby today and learn how to serve our clients better."

"What about our patients? We gonna serve them too?"

Sally is just spoiling for a fight.

"Well, little crab, your patients are your clients. That's what we call them now."

"I am not your little crab, dude."

Ignoring Sally, he began singing the Get Crabby theme song. He also began the silly dance. He beckoned us to join in. As we sat there like bumps on a log, his eyes pleaded with me.

Take another one for the team. I stood up and began to dance, pinching my fingers and swaying my hips. I also felt my face flush. It was probably as red as a boiled crab.

"Oh, my God." Sally was in stitches, tears rolling from her eyes. Dr. Wurst entered the office at that very moment, and my blush deepened.

"What is going on here?" Seeing us dancing and pinching, Wurst grinned, then joined in. This excited the consultant.

"Excellent, Doctor. You got crabby!" The consultant beckoned Sally forward. "Come on, join in. Do the crab dance."

Sally, obstinate as ever, did not move. Finally, the song and dance ended.

"Movie time," the consultant announced. Directing our attention to a video screen, he showed us a cartoon featuring Crabby the Crab. In the cartoon, Crabby lectured us about good client service—smile, make good eye contact, and always shake hands. But don't pinch them! These and more pearls of wisdom flowed from Crabby's chitinous lips as the cartoon dragged on. The advice was very general. Neither doctors nor medical practices were specifically mentioned.

When it was over, the consultant asked, "Are there any questions?"

Sally's eyed glowed as she raised her hand.

"Yes! What's your question?"

I held my breath, waiting.

"This little crab wants to know how much the hospital is paying you to shovel this horse shit?" Her voice rose in anger. "You should use Crappy the Horse instead of Crabby the Crab."

Dr. Wurst blew air through his lips to make a horse sound.

I sighed deeply. *This isn't helping.*

"That is not a Get Crabby attitude." The consultant frowned. "You really have to buy into this. Read the *Get Crabby!* book, for starters." He handed Sally a copy. On Amazon, the book sold for $29.99. Skip had bought hundreds, if not thousands, of them.

"Oh my fucking God." Sally's eyes went wide when she saw the book cover. "Is this a joke? You want me to read *this* book? Seriously?"

"You'll love it." He handed her a stuffed crab toy.

"Well, this is something." Sally had a wry grin.

"Glad you like your toy Crabby. He can inspire you at work every day."

"I am giving this to my three-year-old niece. Your Crappy doll is perfect for babies, just like your program. I have work to do, and Crappy the Crab sure as hell isn't going to do it for me." Sally turned her back to the consultant and started working on a stack of papers piled in the corner of the nurse's station.

The consultant tried to move on, but now it was down to just me. Dr. Wurst had left as soon as Sally had turned her back. Phones were ringing. People were coming into the office. Even with patients blocked from appointments, certain things still needed to get done. Surrendering, he cut the presentation short.

On his way out the door, his assessment was, "I think that went pretty well except for the disruptive nurse."

"She is a little rough around the edges," I said, coddling him a bit. Sally was an excellent nurse, and she was the main reason things functioned as well in the clinic as they did.

"Well, she needs to have more buy-in."

"I will talk with her about that. Rest assured, we'll all be on board with the Crab program soon." This office wasn't going to be the squeaky wheel. Let Slenderman's office do the squeaking.

"Well, Doctor, I appreciate your support. And I'm glad that you and Dr. Wurst got up and danced the crabby dance." His hands made little pinching motions.

Good grief.

As the consultant was leaving, the panic button installation team arrived. Despite Skip's promise, I was surprised. Apparently, Skip was quick to follow through on what he considered a bribe for unethical behavior. Panic buttons were installed at the front desk and in the nurse's station. Several large necklaces, each with a large triangular device with a button, were also provided by the installation team. We were to wear these around our necks and press the button in an emergency. Sally shook her head when she saw them.

"Moo!" she said. "They look like cowbells. I'm not wearing one of those God-awful things."

"I'll wear one when I have a high-risk encounter," I said. While you could never tell with certainty when a patient visit would be high-risk, you could often make a good guess. A new patient coming in for pain-pill refills—high-risk. A well-known and established patient coming in for a follow-up—low-risk. And Ms. Geras delivering a freshly baked pie or tray of cookies—no-risk.

✦✦✦

"Did the visit have to be listed this way?" I slowly shook my head.

"You know that's the rule, Wavesticks. Consultants said so," Sally answered in singsong.

"He actually said, 'I was a bad dog'?"

"His exact words."

"Any indication as to what the actual problem is?"

"No, but I'm rooming him now, so we'll find out soon."

A few minutes later, she returned looking utterly bewildered. "You are not going to believe this. He's here because a metal collar is stuck around his neck."

"What?"

"It's like a big handcuff, but it's around his neck. They can't get the collar open."

"Good God, man!" I said, imitating Doctor McCoy from the old *Star Trek* TV series. "I'm a doctor, not a locksmith."

In the exam room, a bare-chested gentleman in his mid-thirties with curly blond hair and numerous tattoos on his face, chest, and arms, was sitting on the exam table. The large metal cuff around his neck had a long chain dangling from it. Next to the exam table, his girlfriend—who was heavyset, dressed in black, and clearly projecting a Goth look—sat quietly with a bemused look on her face.

"So what exactly happened?" I asked. The patient didn't reply. As he sat there, I noticed he had an impressive tattoo on his abdomen of a man who looked a lot like the patient being walked on all fours while wearing a chained collar. *Looks like Saloon Sally's handiwork.*

"Tell him!" the girlfriend commanded in a loud, stern voice that made me jump.

"I was a bad dog," he whined, looking down at the floor.

"I can't hear you. Louder!"

"I was a baaaaad, baaaaad dog," he whined again.

The girlfriend mockingly smiled.

"Perhaps you could explain why he's here and what I can do for you today?" I asked the girlfriend.

"When he's a bad dog, I put a metal collar on him and walk him around like the dirty, leg-humping animal he is." She began to laugh. "But today the key didn't work when I decided to take the collar off."

"Let me take a look." The collar, fortunately, was not so tight as to threaten circulation to his brain. Trying the key, I found the lock remained stuck. Then an idea struck me. I kept a can of WD-40 in the trunk of my car.

"I'll be back in a minute," I said, and fetched it. I sprayed it into the lock, jiggled the key, and it clicked. The lock released and the collar popped open.

The girlfriend's voice remained stern. "What do you say?"

"Thank you, Dr. Wave," the boyfriend replied, his voice pathetic.

"You're welcome. In the future, don't use a locking collar. It's too dangerous. If the collar becomes too tight, it might cut off circulation and cause a fatality."

"We're going to PetSmart now. I'm going to buy a big leather one."

Excellent idea.

And with that, the bad dog left the office.

When I relayed the story, Sally began singing, "Doctor let the dog out, woof, woof, woof…"

It was impossible not to laugh as she sang. *Woof, woof.*

✦✦✦

You'd think ours was a dental office. Every week, two or three patients showed up with a visit reason of "toothache," and they were a mixed bag. Some were drug-seeking, using the excuse of a toothache to attempt to wrangle a narcotics prescription, but not all of them. In Nebraska, Medicaid covered dental visits. But very few dentists would accept the insurance, so poor patients often came to my office instead. And let me tell you, many Martians had horrible teeth. They arrived with infections, sometimes serious, as well as other complex dental problems. Not being a dentist, these cases were difficult, but I did the best I could to help these unfortunate people.

"Your toothache is ready in room one," Sally announced. "He barked at me."

"He *barked* at you?"

"Yes. He told me his teeth hurt, and he wanted some Oxys. I told him you don't write for Oxycontin. Then he started barking."

"Like a dog?"

"Woof, woof, woof," Sally said.

"Great." I slipped the panic button necklace around my neck, and Sally's barks changed to moos that faded as I walked down the hall to the exam room.

"Good afternoon, sir. What can I do for you today?" I made my voice cheerful despite my inner dread.

"I have a bad toothache, Doctor. I need something for the pain."

Good, no barking.

"Which tooth hurts?"

"Huh?"

"Which tooth has the toothache?"

"Oh, um, all of them do. The pain is killing me."

My face no doubt announced suspicion. He looked comfortable, and usually people claiming a toothache can tell you which tooth hurts.

"May I take a look inside your mouth?" He complied, but unlike most Martians, his chompers were perfect. "Everything here looks good to me."

"It may look good, but it hurts, Doc." He grabbed the right side of his jaw and groaned. "I need some Oxys. Probably."

Abominable acting.

"I'm sorry, but I don't feel it's appropriate to prescribe narcotics for you. There aren't any findings to support such a prescription."

The patient immediately started barking.

"Sir, why are you barking?"

He barked louder, then started growling and shaking his head like a dog would do while gnashing on a chew toy.

"Sir, please stop," I begged, but the barking continued. "I'm going to have to ask you to leave."

"Woof, woof, woof!" He replied. Then he howled. Fortunately, I didn't need the panic button. He left the office barking, howling, and growling as he went. The patients in the waiting room looked on in disbelief.

We watched him issue one final loud howl that rose from the parking lot, then he climbed into his car and drove away.

"We should've called the bad dog lady," Sally said. "She'd know how to handle him."

"Leave the poor fellow alone, he's having a *ruff* day," I said, barking the word.

She giggled. "Wavesticks, you're the greatest."

✦✦✦

Even for Mars, "tree frogs in my head" was an especially unusual visit reason. "Sally, did she really say this?"

"Yes, she did. She's going to be a handful too."

My heart sank. "And why is that?" If Sally said a patient was going to be a handful, watch out.

"She claims to have fibromyalgia as well as Lyme disease from a tick bite. She also reports trouble with chronic fatigue."

"The trifecta." Patients claiming to have fibromyalgia, Lyme disease, or chronic fatigue were often mentally unstable. It's an unfortunate stereotype, and these are all real diseases, but nonetheless, it is also true that frequently, for some reason, many patients with mental health issues claim chronic Lyme disease as an affliction. Fibromyalgia and chronic fatigue are also mysterious and hard to diagnose, and this lady claimed all three, in addition to the tree frogs in her head.

She does sound like a handful.

"Oh, and her allergy list is a mile long," Sally added. Patients claiming excessive allergies is often also an indicator of possible mental illness.

Given Sally's warning, the panic button and a chaperone seemed appropriate. "I'm getting the cowbell, and you're coming with me."

"I wouldn't miss it. I forgot to tell you she looks like the Bride of Frankenstein. Don't be surprised when you enter."

"This just keeps getting better and better." Sure enough, the patient had a tall, beehive-like hairdo, and she was also staring into space with an unnervingly odd look in her eyes.

"Good afternoon." I tried to sound as cheerful as possible. "What can I do for you today?"

"Doctor, there's chirping in my head that sounds like tree frogs. I need my fibromyalgia medication refilled because it treats my pains and also helps quiet the tree frogs."

"What medication is that?"

"Oxycontin."

"Who has prescribed this medication?"

"My doctor from Florida. But he got arrested. I also need more antibiotics for my Lyme disease." Florida is known as a hotbed of inappropriate narcotics prescriptions.

"Can you tell me how you came to acquire Lyme disease?" Skirting the narcotics issue for the moment seemed wise in order to learn more about her medical conditions.

"I was frolicking naked through the woods last year, and a tick bit me on my ass." She started shaking her head side to side, no doubt due to the tree frogs. The patient handed me a stack of photocopied medical records. Instead of pursuing why she had frolicked naked in the woods, it seemed wiser to review her chart.

"Let me check your records." She'd been tested for Lyme on several occasions, but all had come back negative. "I see that the testing was done, but that you were never diagnosed."

"Yes, but the doctor said you can have Lyme disease and get a negative. I need more antibiotics." While this was sometimes true, it did not justify antibiotics. "And don't forget the Oxycontin. Doctor said it's the best treatment for fibromyalgia."

What a quack. Narcotics were the worst treatment for fibromyalgia and not recommended. *Gee, I wonder how he ended up in jail.*

"I also need a shot of B12 for my chronic fatigue. Doctor said it's the cure." Vitamin shots are not the cure for chronic fatigue. No cure exists.

"We have a lot to talk about. First off, narcotics are not indicated for fibromyalgia. I recommend an antidepressant and physical therapy. Physical therapy will also help with chronic fatigue. Vitamin B12 injections are not recommended for chronic fatigue unless a deficiency is identified, and I'll test for that. As for Lyme disease, I find no evidence of infection, but I will refer you to an infectious disease specialist for a second opinion. I don't see an indication for antibiotics right now. Finally, regarding the noises in your head, I'll begin a workup." These points efficiently covered her multiple concerns.

"That won't do at all. I don't want an antidepressant. I want my pain pills. And I do not want physical therapy. I'm too exhausted for that."

"I don't think that's appropriate. I would—"

She cut me off and screamed at the top of her lungs. "Give me my pills! I'll report you if you don't give me my pills! I'll call the hospital. I'll call the state medical board. I'll call the newspapers. I'll call—"

"I am not going to give you narcotics." Cutting her off before she got up to calling the president seemed appropriate. "This is because they are not indicated in the treatment of fibromyalgia or your other possible conditions." That was a medical fact.

"Possible? These aren't possible conditions. I have chronic Lyme disease. I have fibromyalgia. I have chronic fatigue." Infuriated by my hesitation to confirm her diagnoses, she screamed even louder. "You are a *horrendous* doctor! Give me my pills!"

"No."

"What did you say?" She screamed again at the top of her lungs. Sally was wide-eyed and frightened.

"I said no. You have two choices. One, we can proceed with the testing and treatment I have recommended and outlined. Two, you can leave." I spoke very calmly, but my calm voice didn't help the situation.

"I'll find a new doctor, you hateful beast!" She spat on the floor and exited the office, slamming doors and shouting as she went. As far as I know, she never called the hospital, the state medical board, the newspapers, or the president.

"She was a real whack job. I thought you were going to have to hit the panic button," Sally said after the patient left. Her voice was shaky.

"I don't think she was dangerous—just disturbed. She needs a psychiatric evaluation, but we never really had a chance to get to that. She's probably also addicted to narcotics now, thanks to some quack in Florida." Sometimes patients travel great distances in search of doctors who will feed their addiction.

"I think you handled things pretty well," Sally said. "I can't believe how calm you stayed through all her ranting and raving."

"It goes with the territory. I see more than my fair share of this sort of behavior here."

"You sure do."

"Be sure to document everything in your notes, including that you were there for the entire visit, that she left against medical advice, and that she refused the care plan I offered. Also, please document her spitting."

"Will do, Wavesticks."

Having Sally present during the evaluation had been a wise decision. The patient could have made any sort of accusation if a chaperone had not been present.

Tree Frogs, as Sally nicknamed her, eventually found Dr. Do, and her narcotics, antibiotics, and vitamin B12 requests were all satisfied.

Sometimes patients don't travel great distances in search of doctors to feed their addiction.

19

DOCTORS' LOUNGE

"Hey, Wave, you're going to love this one," Beats said the moment he saw me step into the doctors' lounge one summer morning. He was sitting at the table with the other two regulars, Slenderman and Rumpsmith. "Guess who I saw in a restaurant over the weekend."

"Slenderman." I quickly answered. Slenderman scowled, while Beats and Rumpsmith grinned. Slenderman was sitting in front of a stack of empty plates. They had been cleaned so thoroughly it was impossible to tell what he had eaten.

"No, I saw one of our doctors having dinner with a patient. And they were getting cuddly too. They must be sleeping together."

My jaw dropped. "Which doctor?" Sleeping with nurses or other employees was unacceptable. Sleeping with patients was a fast way to lose your license. If you ever look at state medical license board records, you'll see there are three main reasons doctors lose their licenses. The most common reason is drugs—either abusing them or inappropriately prescribing them. The second is a felony conviction—usually tax fraud or again, drugs, but occasionally it's murder, usually of a spouse. And the third is sleeping with patients—something psychiatrists seem to do with unusual frequency. Of note, being incompetent is not one of these three main reasons. Doctors rarely lose their license for being quacks.

"Don't tell him, Beats. He'll just make trouble," Slenderman growled.

"Now... Dr. Slenderman," Beats said, stroking an imaginary goatee, "perhaps he *should* make trouble. You can't sleep with your patients. It's Dr. Himeros. Also, one of my nurses knows a nurse in his office, and word is going around about this."

Dr. Himeros had thus far dodged meeting with me. He, like Beats and many other hospital employed doctors, never attended physicians' meetings. He saw his patients in an office far from Mars Hospital, and had good patient volumes.

"I'll have to investigate this matter. If it's true, this behavior must be reported."

"See what you did, Beats? The hall monitor is going to cause trouble."

"The cat's out of the bag," I countered. "And if word is going around, it was only a matter of time until Skip and I found out."

Over the next couple of weeks, evidence confirming the affair piled up. Dr. Himeros was seen in public kissing his patient, and even in the office, embracing her in a sexual manner. My plan was to present this evidence directly to the state medical board. Only after doing this would I, for sake of protocol, share the evidence with Skip. But first, it was appropriate to meet Dr. Himeros in person.

+++

Dr. Himeros's office was located several miles outside of Mars on the very edge of the county. I arrived during the lunch hour and the front-desk clerk's eyes widened when she saw me walk into the clinic.

"I'd like to see Dr. Himeros immediately."

"You can't see him right now. He's in his office with a patient."

"Really?" My tone was suspicious.

"Yes, he's busy and shouldn't be disturbed."

"I think I'm going to go ahead and disturb him."

My walking into the hallway leading to Dr. Himeros's office caused the clerk's voice to rise in panic.

"You can't go back there now!"

Grunts and groans and a suspicious thumping filled the hallway, all emanating from Dr. Himeros's office. Voices also cried out. A female voice yelled, "Yes, give me that cock."

Dr. Himeros's door was locked. After twisting the knob several times, I began pounding on the door. At the same time, his office phone rang. *The clerk giving warning, no doubt.* All grunts, groans, thumps, and dirty talk came to a sudden halt and were replaced by a muffled phone conversation.

"Just a minute," Dr. Himeros breathlessly called through the door.

A few minutes later, the door swung open, and a young lady in a halter top, short shorts, and flip-flops scurried out and rushed down the hall. She avoided eye contact, and she was flushed and sweating. Dr. Himeros unconvincingly called out after her, "I'll let you know the rest of the test results when they come in."

Sweat was beaded on his forehead. And his office stank like dirty armpits. Or worse.

"Dr. Himeros," I said. "We need to talk."

"About what?"

"I think you know."

He blushed a deep red and cast his eyes downward. Dr. Himeros was a single, middle-aged, unattractive, overweight doctor who had lost most of his prematurely snow-white hair. The patient had to be at least twenty years his junior. And she looked good. She had long, flowing red hair and was physically fit. Their physical differences made me suspicious. Was this true love, or were there financial or other motivations in the relationship? Was he trading drugs for sex? I had no evidence he was committing that horrific crime, and typically doctors engaging in that vile act didn't take the patient out to dinner. But, regardless of motivations, she was his patient. Action must be taken.

"I was just going over some things with my patient," he said.

"What things?"

"Some test results."

"What tests were you reviewing? What did she have done recently?"

"It doesn't matter."

"You're sleeping with her."

"No, I'm not."

"You were having sex with her just now, right in the office, for God's sake! You've been seen with her in public, and I have a half a dozen reports from witnesses documenting inappropriate behavior."

The blood had drained from his face. "That's all a lie."

My heart was filled with sympathy. Attraction is human, but a doctor shouldn't act on his feelings. A doctor can't sleep with patients. The course of action was clear.

"I'm going to be reporting this to the state medical board as well as your department chair. I assume action will be taken. I'm letting you know, face-to-face, as a courtesy. Good day, Dr. Himeros."

"You have it all wrong!" he called out as I made my way out of the office.

I immediately mailed a report of my findings to the state medical board and copied this report to the medicine department chair.

A few days later, Skip greeted me with "good news" at the start of a routine meeting.

"Dr. Himeros just got married." Skip sounded overjoyed.

"I was going to inform you today that he's been sleeping with a patient. I assume this means he *married* his patient." I couldn't stop a deep grimace from spreading across my face.

"I know all about your little investigation. And now, she's his *former* patient. I have a contact on the state medical board. I called him and let him know there was no need to investigate this further, since they're married, and the state medical board is dropping the matter. I have, of course, put a report in Dr. Himeros's secret file."

Skip, it seemed, had helped Dr. Himeros find his way out of his problem. And it was unclear what, if anything, I could do about it.

Not long after this, the problem of another inappropriate physician relationship landed in my lap.

+++

"FUCK! FUCK! FUCK!" screamed Dr. Mors, one of the pathologists, as I entered the doctors' lounge. He was rampaging through the lounge kitchen. He knocked over empty chairs. He smashed plates on the floor. And he threw his full coffee cup against the wall, shattering it.

"Calm down, man. Don't overreact." Beats tried to sound calm, but he sounded worried.

"Calm down? I am going to kill that slut. I am going to shoot her." The anger suddenly changed to grief, and the pathologist burst into tears.

My eyes were wide with surprise. "What on Earth is going on in here?"

"Beats opened his flytrap again," Dr. Slenderman replied dryly as Dr. Mors bolted out of the lounge, leaving a trail of coffee and broken glass in his wake.

"What's going on?" I repeated.

"I told him his pathology tech girlfriend was sleeping with one of the paramedics," Beats answered. "I heard it from my wife. He didn't take the news well. I don't know why he was surprised. He's older than her dad."

Great, another sexually inappropriate relationship.

"Why was she going out with him in the first place?" The pathology tech was twenty-three, brunette, and good looking. Dr. Mors was sixty-two, bald, short, and fat.

"He bought her a car," Slenderman replied. Beats grinned.

"Doctors are not supposed to date staff members. He could get fired." *They aren't supposed to sleep with their patients either.*

"Ha! Get ready to fire half the staff," Dr. Slenderman retorted. He gave Beats a hard look.

"Why are you looking at me?"

"Everyone knows you have shown your 'cobra' to half the nurses in the cardiology department."

"Yeah. The other half is too ugly." Beats grabbed his crotch with both hands. Sally's comments about Beats being handsy came to mind.

Should this be investigated? Probably. But one crisis at a time. "Where is our angry pathologist going, by the way?"

"He's on the way to the pathology department," Beats replied. "He wants to have some words with his girlfriend."

Time to call security. This could get real ugly real fast. Picking up the phone and dialing the emergency code, I dispatched security to the pathology department.

"Why did you do that, Wave?" Slenderman asked after my call.

"He's just upset. He's harmless. Why do you have to turn everything into a big deal?"

"I think it's better to be safe than sorry." I left the lounge and proceeded to the pathology department. The sound of screaming, furniture crashing, and glass breaking filled the hall a hundred yards from the department doors.

Dr. Mors was again on a rampage. He threw anything he could get his hands on. As he did this, a stream of vile profanities flowed from his mouth. Pathology techs looked on in fear as they huddled around a cowering, crying woman.

"I am going to kill you, you filthy cunt! I'm going to blow your brains out. I'm going to chop you up into little pieces and feed you to rats." He progressed with more and more macabre forms of murder and butchery, some of which would shock Stephen King. Security arrived and tried to calm him down. They failed. A short time later, the police arrived in response to a 911 call.

About the same time the police took the rampaging pathologist away in handcuffs, Skip arrived. The doctor screamed curses and death threats as the police frog-marched him past our CEO. As I explained what had happened, Skip's bare head starting glowing red. He was angry. At me.

"*Why* did you call the police? What if this gets in the papers? It would make me look bad."

"I didn't call the police."

"Well, who did? I want to know." He began stomping his feet like a child.

"I don't know who called the police, but I'd imagine someone in the department."

"You called security. Slenderman told me."

My hands extended outward to showcase the broken glass, over-turned furniture, and general disarray in the pathology department.

"Yes, I called security. It seemed like the right thing to do. He was out of control and dangerous."

"So he was a little upset. You should have called me. Now we have a situation on our hands."

"I did what I thought was the right course of action."

"Now I'm going to have to fix all of this. Do you know how hard it is to find pathologists?"

I assumed this statement meant Skip would, with difficulty, replace the pathologist. I was wrong. He fired the pathology tech instead. Privately, Skip described her as a "temptress who had to go." Officially, no reason was given for the termination. As Nebraska is an at-will employment state, Skip was within his legal rights, reprehensible as it was, to fire her. And there was no union at Mars Hospital to help protect against Skip's abuse of power. The pathologist was back within the week.

In response to the incident report I filed, the pathologist was required to take an anger management class, and though he never showed up, he passed it. And he was angry at me. Pathology was part of the surgery department, so of course Slenderman handled the incident report and was sure to let him know who had "ratted him out."

As for the local paper, Skip made some calls, and the whole thing was kept quiet.

Skip placed a report in the doctor's secret file.

I mailed a report to the state medical board.

Would Skip's contact on the board block this?

20
THE END OF SUMMER

By the end of summer, I had visited the majority of the two hundred employed physicians in their offices. Some had managed to avoid meeting me, using all manner of excuses, so I had not yet met everyone. But my attempts were worthwhile. Many problems were uncovered through these meetings.

One physician, an excellent and highly qualified board-certified pediatrician, broke into tears at our meeting. She was hired to work in a new office building in Mars. When she arrived, however, Skip had informed her "no space was available" at that office and she was sent instead to an office on the outskirts of town. Skip had a reputation for hiring a doctor for one office, then moving them somewhere else.

Seeing the office had given her a jolt. It was small, old, and in disrepair, and like many other offices, it smelled of mildew. And it was on a street where all other buildings were boarded up. She said it looked like a scene from the zombie TV series *The Walking Dead*. Since she had relocated to Mars from the East Coast, quitting was not an easy option. She'd planned to make the best of things and leave Mars the day her contract was up.

Another physician had commented on the rampant racism in Mars. The physician, a female general practitioner, reported being harassed for her Muslim faith. She wore a hijab, and my first thought was that her patients might be the ones not accepting of her religion, but that wasn't the case at all. Her patients loved her; the Mars police were the problem.

She was pulled over and questioned too many times to keep count, the reasons usually being "drifting off the centerline," "driving too slow in traffic," or some similar nonsense. But she never got a ticket. When stopped, she was typically asked, "What's a Muslim doing in our town?" or "What are you up to?" At night, sometimes the police would pass her car on the road and shine an intense spotlight on her as they passed. Imagining it was very frightening; I'm sure the lived experience was even more so. She started to avoid driving in town as much as possible and went out of town to buy things like gas and groceries to keep her visibility down. She also planned to leave Nebraska as soon as she could. No wonder Mars needs doctors.

Many doctors raised security concerns. One female doctor had been accosted in the parking lot of her practice. Luckily, she hadn't been harmed. Lighting at every office was poor and security cameras were absent. Doors weren't properly locked—the security keypad used the same numerical code at every clinic. And except for in my office, there were no panic buttons.

Several physicians reported serious problems in the electronic medical record. A few years earlier, the hospital had transitioned from a paper chart system, and the change had been rough. Some offices had dreadfully slow internet speeds. A doctor would enter data and wait minutes for the hourglass to finish spinning before they were able to continue. It was maddening. Then there were the order screens. What should have been simple, such as ordering a medical test or a single medication, often required navigation through dozens of menus. The electronic record wasn't user-friendly, and scores of pop-up warnings, rarely of use, would slow things down further.

There were also onerous documentation requirements. Screen after screen demanding data often of no relevance whatsoever had to be filled in while seeing patients. Doctors felt like data entry clerks, and they were for the most part. Patients hated this since doctors spent more time looking at computer screens than at them. The real purpose of these documentation requirements and the EMR itself wasn't to provide better patient care; it was to generate higher bills and more revenue for the hospital.

Doctors complained they were instructed to document, document, document and to bill at the highest level possible. They were warned it was against the law to undercharge. They were even told the ridiculous story they could go to jail if their bills were too small. And if their billing wasn't high enough, doctors were given "help," which mostly consisted of nasty emails and phone calls from the billing department demanding the doctors charge more. On top of this pressure, doctors were forced to see more patients in ever-dwindling time slots.

Doctors felt incredibly stressed. But despite my bringing these matters to Skip, he would change nothing. Doctors, he said, were the problem. A billing consultant had advised these changes, had told him doctors weren't billing enough, and had threatened jail time. According to Skip, doctors also needed to get with the program and stop complaining about the computer, which was fine, as were all the other irrelevant matters they constantly griped about.

By the end of the summer, it was abundantly clear Mars Hospital had one main problem: an incompetent, corrupt hospital administrator, and there was no easy fix to this problem.

FALL

21
OFFICE INTERLUDE

Smiling, Sally showed me the day's schedule. "Dirty drunk follow-up" was the visit reason for the first patient. I couldn't help but sigh.

"Good morning," I said. The patient sat on the exam table, and his wife sat in a nearby chair. Her face was wrinkled in annoyance and her arms were crossed. "What brings you in today?"

"My dirty drunk husband was in the emergency room yesterday. He was falling over." The husband said nary a word.

"Can you tell me what happened?" My gaze focused on the patient. Silence.

"I told you what happened," his wife blurted out angrily. "He's a dirty, filthy drunk. He got so shit-faced he couldn't walk straight."

"What were you drinking?" My gaze did not waver. "Do you understand me, sir?"

"Yes, sorry," he finally said in a quiet voice.

"What were you drinking?"

"I wasn't drinking. I just couldn't walk right."

"Liar!" His wife's face turned red as she shouted. "He's always drunk and staggering around. "He is a worthless, dirty drunk. I should have divorced him years ago."

Something didn't feel right. "Ma'am, if you'll excuse me, I need to go look at the hospital records."

I stepped out of the room and pulled up inpatient records from a special computer terminal. The Mars Hospital outpatient electronic medical record didn't interface with the inpatient EMR—a serious flaw. Eventually, after a patient received treatment in the hospital, a paper copy of the medical record was printed out and mailed to the outpatient office. When it arrived, weeks to months after the hospital visit, Sally scanned it into the outpatient computer system. This was slow, terribly inefficient, and bad for patient care. Several doctors, myself included, had purchased computers at our own expense to link into the hospital inpatient computer system. Skip, of course, would not pay for these extra computers or take the necessary steps to link the outpatient computers. It wasn't in the budget, he'd said. With these computers, inpatient records could be accessed directly. This was just one of the many work-arounds doctors were forced to use at Mars Hospital due to dreadful inefficiencies in our computer system.

On his ER visit, my patient had been diagnosed with alcohol intoxication. He'd presented with a staggering gate and was presumed to be drunk. This diagnosis was wrong. His blood work had shown zero blood alcohol, but the presumptive diagnosis of alcohol intoxication had stuck.

The patient had also received a CT scan of his head, late in the evening after the radiologist had left for the day. The emergency room doctor, with minimal training in radiology, had read the scan as normal. However, it was dangerously abnormal. There was a massive stroke in the cerebellar region of the brain. The cerebellum, located in the back of the brain, is responsible for balance, walking, and coordination. This is the same part of the brain affected by alcohol, and that's why, when someone's drunk, they stagger. The patient was telling the truth. He had not been drinking, but had suffered a massive stroke causing significant brain damage.

In the exam room, the patient and wife listened carefully to my explanation. This was a medical emergency. Immediate hospital admission was required. If the stroke worsened, it could be fatal. The patient and wife agreed to the admission. The wife, however, still held a firm opinion on the matter.

"He's still a dirty drunk. I don't care if he did have a stroke."

The patient did well.

The marriage did not.

Missing this diagnosis was gross malpractice, which I reported immediately to the department chair via an incident report as well as the state medical board. Given my strong suspicion that no action would be taken, I started my own investigation of the department. Over the next several weeks, quietly and hopefully without Skip's knowledge, my investigation revealed widespread malpractice in the emergency department.

+++

My next patient was coming in with back pain, a worrisome reason for a patient visit. Numerous legitimate conditions ranging from minor to life-threatening can cause back pain, but it's also a common complaint doctors receive from drug-seekers.

There were several red flags with this case: she was a new patient, she was young, and her visit reason—"back pain from a spinal tap"—was an unlikely cause.

"She wants Oxys for her back." Sally's straightforward assessment was the biggest red flag of all. "Good luck. You better take your cowbell."

"I will." After I threw the mobile panic button necklace around my neck, Sally sent me off with a moo.

The patient was a twenty-two-year-old woman accompanied by her boyfriend and an infant, sleeping soundly in a baby carrier on the floor. The patient looked anorexic. She had long, brown hair which was dirty and full of burrs. *Is she homeless and sleeping outdoors?* Her clothes were equally dirty and faded. Their original color was unclear. And she had a variety of tattoos, including a nightmarish clown on her right arm.

She gave the following story: She'd delivered her baby eight months earlier. During the delivery, she'd received an epidural injection in her spine for pain. This was what she was calling a spinal tap, though that's a completely different procedure.

In the eight months since the "spinal tap," she'd been suffering from chronic pain at the epidural injection site. She came today because she was changing doctors. Her prior doctor had cut her off from pain pills. I was her next choice.

Lucky me.

"I need a prescription for Oxycontin, and I need it now. My back is killing me," she said after telling me her story. I proceeded immediately to the neurological exam. It was normal. There also was no muscle spasm and no curvature of the spine, and the injection site had healed and was no longer visible. However, my lightest touch to the lower spine and nearby skin caused a violent reaction. She screamed loudly and leaped from the exam table.

"Ouch, stop! See, Doc? It hurts like crazy. I need those pills." Her acting was hideous. Her acrobatics, however, were impressive for a patient with back pain. She leapt up from the exam table, landed on her feet, and stood straight and tall.

"I need to investigate a bit further." Her pain was almost certainly bogus. But it is important to work up all complaints and not make assumptions. Several tests to evaluate her pain came to mind, but placing orders in the computer while in the room with a patient was too distracting and time-consuming. As a work-around, I wrote all necessary tests on a piece of paper attached to a clipboard, which I'd brought into the exam room instead of my laptop. These orders, along with a few notes written during the visit, could then be wrestled into the computer later. Sometimes this fight occurred in the office. But usually, it occurred late at night, at home, long after the office had closed. Doctors call working at home to finish chart documentation and orders *pajama time*. Doctors in the US average about two hours per day of pajama time.

Many Mars doctors took this work-around a step further. They didn't just write down a few notes and orders; they kept entire secret paper charts on patients. These secret charts were usually for more complex patients. The charts held useful information that was difficult and time-consuming to extract from the electronic medical record. And while I neither kept nor approved of these secret charts due to the complex ethical and legal issues of double-charting, I understood their utility for good patient care given our abysmal records system, so I'd taken no action to end the practice. These secret charts were, of course, kept hidden from Skip. He would certainly disapprove of such clandestine documentation.

"Fine. Investigate away. But give me some Oxys now for the pain."

"I recommend ibuprofen for now. It's an anti-inflammatory, and it works well for back pain. I can prescribe the eight-hundred-milligram tablets, or you can take four of the over-the-counter ones. Take them with food to avoid an upset stomach, no more than three times a day."

She blinked. "Ibuprofen?" A moment passed, then she exploded.

"I don't want ibuprofen! I want Oxycontin!"

"That's a controlled substance and not appropriate at this point."

"It's what I need. Ibuprofen doesn't work for me."

"I'm sorry. I am not comfortable prescribing you Oxycontin. I recommend anti-inflammatory medication. It's the first-line medicine for this type of pain."

She was still standing, but now her arms were crossed, and she was scowling. Her boyfriend, who had been quietly sitting this whole time, joined the fray. He began yelling at the top of his lungs.

"You bastard! I need those pills!" He got right up in my face. His dilated pupils, watery eyes, and runny nose indicated he was going through opioid withdrawal, and the pills clearly were for him. Stepping backward toward the wall, I grasped the panic button necklace.

"Sir, please calm down and sit back down." My voice was calm and quiet despite the terror I felt.

He balled his fists and stepped forward, inches from my face, eyes full of fury. "I want those pills, damn it!" He was a big guy, over six-foot-four. He was covered with tattoos, including small teardrops below his eyes. As I envisioned his muscular arms and shoulders propelling his fists into my face, I squeezed the panic button. Stepping back again put my back flat against the wall. The angry boyfriend stood between me and the door.

"Sir, please leave. This behavior is not appropriate." My voice trembled.

"I'm not leaving until you write for those pills!" His face took on a red color, and I could smell his sweat.

"You need to leave, sir. I've already called the police."

"I am fucking sick and tired of doctors not treating me and giving me the medicine I need!"

The woman yelled at the top of her lungs. "You asshole, you got my man all upset. I hope you're happy." All the commotion had woken the baby, who also screamed, adding to the general chaos.

Sally entered the exam room, eyes wide, and said, "Is everything alright in here?" The boyfriend turned toward her, and the distraction allowed me to quickly side-step him and move out into the hall.

"The police are on the way," I said. "I suggest you both leave right now." My heart pounded even harder after escaping into the hall.

The police must have already been close by. Sirens were already blaring. The boyfriend grabbed the baby carrier and swung it wildly, almost slamming it into the wall, while heading for the door. Both the woman and the man quickly exited the clinic.

The police stopped the couple's car before they left the parking lot and arrested them. They both had outstanding drug warrants and had skipped bail. Charges were also added for the boyfriend when they found an illegal gun in his car. Thank God for the panic button. *Had he carried that gun into the exam room?*

The boyfriend didn't get released from jail before trial, but the patient did. Shortly after she bonded out, she filled out a physician review online: *I saw this doctor for back pain from a spinal tap. Do not go see this doctor. He is a pig! He is hateful! He is mean! He will not give you the pain medicines you need!* A variety of other nasty exclamation-pointed comments continued for a full page, and she gave me one star, the lowest possible rating. There went my patient satisfaction score and chance for a bonus as Skip had tied all bonus payments to patient satisfaction scores. And nothing could be done about this review. Patient confidentiality laws prevented me from telling my side of the story. So, for refusing to prescribe narcotics inappropriately, my pay would be cut and my reputation harmed. What a detestable way to compensate and rate doctors.

+++

One afternoon, a husband and wife came to see me because they couldn't have a baby. Though I was a general internist and not an obstetrician, seeing obstetrical cases wasn't uncommon at the Mars Clinic. Obstetricians were few and far between in rural Nebraska, and patients needed care.

Infertility is a common problem, but preliminary testing was negative. The pap smear, pelvic exam, ultrasound, and blood work were all normal. Consultation with an infertility specialist was the next step. Almost miraculously, Sally was able to get the patient an appointment at the University of Nebraska medical center with a wait of only a couple of weeks.

A month later, the specialist called in a follow-up. She, too, was unable to figure out the problem. The patient and her husband returned to my office for further discussion.

"Everything on the testing was normal—normal sperm, normal diagnostic imaging, and normal hormones. This happens sometimes. We are unable to find the cause of your infertility."

"Should we just keep trying?" the husband asked.

"I would say yes. Sometimes it just takes time."

"We've tried enough. My asshole is sore," the wife said, scowling.

Wait a second. "You have soreness in your anus?"

"Yes."

"Why is that?"

"I don't know. You're the doctor. You tell me. Too much sex, I guess."

"I'm afraid I need you to be rather explicit. When you are having sex, how exactly are you doing it?"

The wife silently frowned but the husband spoke up.

"Huh? I stick my dingy up her butthole and pump away." His hands grabbed imaginary hips and he gave a few thrusts to demonstrate his technique.

My eyes widened in surprise. *Could they really be this ignorant?* The couple was equally surprised when told where the dingy was supposed to go.

"It goes there? That's where the pee-pee comes out!" The wife's voice was distressed, and her face showed confusion and disbelief.

And what comes out of where you've been having sex? "Well, not exactly." A basic anatomy lesson followed. They both listened in rapt attention.

"Are you sure, Dr. Wave?" The husband sounded suspicious.

"I'm certain. Trust me, I am a doctor."

"If you say so. We can try sex the new way."

The new way!

After they left, I told Sally what had transpired.

"No fucking way," she replied in a most animated fashion. "That's too crazy even for Mars."

Later that day, the university specialist called and couldn't believe the story either. "What's wrong with these people?" The specialist had never heard a story like this.

"Education. Or lack thereof," I replied. "There is no sex education in Mars."

"I guess, but how the hell can you possibly think *that* is how you make a baby?" The specialist had a point. But such was life on Mars.

Nine months later, my patient gave birth to a healthy baby boy.

Sex the new way had worked.

22

SKIP MEETING

This Skip meeting was certain to be difficult. Entering his office, the Crap Man, the moniker the medical staff had given the consultant, was sitting next to Skip. Both were pictures of unhappiness. Over the past several weeks, the Crap Man had tried to implement his Get Crabby program in physicians' offices, but it had been a disaster. Doctors refused to play along. No one would sing songs or do the crab dance. And to make matters worse, Sally's nickname Crappy the Crab had caught like wildfire. This infuriated Skip.

"Dr. Wave, today we will do a deep dive into the Get Crabby program." Skip was already holding his goatee. His hand bobbed as he spoke. "We are going to start this deep dive with your office." *Deep dive* was a catchy consultant phrase even more annoying than *thinking outside the box*, another favorite. "Our advisor says the Get Crabby rollout in your office did not go well. Your nurse didn't buy into the program."

"It went better than the rollout in any other office." In Dr.

Slenderman's office, the staff had refused to participate. Dr. Slenderman had literally pulled the plug on the DVD player while the consultant was screening the crab cartoon. And he'd gotten so upset
when the consultant had started doing his song and dance, that Slenderman had shouted, "Get the fuck out!" at the top of his lungs. The
consultant had quickly scurried out of the office in the face of Slenderman's fury. Other offices had behaved similarly, albeit with less
yelling and cursing. No one was buying into his ridiculous program.
By comparison, things in my office had gone swimmingly.

"That may be. But your nurse is disruptive. She's the one who
started using *crap* instead of *crab*." Skip's bare scalp turned red after
saying the word *crap*.

"I doubt my nurse was the first one to use that term." She had
been, but no harm in trying to protect her.

"No, she was definitely the first," the consultant said, sounding
like an annoyed teacher giving a lesson. "She even said we should
use Crappy the Horse instead of Crabby the Crab." My hand went to
my mouth to hide my smile and stifle the urge to make a horse sound.

"Now we have people all over the hospital calling our advisor
the 'Crap Man,'" Skip continued. He was turning redder by the second. "We've heard employees saying they're going to do their job
like crap. And worst of all, we have people doing the crap dance."
My hand remained over my mouth. By now, Skip's bald head was
redder than Rudolph's nose.

Lately, doctors had been doing the crap dance in the doctors'
lounge. It was embarrassing to watch. It involved putting "your ass
cheek in" and "your ass cheek out" and then "shaking it all about."
This was followed by doing the "crappy crappy," during which a
squatting position was assumed. The dance then concluded with a
variety of maneuvers with the buttocks.

Beats especially liked this dance. "Where is Stercus when we need him?" Beats often added at the end of the song.

"It's unfortunate people are doing the new dance," I said to Skip when I gained my composure. "I think it's best to just ignore it. It's juvenile and will stop on its own." The more fuss Skip made about the dance, the more doctors would do it.

"It's beyond unfortunate; it makes me look bad," Skip said.

"It's not your fault people aren't accepting the program. It's hard to get professionals to buy into a cartoon crab. And some people are uncomfortable with the singing and dancing." *Always be the diplomat.*

"They don't seem uncomfortable doing the crap dance." Skip's voice increased to a yell. "They need to buy into the program. It's supposed to be *fun* to sing and dance like the Boston crab sellers. It would boost morale if they participated. Has anyone read the book? Is anyone getting crabby?"

"Well, I have given out the books. I will confess that there hasn't been a lot of interest."

"Every single doctor needs to read that book. Do you know how many hundreds of those books I bought? Half of them are still sitting in boxes, and the other half are unread."

No point in arguing. Skip was incapable of grasping that no one was going to read the book. It was silly, and Crabby the Crab just didn't translate well to a medical office.

"And our patient satisfaction scores are going down, not up. We also did an employee satisfaction survey, and those scores went down too. *Down!* If employees would buy in and start thinking outside the box and getting crabby, employee satisfaction would go up." Skip twitched with agitation while the consultant silently nodded in agreement.

"Skip, there are reasons for the decline in employee satisfaction. Our patient volumes are going up, as are the demands on time. Meanwhile, you keep adding more and more requirements on the staff."

The additional requirements had hit the nurses especially hard, spanning from more data entry and more time on phones getting authorizations to requiring nurses to act as phlebotomists, patient schedulers, and housekeepers. But every staff member, not just nurses, was being given an ever-longer list of required job duties. "Despite the increase in the amount of work, there is no increase in the number of staff."

"We need to keep a lean staff. They just need to work smarter. That's where the çrab program is supposed to come in," Skip said. *Lean staff* and *working smarter* were another couple of favorite consultant catchphrases. They meant piling more work on employees without paying them more.

"I think morale would improve if the staff had more help. The same is true for doctors. Doctors are acting as data entry clerks for the electronic medical record and must spend ever-increasing amounts of time dealing with insurance companies for the approval of tests as well as an array of other nonclinical tasks. This wastes a valuable resource—their clinical skills. Every second they spent *not* directly caring for patients is an inefficient waste of resources. If we added additional staff for the offices and added in scribes for the doctors, I'm sure patient and employee satisfaction would increase as would productivity and quality of care."

Scribes were becoming quite common nationwide. A scribe is an individual who follows the doctor into the room during an exam. Under the doctor's supervision, the scribe handles documentation, data entry, and test and treatment orders. This allows the doctor to focus on the patient. Scribes are well accepted by patients, and doctors love them. It dramatically improves efficiency and productivity and also gives the doctor the security of a witness to all patient encounters.

"So if they work less, they'll be happier? We don't have the budget to hire more staff." Skip dismissed my proposals out of hand. "Money is tight, and they'll just have to make do."

The tens of thousands of dollars you're spending on the crap program would have paid for this, as would firing scores of useless administrators on the payroll. The hospital had more than tripled the number of administrators in the last few years. *How about, instead of managers, hiring people who do productive work?*

"The staff would still work extremely hard," I explained. "It just makes sense that as you add more work requirements and as patient volumes increase, you increase efficiency and change the workflow."

"The answer from doctors is always the same. Hire more staff. We don't need more staff. I've decided to require all employees to read the book. It's no longer optional. We are sending out an online test that cach employee will have to take that quizzes them on the book's content. You will announce this at the next physicians' meeting."

"Okay." *The floggings will continue until morale improves.*

"Now, I want to talk about your patient reviews. You received an atrocious online review. This is a big problem." It was the drug-seeker's review.

Sighing, I slowly shook my head no. "Skip, the review was done by a patient seeking an inappropriate narcotic prescription who was arrested by the police after her visit. Of course she's unhappy. I should also point out that a gun was found in the patient's car. This is frighteningly similar to a situation that recently occurred in Indiana. A patient was refused narcotics, returned with a gun, and shot and killed the doctor. This could have happened here."

"Doctor, this is exactly where the Get Crabby program comes in," the consultant said, speaking in an excited tone. "Did you get crabby with that patient?"

Getting crabby, as we well knew, had the magical ability to turn an angry, dissatisfied, gun-toting "client" into a happy one with but a wave of the pincers.

"You could have explained things in a friendly, joyful, and crabby way and turned the situation around." The consultant's voice became more animated as he spoke. "The patient would have left happy and joyful and would have written a great review if you'd followed the program and acted like Crabby the Crab."

An addict going through withdrawal responding to Crabby? And he's talking about Crabby like it's a real person? What planet is this guy from? Flabbergasted, I said, "I don't think there's anything I could have done to make this patient happy."

"Well, Dr. Wave, that's the problem. You aren't buying in! Crabby would not have let the patient leave unhappy. Crabby would have considered writing the prescription. Then the patient would have left happy and would have written a good review," the consultant continued. He then started pinching his fingers like a crab claw.

"*What?*" My voice was rising in anger.

"What he means," Skip interjected, "is that perhaps with more exploring, you could have found an indication that would have allowed you to feel comfortable writing the prescription. That's what Crabby would have done. Maybe it was indicated, and you didn't spend enough time getting crabby to find that reason."

Good Lord. Now Skip was talking as though Crabby were real. And he was supporting inappropriate narcotic prescriptions. Many doctors have found themselves in deep trouble going down this road. *I hope Crabby has a good lawyer.*

This attitude is one of several reasons why the nation has a shocking narcotic addiction problem. One hospital accreditation body, the Joint Commission, had begun to pressure hospitals and doctors to better treat pain and in 2001 required hospitals to measure it as a "fifth vital sign," though pain is really a symptom. This problem was further compounded by drug companies who marketed their new narcotics like Oxycontin as having a minimal risk of addiction. And on top of this, to increase patient satisfaction, hospitals had pressured doctors to keep patients satisfied and had linked doctors' pay to these satisfaction scores. All these factors led to the increased prescription of narcotics, which was disastrous for the nation.

"Skip, with all due respect, no reason whatsoever justified writing the script. I explored the matter very carefully."

"Well, you still could have tried to get crabby. And you must stop hitting that panic button. It looks bad."

"I will try to avoid using the panic button." *Agreeing with Skip on this is harmless and hopefully will shut him up.* "I will also be more mindful of the crab program and try next time to get crabbier." *Crabbier? Is that even a word?*

"Excellent." A satisfied grin appeared, and the redness quickly faded from his bare head. "I now want to talk about a variety of things we can do to help get more crab program buy-in."

Skip and the consultant outlined a variety of planned events, all silly and unlikely to work. The most hilarious were a puppet show followed by a pantomime.

Slenderman will just love that.

23
THE OLD OFFICE

Dr. Do was hired despite my recommendation to the contrary, and Dr. Essex continued to practice despite my demands he be immediately suspended. Nothing out of the ordinary happened for a few months. Then all hell broke loose.

The trouble started with Dr. Do. She had full hospital privileges despite her criminal conviction and no board certification or controlled substance license. Dr. Do frequently showed odd behavior. There were wild mood swings. She was often late for hospital rounds or failed to show up at all. She frequently appeared wired. These were all tell-tale signs of substance abuse, which I relayed to Skip as well as the department chair.

Skip scoffed at my suspicions. He supported Dr. Do and frequently pointed out her patient satisfaction scores were higher than mine. Dr. Do had a reputation for being easygoing with her prescriptions for narcotics though she wasn't authorized to write for narcotics. Dr. Do was using Dr. Essex as a cosigner to make it happen, a dubious practice at best. Indeed, many drug-seekers, including the one who'd given me a loathsome review, found a happy home in Dr. Do's office. She'd received many glowing reviews and five-star ratings for writing generous Oxycontin prescriptions. And Skip rewarded her high satisfaction scores with cash bonuses.

One afternoon, a ward nurse called into my office. She relayed that she had noticed Dr. Do sitting in the corner of the nursing station that morning, furiously turning pages in a large medical tome. She didn't think much of it. Later in the day, Dr. Do was still flipping pages with glazed eyes and mouth open and drooling.

Dr. Do began babbling when questioned by the nurse, who in turn called me. Per my instructions, the nurse called the ER doctor on duty who reported, "She's high as a kite."

Dr. Do, escorted to the emergency room, lit up her drug screen like a Christmas tree. She was transported to an inpatient drug rehab program and placed on a medical leave of absence. Her patients were assigned to other physicians.

At our next meeting, Skip was unperturbed.

"Dr. Wave, drug addiction is a medical condition. When she finishes rehab, we'll put her right back to work."

Drug addiction *is* a medical condition, but patient safety comes first. "I'm in no rush to see her return to work. She's a danger to patients."

"We need her back. We need her in the old office." Skip's eagerness for her return was disheartening but not surprising.

The DEA subsequently raided Dr. Do's office, and the Feds seized a variety of records in addition to a supply of narcotics. Dr. Do had been dispensing narcotics right from her office.

Dr. Essex was also interviewed. He'd thought the DEA agents were from the local police department despite being told otherwise numerous times. He kept asking them if they were there to sell tickets to a fall festival called the Mars Nut Fest. The DEA interview of Dr. Essex must have been priceless. Skip's reaction to my suggestion that Dr. Essex should not be signing narcotic prescriptions was typical.

"If we must, we'll get another doctor to write controlled substances for her when she gets back."

"Assuming she isn't arrested on criminal charges."

"Now... Dr. Wave, I'm sure she isn't going to get arrested. You're overreacting." He began gently caressing his goatee.

"Am I? She's writing thousands of narcotics prescriptions without a license and dispensing them from her office. It's a wonder she's not already behind bars."

"Dr. Essex cosigned those scripts." His goatee caresses picked up speed.

"Dr. Essex has Alzheimer's. He has no clue what's going on or what he's signing. He shouldn't be practicing."

"We aren't going there, Dr. Wave. Dr. Essex is an institution around here." Skip had blocked all my efforts to suspend Dr. Essex's medical and surgical privileges. And as the state medical board had also taken no action, he was still operating. And there was nothing I could do about it.

A few days later, that institution came crashing to the ground. Dr. Essex was performing surgery to remove a gallbladder, which he'd done countless times. With the operation well underway, he asked the surgical nurse an alarming question.

"What are we doing today? Are we removing the colon? Or are we doing something else?"

"Doctor, it's the gallbladder."

"Are you sure about that? I thought we were removing the colon." He started telling a story of how he'd been a surgeon during the Vietnam War. "Back then, you had to be ready to do any kind of surgery. I removed many colons at the army field hospital in 'Nam."

"Doctor, you are removing the gallbladder. The patient is under anesthesia and on the table. Can you continue? Should I call someone else to finish the surgery?"

"Oh. Oh, yes." Looking down, he saw the patient and snapped back to the present. "The gallbladder it is!"

He completed the surgery perfectly. Luckily, the part of his brain that controlled motor skills was still working fine. His memory was shot, but his hands still held a lifetime of experience. That carried the day. This time.

After the surgery, the surgical nurse went straight to the director of nursing, who went straight to Skip, who went straight to me.

"Dr. Essex seems to be having some trouble with his memory," Skip said. "I think we're going to have to get a formal neuropsychiatric evaluation." Apparently, with nursing in an uproar, he'd finally decided to act.

"Excellent idea," I said.

He caught my sarcasm and didn't like it.

The evaluation, performed at the University of Nebraska, concluded without a doubt that Dr. Essex had advanced Alzheimer's disease. The evaluating neurologist was stunned Dr. Essex was in active practice and performing surgeries. His condition was so advanced, it had to have been progressing for years. In fact, it was discovered that his wife had attached a monitor to his ankle since Dr. Essex would often wander off and get lost. She'd even reported this to Skip. Of course, he'd ignored her report. Or maybe he had put it in the secret files.

When the university hospital failed to rubber-stamp an immediate return to practice, Skip was thoroughly annoyed. "Well, I hope you're happy, Dr. Wave. I have no choice but to suspend his privileges until he improves."

"Skip, it's Alzheimer's. He isn't going to improve. He's going to get worse. And I'm happy we're keeping our patients safe. He could have killed someone. But, I am not happy this doctor must retire under these circumstances. He had a long and distinguished career. It's sad to see it end this way. It would have been much better for him to have ended it with a retirement party rather than with a suspension."

"And now we have no doctors in the old office. Revenues will fall!"

Money, as usual, was Skip's only concern. My face must have showed the contempt I was feeling, but he gave no indication he'd noticed.

24

OFFICE INTERLUDE

Not long after Dr. Do had gone to rehab, the first of what was to be many of her former patients arrived at my clinic. The visit reason, "the nerve pills aren't working," seemed straightforward. Anxiety not responding to treatment isn't unusual.

"She's ready," Sally announced. "And she is a very sweet old lady."

The patient was seventy-seven. She had a round face, white hair, looked very grandmotherly, and was even knitting as she sat waiting in the exam room. The record review revealed Dr. Do had recently started her on Oxycontin, a narcotic pain killer, and Ativan, a tranquilizer. Neither of these medications are first-line treatments for anxiety, and both were dangerous when used in the elderly.

"Good morning. What seems to be the trouble?"

"Doctor, the pills prescribed for my nerves are just not working. I'm still getting the pains in my chest when I walk."

"You're getting chest pains?" Chest pain, especially in an elderly patient, was a different can of worms entirely.

"Yes. When I walk a half a block or so, I get a crushing pressure in my chest. Sometimes I can't even breathe."

"Do you feel anxious, nervous, or worried?"

"No, but sometimes the chest pains make me a little worried."

"Are you getting sweaty? Are there any pains shooting into your left arm?"

"Why, yes. That's exactly what's happening. Dr. Do said it was all due to my nerves, and I needed some nerve pills." This was classic cardiac angina. A third-year medical student should be able to make the diagnosis that Dr. Do had blown. This patient needed cardiac treatment, not narcotics and sedatives.

"You don't have a nerve problem. The problem is your heart."

"Really? Why didn't Dr. Do tell me that?"

"Let's focus on what to do now." *Diplomacy*. Doctors aren't supposed to speak ill about other doctors in front of patients. But my face certainly showed the anger I was feeling. *What a quack.* "I will immediately refer you to our cardiologist."

"Whatever you say, Dr. Wave."

Beats agreed to see her right away. A treadmill stress test, which she failed impressively, confirmed my diagnosis. She went to the cardiac lab early the next morning. There, an angiogram—a procedure where a catheter is inserted into the right femoral artery at the groin and dye is injected to highlight the blood vessels feeding the heart—discovered blockages. Beats inserted a metal stent to open them. Problem solved.

The patient's chest pain from "nerves" cleared up immediately. I reported Dr. Do's malpractice and discontinued the useless and dangerous Ativan and Oxycontin prescriptions. The only wrinkle was her groin. She complained of pain at the site of her angiogram. Testing didn't reveal a cause, and Beats claimed it was likely all psychosomatic.

The patient then asked Dr. Lyssa about the groin pain, and she prescribed her Oxycontin and Ativan.

I reported this too.

✦✦✦

My next patient had arrived. The schedule listed the visit reason as "dirty drop."

"Sally, do you have any idea what a dirty drop is?"

"You are so innocent. It means he flunked a urine drug screen."

The patient soon confirmed this was indeed the case. "Doc, you got to help me out." The patient was on parole. He worked at a nearby factory and had crashed a forklift into a wall. Company policy required all accidents be investigated with a drug test, and his failure would not only cost him his job but also be reported to his parole officer. It might land him back in prison.

"If you failed the test, how is it that I can help you?" It wasn't clear to me what he wanted me to do.

"My lawyer said I need to get a new drug test right away. A negative test might keep me out of jail."

"Have you been using drugs?"

The patient's face lit up in surprise. "What?"

"Are you using drugs?"

"Um, no." He avoided eye contact, and his body language screamed that he was lying.

"Alright, we'll do another urine drug test."

After handing him a urine collection bottle, he went to the bathroom. He came out quickly with the sample. A temperature measurement revealed the sample was at room temperature, not the normal 98.6 degrees. This was a planted urine sample.

"This test is no good," I said. After I explained why, he looked guilty but said nothing. "You need to do another test under my direct observation." Watching him urinate into the bottle was the only way to ensure no cheating.

"I don't want to give another sample." At least he didn't try to argue. "Can't we just use the sample I gave you?"

"No. It isn't a valid sample."

"Ah, come on, Dr. Do. No one will know. My lawyer said I had to get this. He said you wouldn't give me a hassle."

"I am not Dr. Do. I am Dr. Wave." *What an insult!*

"Huh? I made an appointment with Dr. Do. I called the office and was told to call here for the appointment. I thought the location had just changed."

"Dr. Do is out. You called here yesterday, spoke to Sally, and made an appointment to see me." Dr. Do's office staff was giving out my number when her patients called. This was fine, but they weren't making it clear that patients would be seeing a different doctor. And unless the person calling mentioned they were one of Dr. Do's patients, Sally had no way to know they were expecting to see Dr. Do and not me.

"Oh. Whatever. Are you sure you can't use this sample?"

"I am sure."

The patient left the exam room, sat down in the waiting room, and called his lawyer. After talking to his lawyer a few minutes, he asked Sally for directions to Dr. Lyssa's office.

+++

Ms. Geras arrived with a freshly baked coconut cream pie, my favorite.

Sally was also delighted. "She loves to bake, and I love what she bakes." But when Sally returned from rooming Ms. Geras, fury had replaced delight.

"Those fuckers at the hospital are threatening to take her house. She is terribly upset. Fuck! *I'm* upset. You made payments on that bill. And who takes a little old lady's house over a hospital bill anyway? What a bunch of heartless bastards." Sally fumed as I frowned and slowly shook my head.

Payments were made. How can this be happening?

"Good morning, Ms. Geras. What is this about your house?"

She produced a letter from a local collection agency. It threatened a lien on her home and foreclosure. The hospital had cashed the money order sent a couple of months earlier, but they had sent the bill to a collection agency anyway. The collection agency's comment about this payment made me tremble with rage.

The hospital received your money order making partial payment. As payment plans must be started within 30 days of bill issuance, this payment was credited to your balance. The remaining balance is now past due.

"When did you get this letter?"

"It came in the mail a few days ago. The collection agency has been calling me nonstop. I tried to pay them more. I even cashed two old savings bonds I had and gave them the money. But they still want my house."

"Did you call the hospital?"

"Yes."

"What did they say?"

"They said the payment arrived too late for a payment plan as payment plans must be started within thirty days of discharge. I didn't even receive the bill until more than thirty days had passed. How can someone get on a payment plan within thirty days if you don't even get it in time?"

They can't. My bile rose. "This is unacceptable. I'm going to make some calls." After I raged from the exam room to my office, I began my calls.

Unsurprisingly, a conversation with Skip yielded no results. But at least he spoke to me. At the sound of my voice, the billing department hung up immediately. I then called several local law offices with Sally's help. It was time to hire a lawyer for Ms. Geras, but lawyer after lawyer refused the case. Finally, after innumerable calls, one lawyer agreed to take the case for $500.

Ms. Geras left with a referral to a lawyer instead of a doctor.

And Sally insisted on paying part of the retainer.

I paid the rest.

25
SKIP MEETING

Billing irregularities weren't the only money-related problem at Mars Hospital. The hospital's 401(k) retirement plan was also a mess. This plan allowed employees to invest a portion of their wages into the stock market. However, the plan was performing poorly. When the stock market went up, the plan's fund barely increased in value. When the stock market went down, the fund plummeted. But why? After obtaining a copy of the plan documents, with great difficulty, the answer was clear at once. Fees.

The plan charged the hospital and employees incredibly high fees. Index funds that should be charging a few tenths of a percent as a fee were charging ten to twenty times as much. And the employees paid extra fees on top of this, for advertising, consulting, and education to name a few. And additional fees were charged directly to the hospital to manage the retirement accounts. It was criminal. As Skip listened to this information, his mouth dropped open, then his eyes wrinkled in disbelief.

"Dr. Wave, there's no way they charge fees that high."

I set a stack of plan documents before him. "These documents clearly show the excess fees," I pointed out.

He glanced through them and scratched his head. "That can't be right. This plan was picked out by advisors I hired a few years ago. They said the plan was terrific."

That explains it. Some consultant had foisted this crappy plan on Skip. They must have made a fortune.

"The documentation speaks for itself, Skip."

He shuffled through the papers with a deepening frown. Sure enough, a hand went to his goatee. "I'll have an advisor look at this."

"You can see it all spelled out right here! You don't need an advisor."

"You're wrong. I do."

"Perhaps you could call Vanguard directly." Vanguard was an excellent low-fee mutual fund company that could replace ours.

"No, I must talk to an advisor."

Do you need a consultant for everything? "The sooner we change plans, the better. This plan is costing the hospital and employees a fortune."

"I'll get back to you." Skip stacked the documents in a pile on the corner of his desk.

"There's another problem," I said.

"More problems? What else?" Clearly annoyed, he refused to release his grip on the goatee.

"It was reported to me that there is a theft ring operating out of the hospital, stealing various items and selling them to businesses in other towns."

"That's impossible," Skip said.

A patient had told me otherwise.

The patient worked at a business in a town forty miles from

Mars. According to him, someone at the hospital was "robbing the place blind." The owner of the business was buying equipment stolen from Mars Hospital. "Doctor, someone is selling water heaters, industrial cleaners, tools, air conditioning units, all sorts of things from the hospital. It just isn't right. I had to report it to you."

The theft ring had been operating for years, according to this patient. He'd left with a thank you and a promise I'd bring the information straight to the CEO. But Skip refused to believe a word of the story.

"Impossible! People wouldn't steal from the hospital. They'd get caught."

"Have we ever done any inventory audit? If there is a theft ring operating, any irregularities should turn up."

"No. We don't need an audit. There is no thievery in this hospital."

"You should order an audit immediately."

"Don't waste your time on this nonsense. You are the medical director, not an auditor. You should be focusing on the crab program."

"An audit would—"

"There is no thievery in this hospital. This discussion is over." Skip's tone sounded worried. His hairless scalp began to sweat.

Is he in on it?

The retirement plan never changed.

And, of course, there was no audit.

26
OFFICE INTERLUDE

"Patient's ready. This one will be interesting," Sally said with a smirk. "Mom brought her nineteen-year-old son in, and she says he's the devil."

I rolled my eyes. *Terrific.*

I entered the room with trepidation and saw the patient sitting quietly on the exam table. He had bright yellow hair fluffed up and was wearing a *Metallica* t-shirt, all of which made him look like Beavis from the old MTV series *Beavis and Butt-head*. His mom sat in a chair across from the exam table.

"Hello. What may I do for you today?"

Mom spoke right up. "My son is drinking our cat's blood. He's possessed by the devil."

My eyes widened, and my gaze turned toward the patient. "Is this true? Are you drinking your cat's blood?"

"Why do you think the cat runs away from me?" he answered.

I guess that's a yes.

"Satan. Satan," he shouted in-between cackles.

"You see? He's possessed!" Understandably, mom's tone was distressed.

"I am building the Ultrafire. I will be gone soon."

His mother explained her son was trying to build a spaceship he called the Ultrafire. He had taken apart her washing machine to construct it. He planned on flying from the city Mars to the planet Mars, where his wife lived. She was a true Martian.

He denied taking drugs. Later, testing confirmed this to be true. On further questioning, the mother added the following history: Over the past few years, her son's mental condition had steadily deteriorated. He had been an active, normal kid but around the beginning of his adolescence, he changed. He developed odd, ritualistic behaviors. He talked to himself. His grades in school plummeted. And, of most concern to his mother, he worshipped Satan. Of most concern to me, his mother reported he heard voices.

"This could be schizophrenia." While treating anxiety, depression, and other common mental disorders was in my wheelhouse, schizophrenia was beyond my level of training. I ordered an immediate psychiatric evaluation. The psychiatrist agreed with my preliminary assessment, and the patient was hospitalized at the Mars Mental Treatment Center, an inpatient psychiatric facility adjacent to Mars Hospital. The center had a poor reputation, but it was the only center that would take him. Inpatient treatment for psychiatric conditions is difficult to obtain unless you have a lot of money or very good insurance. He and his family had neither.

I hoped hospitalization would make things better for this troubled young man, but alas, it only made things worse.

A couple of weeks after his visit, Sally read an online news report. "Guess who got arrested last week?"

"A patient scheduled to come in today?"

"You wish. It's the devil himself." On her phone, Sally showed me a local news story about my young patient. He had been arrested at the mental hospital. According to the story, he'd assaulted two orderlies when they tried to prevent him from building an altar in his room. Staff had called the police, but before they'd arrived, he had barricaded his door using the bed and two chairs and had tried summoning Satan.

The police arrived, busted down the door, and forcibly restrained him. He became combative in the process and allegedly punched an officer in the face, all the while screaming, "Satan will kill you all!" The punch had broken the officer's nose. My patient was subsequently charged with attempted murder of a police officer. Bail was set high, despite his mother's pleas. He was currently in the county jail, in solitary confinement.

According to the report, he'd pleaded not guilty and claimed he hadn't hit the officer. His defense was mistaken identity. Satan himself had broken the officer's nose, not him.

"How can they charge him?" I asked. "He's mentally ill." *Unbelievable.*

"Oh, he is batshit crazy."

"Surely this won't go to trial. The police arrested him inside a mental hospital, for crying out loud. He was there for schizophrenia. There's no question he's mentally incompetent. And attempted murder? For a broken nose?"

"This is Mars, Wavesticks. He slugged a cop, so he's going to prison. You'll see."

"This can't stand. I'm calling his public defender."

What the public defender said shocked me. "I'm not his public defender. He's representing himself."

"But how can that be?" I asked.

The public defender explained. He had initially been assigned to represent my patient, and he had demanded a competency hearing. He'd presented affidavits to the effect that his client had schizophrenia and wasn't fit to stand trial. His client, however, had taken issue with this defense. He'd told the judge he was just fine and wanted to represent himself. Shockingly, the judge had ruled in his favor. It was a travesty.

Next, I called the mayor. She wasn't only Skip's boss, but also the chief of police's. While the county prosecutor didn't answer to her, without support from the police, the charge of attempted murder, or any charge for that matter, wouldn't stick. As I began to explain the situation and how attempted murder was clearly an example of overcharging and that it was wrong to charge an untreated, schizophrenic young man, she hung up on me.

A short time later, the case went to trial. It was a spectacle. People were lined up early in the morning at the courthouse to get a seat to watch the show. And what a sad show it was. My schizophrenic patient sat alone at his defense table. The judge allowed him to wear a black hooded cloak with an upside-down cross necklace so he could look like a Satanist, which he claimed was his religion. That must have played well with the jury in this born-again Christian town. During the trial, he motioned to call a coven of witches as character witnesses. Motion denied. He motioned to be allowed to build an altar to Satan in front of the witness stand in order to summon the devil. Satan, he proclaimed, would then take the stand and, under cross-examination, confess to committing the crime. Motion denied. He motioned to call his wife, currently on the planet Mars, as an alibi witness. Motion denied. When the arresting officer testified against him, he motioned to be allowed to slug the officer in the face in order to prove it was not his fist that had hit the officer but the "fiery fist of Satan." Motion denied.

The jury quickly found him guilty. The judge gave him fifty

years, the maximum sentence. The earliest he would be eligible for parole, according to Nebraska law, would be in twenty-five years, assuming good behavior. Given he was dragged kicking and screaming out of the courtroom, good behavior seemed unlikely.

Sally was right. This was Mars justice, at its finest.

+++

"Hey, Wave, I heard you had the devil as your patient," Beats commented one morning shortly after the trial as I entered the doctor's lounge. He was there with Slenderman and Rumpsmith, of course. All the doctors had plates of food. The drug reps had ordered catering from a fancy Italian restaurant and had set up a sumptuous spread in the hallway outside the doctors' lounge. Slenderman had two plates of food piled up with enough lasagna to choke a horse.

"The kid is mentally ill," I said. "He should not be in prison. How the judge ruled him competent is beyond me."

"If you can't do the time, don't do the crime," Slenderman remarked while digging into a huge portion of lasagna. There was already sauce clinging to his beard. "Hey, Rumpsmith," he mumbled, his mouth full of lasagna, "tell him about your nutcase."

"I have a patient coming in from the prison at least twice a week. She's eating strange things, and I just removed part of a light bulb from her stomach."

"She ate a light bulb?"

He nodded. "Usually, when I remove a light bulb, it's from the other end," Rumpsmith dryly added. Rumpsmith had told many a doctors' lounge story about things patients had shoved into their own rectums. He had removed dildos, a garden's worth of vegetables, Coke bottles, beer cans, and once even a light bulb. "And now other inmates in prison are giving her stuff to eat. They get a laugh out of it."

"She sounds mentally ill. Why is she in prison?"

"Arson. She started a fire in a garbage can here at the hospital, then stood there, watching the fire. She's doing hard time now—twenty years, I think."

"Twenty years for setting a garbage can on fire? That doesn't sound like arson. Was there any damage to the hospital?"

"They put out the fire in the can. No harm done."

"I can't believe she got twenty years for that." *But that's better than the fifty my patient received.*

"I'm glad they locked the firebug up. She's right where she belongs," Slenderman commented, his mouth still stuffed with lasagna.

"She costs the state a fortune," Rumpsmith said. "She keeps eating anything she can get her hands on. She's been placed in solitary confinement and is allowed to wear only a paper gown, but she keeps finding things to eat. She ate the light bulb by taking apart the fixture in her cell."

"And this is how we treat the mentally ill." I shook my head sadly. Jails and prisons are the mental hospitals for the poor.

"Oh, boo fucking hoo, you bleeding-heart liberal," Slenderman said as he walked out of the lounge to get another plate of lasagna.

27
OFFICE INTERLUDE

The patient, a morbidly obese man, got right to the point. "I need some diet pills, Dr. Wave." His wife, sitting nearby, listened intently.

"Well, let's talk about that."

"There's nothing to talk about. Look at me, I'm fatter than fuck!" He grabbed one of his fat folds. "Look at this fat. When I wash it, I gotta use a blow dryer." He was not one to mince words.

"Have you tried to diet?"

"I am immune to diets. They don't work."

"What do you mean you are immune to diets?"

"Doc, I don't eat."

His wife laughed out loud.

"Bitch, shut your pie hole or get the fuck out. I don't eat!"

His wife grimaced but said nothing.

"Please calm down. Let's talk about what you eat." It turns out, in addition to a chocolate bar and a box of oranges, he'd consumed a dozen Krispy Kreme donuts, a frozen pizza, an entire two-liter bottle of cola, and an undefined quantity of "snacks and goodies." All before noon today.

This guy must be consuming more than 10,000 calories a day.

"It doesn't seem like you have been trying to diet at all. And, clearly, you have been eating."

His wife silently nodded. He shot her an angry look.

"Diets don't work, Doc. I've tried to diet. I gave up. I am immune to them." He shot his wife another stern look. "And what I mean is that I don't eat except when my blood sugar goes down low."

"Have you had your blood sugar checked?"

"No, but I can tell. I feel weak and dizzy. That's low sugar."

That could be a lot of things.

"Do you exercise?"

"No."

What a surprise.

"What kind of work do you do?"

"I'm out of work. I used to work construction, but I got laid off."

"Ten years ago," his wife interjected. "All he does is sit at home on his fat ass, eating Little Debbie snack cakes. I work. I clean houses."

"Shut up, Missy. Doc doesn't want to hear your yapping."

Her information was pretty helpful, though.

His physical examination was unremarkable, aside from morbid obesity. After ordering blood work, including sugar and thyroid levels, and a cardiac workup, the discussion turned to treatment.

"I recommend a diet and exercise program. Even cutting him back to a standard two-thousand-calorie diet could lead to massive weight loss."

"What about the diet pills?"

"I do not recommend diet pills. Diet is where we start."

"Doc, I told you they don't work for me. Honey, tell Doc diets don't work for me."

"Diets don't work for me, I am immune to diets," she parroted in a singsong voice.

"Bitch, you're fat too! Why don't you go on a fucking diet?"

"I may be fat, but you're a fucking blob. Tell the doctor how you collapsed our bed. He sprained his ankle when he plopped down, and it busted."

"Folks, please. Stop this bickering. Diet pills are stimulants. They are dangerous. They can stimulate the heart, leading to a heart attack." *Time to get crabby. Will he write a negative review?*

"Well, being a fat ass is also dangerous," he countered.

"That's why we're starting with a diet. Start with cutting out sugar. Things like soda, chocolate, and donuts are out. Foods like vegetables, fish, and lean meats are in. I'll give you a detailed brochure before you leave."

"You make it sound like I'm eating too much. That's not the problem."

"That is, at the very least, part of the problem. You need portion control."

"That's ridiculous. My portions are just fine."

"Yeah. Your portions are fine for Jumbo, the circus elephant," the wife said with a laugh.

"I have had just about enough of your shit."

"Shit? Your elephant-sized shits are so big they clog the freaking sewer pipe."

"Please, folks. No more arguing."

"Tell Doc about the jelly dogs," the wife continued.

The patient's eyes narrowed. "What about them?"

"You eat an entire pack of hot dogs, and instead of mustard and ketchup, you slather grape jelly on them."

"That's cause my sugar drops down low."

"You eat jelly-covered hot dogs?" I asked in disbelief. *How vile.*

"Doc, he could win a hot dog eating contest. He stuffs those babies in his mouth so fast he must think someone is gonna steal them if he don't gobble them down right quick."

"Shut up, woman!"

"Tell him about the Pop-Tart sandwiches."

"There ain't nothing to tell."

"He takes two Pop-Tarts and slathers white cake frosting between them before stuffing them into his fat face and eating them like a sandwich."

A small gasp escaped from my lips.

"Goddamn it. That's enough!" The patient's face turned crimson. "I'm going to smack you in the mouth."

"Sir, please calm down. Ma'am, I think it would be best if you could step out of the room."

"Before you could smack me, you'd have to catch me. *Fat* chance of that." She walked out of the room.

Thank God.

"You see what I have to put up with, Doc?"

"Perhaps you should consider marriage counseling."

"Just give me the diet pills, okay?"

"Let me explain something to you." I provided a long and detailed explanation regarding the risks of diet pills and how diet and exercise would improve his energy and mood as well as reduce the risk of several diseases. Additionally, I offered a referral to a dietitian. Although all this took much longer than the ten minutes allocated for the visit, Crabby would be pleased.

"You're not going to give me the diet pills, are you?" he asked when I'd finished. His voice was sad and dull.

"Don't you see how the plan I outlined is better?" *Don't say no. Crabby never says no.*

"No, I don't see that."

"Will you at least try the diet?" My tone was pleading.

"Sure, Doc, whatever you say. Are we done now?"

"Yes. Let's make a follow-up appointment before you go." *Always sound cheerful.*

He no-showed for the appointment and never did the testing. Luckily, he didn't write a negative review online, either.

A few weeks later, while I was filling my car with gas, he walked out of the gas station convenience store carrying a case of soda, a few frozen pizzas, three boxes of Pop-Tarts, and several boxes of Little Debbie snack cakes.

"Doc, you caught me," he stated in a matter-of-fact tone.

So much for the two-thousand-calorie diet.

I never saw him again.

✦✦✦

Sally informed me we had a "dirty birdie" ready to be seen. His visit reason was, "I got worms."

Better wear double gloves before seeing this dirty birdie. When I entered the exam room, it was empty, so I returned to the nurse's station.

"Sally, no one's in there. Did you see where he went?"

"Nope. Maybe we got lucky and he left."

Occasionally, patients would walk out before being seen. It happened once or twice a month.

"Do you hear that, Sally?"

Music echoed through the hall. It was the song "Yankee Doodle."

"Sounds like a harmonica," I said. The music was coming from the staff bathroom. The door was closed and locked. The harmonica music stopped when I knocked and called the patient's name.

"Hey, Doc. Give me a minute. I'm taking a mighty shit." "Yankee Doodle" resumed.

Sally looked on in horror. "Nasty! Tell him to get out of our bathroom." A loud expulsion of gas briefly drowned out the harmonica. "Yuck!"

"Sir, this is the staff bathroom. You must use the patient bathroom down the hall."

"Too late. The shit's a-flying. I'll be out in a little while."

"Not much we can do now, Sally."

"I am never using that bathroom again," she declared. A foul odor became apparent. Sally gagged, then pinched her nose. As Yankee Doodle rode his pony, we retreated to the nurse's station. His harmonic bowel movement continued for the next ten minutes, the entire time allotted for his visit, putting me way behind schedule. Finally, he emerged from the staff bathroom, harmonica in hand.

"Man, I dropped a bomb in there."

Even down the hall, the odor remained strong. The patient, dressed in a fast-food restaurant uniform, vigorously scratched his rear. When he'd finished, he sniffed his index finger.

"Ugh," Sally gasped. "I am never eating fast food in this town again. That is sooooo nasty."

"Now we know why there are so many cases of food poisoning in Mars." On one occasion, food from a local restaurant had arrived in our office with dead cockroaches inside the Styrofoam container. Insects were one cause of foodborne illness in Mars restaurants; butt-scratching employees apparently was another.

Back in the exam room, I asked about his problem with worms. "What exactly is going on?"

"Every night, worms come crawling out of my ass. And my ass itches like hell. I've been digging through my shit and finding all kinds of strange things in there. Yesterday, at work, I dug through my shit and found baby worms."

Envisioning him digging through feces while at work made my stomach churn. "With the itching, the problem might be pinworms." Pinworms are a common pediatric infection, but they can occur in adults. Live worms exit the anus, typically at night, to lay their eggs around the anus, and there is intense itching. Tapeworms were also possible but less likely. These are rarer and itch less, but can also poke out of the anus. And those worms are larger and more noticeable.

Immediate treatment was instituted and stool tests ordered to confirm the diagnosis.

"Take this medication, and take off work until your symptoms have resolved and any infections have cleared. I'll write you a note."

"I can't take off work. I need the money."

"If you have worms, you're highly contagious. You especially can't work in a food-service job."

"Whatever you say." He left, my doctor's note in-hand. While walking out, he again furiously scratched his rear, this time using the harmonica, which he held in the other hand.

A few days later, the test came back positive for pinworms as well as three other types of worms and parasites. On top of this, he had salmonella. This guy was a walking petri dish.

His infections were automatically reported to the Department of Public Health. They found him still working at the fast-food restaurant, which was shut down immediately.

From that point on, I never again ate at any restaurant in Mars. It was weeks before Sally would use the staff bathroom.

+++

"The mail-order bride is ready to be seen," Sally said, a big smile on her face.

"Excuse me?" *This must be a joke.*

"Her husband picked her out of a catalog. He ordered her up from Russia. She's a real beauty, too. I bet she was thrilled to be delivered to this joker." Sally grimaced.

"What's she here for?" It was hard to believe there were mail-order brides in this day and age.

"General checkup."

"You're coming with me."

"This should be interesting."

A beautiful young woman with long, golden brown hair sat on the exam table. She was accompanied by her fifty-five-year-old husband. He too had long brown hair, which was oily and tangled in knots. He smiled when we entered. His grin was nearly toothless.

"Hey, Doc, what you think of my bride?" He seemed immensely proud.

"How do you do?" I said. My gaze focused on the patient. "What brings you in today?" She tried to answer, but her husband cut in.

"She's just here for a checkup. I want to make sure my mail-order bride is in good shape. Otherwise, I'll have to return her." He chuckled.

"What do you mean by mail-order bride?" My voice held doubt.

"I ordered my wife right off the internet. I mean, let's be real. Look at me. There's no way I could get a lady like her in Mars."

No doubt about that.

The man said he'd paid a fee to a company he'd found, and had then flown to Moscow, where he'd gone to a mixer with several other men from around the world to meet a variety of Russian women. The lady he'd selected from the online catalog was there, but several other women were too. This was to ensure an adequate number of selections in case the preselected lady "wasn't a good fit."

He'd spent a few hours at the mixer and had decided to stick with

his first choice. She returned to his hotel room with him. "By morning," he said, "I knew I picked the right lady." They were married
the next day, and paperwork was started for a visa. He flew back to
America. A few months later, after obtaining her spousal visa, his
bride arrived.

"She was pretty surprised when she got to Mars. She said this
was not how she'd pictured America. She said Mars was worse than
her hometown in Russia."

I know the feeling.

"But I'm happy. She cooks. She cleans. And she does all the
wifely duties." He glowed and a broad smile slowly formed. Sally
and I both grimaced. We later reported this case for possible traffick-
ing to the Department of State.

The young lady's medical evaluation came back completely normal. He was happy and did not return her.

28

THE DOCTORS' LOUNGE

"I heard something the other day about your patient, Ms. Geras," Beats said one fall afternoon.

He was sitting with Slenderman, the same as always, but today Rumpsmith was absent. Drug reps were handing out free pizza slices outside the doctors' lounge. Beats had one slice; Slenderman, an entire pie. In addition to pizza, they also were handing out gift certificates to local stores.

How can I report these drugs reps? Doctors are being bribed to prescribe new, expensive medications. This is wrong. I sent a letter to the Inspector General's office the next day. I was writing letters to various agencies about something every week now.

"What did you hear?" I asked.

"I heard the hospital was trying to take her house. Is that true?"

"Yes. She owed money on a bill, and a collection agency is playing hardball. She tried making partial payments, but the hospital said the payments arrived too late. She's got a lawyer now to fight the foreclosure." *No reason to say who is paying the lawyer.*

"See what a bunch of asshats they are around here? They blow money on dumbass shit like the Crap program," Beats said. "And to pay for it, they take homes from little old ladies."

"Deadbeats should pay their bills," Slenderman interjected. "She should pay up. Hell, I waived her bill. She probably wants free care from everyone now, thanks to Wave."

Is he trying to sound magnanimous for dropping his fraudulent bill? Pathetic.

"Hey, Wave. Take this." Beats tried handing me something small.

"No, thanks. What is it?"

"It's a Cobra pin."

"What's it for?" *I know you nicknamed your penis Cobra.* Beats walked over and pinned the tiny enamel cobra to my lab jacket.

"It's good luck." He and Slenderman both wore the pin. "You're one of us now."

"Ha." Slenderman barked.

"Thanks." Once I was out of the lounge, I removed the pin and put it straight into my pocket. My gut warned me the insignia was trouble, and it was right.

✦✦✦

The next day, Skip called me in for an emergency meeting. Before even sitting down in his office, he pranced forward and took hold of my lab coat. He started flipping it back and forth while carefully inspecting the fabric.

"Where is it?"

"Where is what?"

"The Cobra pin! I was told you are in the Cobra Club."

"Well, you were told wrong. I'm not."

"Thank God." Skip sighed deeply, pranced back to his chair, and sat down.

"Skip, what on Earth is going on? What is the Cobra Club?"

"Beats and Slenderman started the club to undermine the hospital and bad-mouth me. Do you know what the pin stands for?"

This ought to be good. "No, I do not."

"A penis! An erect penis. That's what it symbolizes. How dirty. How disrespectful." Skip gently caressed his goatee.

"How silly. That sounds like something guys might do in junior high."

"It's a lot more serious than you think. They aren't supporting the Get Crabby program. They're mocking my initiatives. And they're bad-mouthing me. *Someone* has even gone so far as to report us to the state, saying we should lose our nonprofit status because we aren't giving charity care." Skip cast a suspicious look in my direction.

Does he know? I'd sent a letter stating just that.

"It's just bluster," I said. "The hospital isn't likely to lose its tax-exempt status." Hospitals around the country frequently abused their not-for-profit status. Only rarely did the state take action, sometimes not even when hospitals bullied little old ladies and tried to take their homes. My numerous letters had been met with silence.

"Your patient is part of the problem. She told Beats we are trying to take her house. That's ridiculous."

"The hospital is trying to take her house."

"Now... Dr. Wave, you know that isn't true. That bill was turned over to a collection agency. *They* are the ones trying to take her house, not us."

"The hospital will get half of any money collected." The hospital used an aggressive local agency to try to stay clean. The collection agency took little bills to small claims court, and the county docket was clogged with these cases. Larger bills, like Ms. Geras's bill, were handled even more aggressively with civil debt collection lawsuits.

No matter the judgment, the agency would apply bank liens, wage garnishments, and home foreclosures. The collection agency also pushed for contempt of court and body attachment orders against the debtor whenever possible. They would use things such as failure to show for an investigation of assets deposition or inability to follow a court-ordered payment plan to have the debtor arrested and thrown into jail for contempt of court. Debtors' prisons are alive and well in Mars, Nebraska, and many other places in America using contempt of court as the loophole.

"Well, fine point or not, technically, it isn't us." Skip crossed his arms. "And this is just one example of the Cobra Club causing trouble. They're bad-mouthing me. They're out to get me. And they are also the ones mocking me with the crap dance."

It was true the Cobras were mocking the crab program. But they weren't the only ones.

"I want you to tell everyone that anyone wearing a Cobra pin will be disciplined," Skip demanded.

"Alright, I will pass it on. No Cobra pins."

29
OFFICE INTERLUDE

Every year in the fall, Mars celebrated the Nut Fest, a fall festival like many held in cities around the country, with a few unique Mars twists. Sellers sold a variety of nuts—roasted, salted, and chocolate-covered. Also, there were the deep-fried bull testicles. T-shirts announcing, "Cold Beer and Hot Testicles" were ubiquitous.

Interestingly, patients presenting with complaints relating to their testicles increased substantially during the Nut Fest. A twenty-year-old patient presented for the visit reason, "I am growing a third nut." Appropriately, he was wearing the festival's famous shirt. He spoke up the moment he saw me.

"You've got to check my nuts. Something ain't right." His voice was distraught. Testicular masses can indicate testicular cancer. And this can occur even in young men. He had reason to worry.

Examining the patient, I discovered he had a small varicocele. The patient listened intently to the verdict, but he didn't understand. "A what? Is it cancer? Is that why I am growing a third nut?"

"It's a collection of veins, and it's harmless. You aren't growing a third testicle, either."

"It sure feels like a nut. You sure I'm not going to die?"

"Not any time soon. I'll order an ultrasound to confirm, but I am almost certain." An ultrasound of the testicles was a standard precautionary measure in this situation.

"Is this ultrasound going to squeeze my nuts?"

"There will be no squeezing."

"They aren't going to cut my nuts off, are they?"

"No cutting, either."

He looked skeptical, but nonetheless, he agreed to the ultrasound. "By the way, when will you cut out that third nut?"

"As I said, it's a varicocele, and we're going to leave it alone. It won't hurt you at all."

"So I gotta go through life with three nuts?"

Sigh. I repeated my entire explanation once again.

"What if it keeps growing? I saw a picture on the internet of a guy who had a huge nutsack. It was bigger than a freaking basketball."

"It won't keep growing. That picture was from a different disease." Certain rare diseases of the lymph glands can cause such swelling, but not a varicocele. *Thanks, Google!*

"You sure?"

"I'm sure." The ultrasound was negative for cancer and confirmed a small varicocele. The patient was delighted.

"Great news. I guess I can live with three nuts."

Sigh.

He enjoyed the rest of Nut Fest without fear or worries.

✦✦✦

Sally was grinning like the Cheshire cat. "This one's here

because he says he squeezed his balls too hard."

"He squeezed his own testicles?"

"Yes."

"Did he mention why?"

"I didn't ask. Be sure to let me know."

I walked down the hallway and entered the exam room.

"Good morning. I understand you're having some discomfort."

A young gentleman with a mop of black hair was sitting on the table. He looked just like Moe of *The Three Stooges* fame.

"Doc, I busted my balls. They hurt like hell." He kind of sounded like Moe too.

"What happened?"

"Well, I shot my load, grabbed my nuts, and squeezed. I guess I squeezed too hard this time."

"Why did you squeeze your testicles?"

"Huh? I did it to get all the stuff out."

"What stuff?"

"My spunk. My goo. I wanted all the goo out of my nutsack. It ain't healthy to leave it in there. I squeeze them every time to make sure it all comes out."

Good lord. This fellow's understanding of human anatomy and biology was nonexistent. It seemed the good townsfolk of Mars considered anything related to sex sinful, including sex education or anything pertaining to reproductive anatomy. Ignorance, however, was just fine.

I began a lecture on basic male reproductive anatomy, emphasizing that no squeezing of the testicles was required as this would cause only unnecessary pain.

"My buddy at Sal's told me you had to squeeze it all out." He had a doubtful tone.

"Your bar buddy is wrong."

"Huh. Well, what do you know? Okay. Thanks, Doc!" The patient left happy.

And as a nice bonus, he gave a good review: *Doctor knows everything about your nutsack. He's a nut expert!*
Crabby would be pleased.

+ + +

"What's a 'big ball?'" I asked Sally.

"He pointed down to his groin when I asked," Sally said. "Have fun."

The lyrics of the old AC/DC song "Big Balls" went through my mind as I entered the room. The patient, a forty-five-year-old, obese, brown-haired man who looked like the actor John Candy sat expectantly. Mars seemed to be filled with movie star look-alikes.

"Good afternoon. So what exactly is bringing you in today?"

"My big ball. The dog bit it."

"And what do you mean by that?" I asked.

His explanation indicated he had a large hernia in his groin. It bulged out, and he called it his "big ball."

"How was it the dog came to bite your big ball?"

"I was teasing him with it. Dog got mad and bit it." He explained he was taking his big ball and smacking his dog's nose with it.

This was potentially serious. Dog bites can cause serious bacterial infections. The hernia, which contains intestines, could become infected. And the intestines themselves could have been punctured.

"I'm starting you on antibiotics and sending you for a surgical evaluation." The referral was to a university surgeon, not Slenderman or any of the other clowns in the Mars Hospital surgery department.

"And don't ever again use your hernia to tease the dog," I added.

He promised, and the patient did well. The hernia was repaired at the university without complication.

The dog, undoubtably, was also happy.

+++

"Thunder Nuts is ready."

Sally sure had a knack for nicknames. "Why do you call him Thunder Nuts?"

"That's what everyone in town calls him, Wavesticks." She explained the patient had picked up the nickname from a large tattoo on his abdomen—a cloud surrounding the words "THUNDER NUTS" in large, bold block print. A lightning bolt shot out of each side of the cloud, each terminating at his groin near his right and left testicles, respectively. Saloon Sally, of course, was the tattoo artist.

The reason for Thunder Nuts' visit was unclear. His listed reason was, "How long to soak it." Soak what? Sally made a guess based on his nickname. My prediction was more mundane: a rash or skin lesion needing a cleaning. We were both wrong.

"What brings you in today, sir?" I took great care not to call him Thunder Nuts accidentally.

"Hey, Doc. Can you tell me, how long do you soak after sex? I want to make a baby with my girlfriend."

"You are soaking after sex? You mean in a bathtub?"

"No. How long do I soak my cock?"

"Why do you soak your penis? Does it hurt? Do you have some sort of a rash?" *Is this an STD visit?*

"No. I want to make a baby. How long do I soak it when I'm done?"

"Please explain precisely what you mean."

He had a strange idea about conception. He thought that, after sex, he needed to leave his penis soaking inside the vagina.

"You don't need to do that," I informed him. "You can take it right out."

"What? That can't be right. My buddy at Sal's told me you had to leave it in there soaking."

"Well, your buddy is wrong." Since Mars schools offered no sex education, it seemed there was some barfly teaching classes at Sal's Saloon, with predictable results.

"Well, ain't that a kick in the teeth. You absolutely sure?"

"Trust me. I am a doctor." His physical exam was normal, except for the large Thunder Nuts tattoo, which appeared exactly as described.

After the visit, Sally made the excellent suggestion of putting in a consult for an obstetrician to see his girlfriend. If she was as ignorant as he was regarding sex, she would need all the prenatal education and support she could get.

30

THE NUT FEST

One afternoon, Beats talked me into going to the Nut Fest. "There's a really good stand that sells corn dogs and salty nuts."

"No, thanks." Neither corn dogs nor salty nuts sounded appealing.

"Come on, Wave. You've got to try them. I'll drive. And I'll buy!"

"Alright. What the heck."

Beats drove a red, four-door 1980 Corvette convertible. Though it was an expensive car, it was rather ugly in my opinion. Inside, a Cobra ornament hung from the rear-view mirror. As he drove off, Beats's blond hair flew wildly in the breeze and the ornament swung like a pendulum.

"This must be the cobra-mobile."

"Yes, it is. You need to get a decent car, Wave. You'll never get laid driving a Honda Civic. There are a bunch of hot new physical therapists getting hired. You better hurry or you'll lose your place in line. Doctors are swarming. It's feeding time at the zoo."

"I didn't hear you say that. I've dealt with enough doctors swarming

inappropriately. You'd be wise to stay away from the physical therapists and all other hospital employees. As for cars," I continued, "I
invest my money. I don't spend it on cars." We talked about investments, a much more comfortable topic, as he drove. "Beats, my
investments are all in index funds, period. And not crappy ones like
the hospital's."

Beats laughed. He invested in all manner of high-risk, specula-
tive ventures. He reported he had invested in an oil well in Iowa
which was dry and a Hollywood movie which had flopped.

We arrived at the corn dog stand, Beats parked, and we found
our place in the long, snaking line.

"How many corn dogs and salties you want?" Beats asked when
we finally reached the front of the line.

"One of each."

He ordered the same. "They don't take credit cards. You have
any cash?" Beats carried no cash.

"Here's a twenty."

"I'll pay it back. I said I was buying."

"Don't worry about it."

The corn dogs were excellent. The salties, not so much.

+++

The next morning, an urgent message arrived from Skip instruct-
ing me to report at once to the administrative suite.

"There he is." Skip shouted the moment he saw me. He was agitated and huddling with several vice presidents.

"Good morning. What's going on?"

"What is this?" With both hands, he raised a white envelope over
his head. My name was written on it.

"It looks like an envelope to me."

"Yes! Beats dropped it off here this morning. He asked my secretary to give it to you. He said it contained money!" Skip scowled.

"Well, let's take a look." Tearing the envelope open revealed a crisp, new twenty-dollar bill.

"Kickback cash," Skip bellowed. "You can't take kickback cash from Beats. That's illegal."

"Skip, this is corn dog money. I gave Beats twenty bucks to buy corn dogs. He's repaying me."

Skip blinked and looked confused. "I thought it was kickback cash for sending him patients," he mumbled.

"No. He didn't have any cash on him, and the stand didn't take credit cards. It's corn dog cash, not a kickback."

Skip's cheeks turned red. "Well, I don't think you should be loaning money. It's not proper." He tried to sound righteous.

Unbelievable. "I promise not to loan corn dog money ever again."

I went to the doctors' lounge next and told the story to the usual crew. They all laughed except Slenderman.

"The things Skip worries about," he said. "What a useless sack of shit." Today Slenderman was eating donuts. Powdered sugar was once again changing his beard from black to white in small increments.

"It shows how his mind works," Beats said when he stopped laughing. "He's suspicious of kickbacks, which probably means he's getting them himself."

That wouldn't surprise me in the least.

31
THE HOSPITAL

One afternoon, a physician named Dr. Peitho called me, terribly upset. He was a Mars primary care doctor who worked in a remote office with a low patient volume. Skip was considering closing the office because it was not generating enough revenue.

He explained, "The visit was a simple follow-up. I had seen this female patient in the hospital for a lung condition. I was in the exam room listening to her lungs. Her husband was sitting right next to her when she made the accusation."

"What exactly was the accusation?"

"She said I reached around from behind and pinched both her nipples! And the husband said he saw me do it."

"Did you do anything that could have been construed as a pinch? Did you examine her breasts in any way or examine her chest?"

"I was listening to her lungs with my stethoscope. I never even touched her."

"Had you seen this patient before, or was this a new patient?"

"Other than at the hospital, no. She was a new patient, and this was her first office visit."

"Did you have a chaperone?"

"Of course not. Why would I?"

"To avoid accusations like this one." More and more doctors are subject to accusations. While accusations certainly must be taken seriously and the benefit of the doubt given to the accuser, sometimes accusations are made for gain. There are people out there who will use an allegation as a lever to obtain narcotics. There are people out there who are looking to gain money through a lawsuit. And there are people out there who are just plain crazy.

But there are also sick, perverted doctors. In the news, there have been many cases where doctors, sometimes for years, abuse patients. Because of this fact, any claim of abuse by a doctor must be taken seriously.

"What should I do?" Dr. Peitho asked, his voice full of distress.

"Do nothing. I need to file a report immediately with the medical staff and inform Skip."

His voice dropped. "If you say so."

After hanging up, I immediately filed a report of this incident with the medical staff office, the office of risk management, and the hospital's legal counsel. No prior accusation had ever been leveled against this physician. Of course, sometimes after one accusation, an avalanche of allegations follows.

The next step was calling Skip to report it. I expected him to do nothing.

"Do you think he did it? Did he grab her boobs? Did he pinch her nipples?" Skip's voice rose in anger. "We can't have doctors grabbing boobs and pinching nipples!"

"He denies it. It is an odd accusation. I mean, would he really pinch nipples with her husband sitting right there?"

"Her husband is a witness. It'll be the word of two against one." Skip's voice became animated.

In my mind's eye, he was holding onto his goatee for dear life.

"He has no history of other accusations," I said. "And he's horrified she's making this claim. I'll admit it's hard to believe. But, bottom line, you're right. It will be his word against hers."

"And the word of her husband," Skip added.

"Yes. There was no chaperone." *Too bad there wasn't a nurse or scribe present to act as a witness.*

"He's got to go. I'm firing him, effective immediately."

My jaw dropped. *No secret file this time.* "What? That doesn't seem fair. There should at least be some due process. We should have someone talk with the patient and her husband. There should be an investigation."

"No. He's gone. We have to fire him so we aren't liable."

We?

"I don't think it's a question of liability—"

Skip cut me off. "Of course it's a question of liability. As his employer, we might be liable for his criminal activity. If we fire him now, we'll have a better chance to avoid paying a legal settlement."

"He claims he's innocent. Perhaps we—"

"No. He's gone. Call him now and tell him I fired him for cause: licentiousness." Skip's voice beamed with pride as he used his big words. There is a clause in the standard Mars Hospital contract allowing immediate termination for licentiousness, but the term wasn't clearly defined and gave Skip an easy way to get rid of doctors when it suited him.

"Skip, don't you think—" The line clicked and went dead.

Calling the doctor back and doing Skip's dirty work was painful. Hearing the news, the doctor broke down and cried.

The patient filed a police report. An investigation of the complaint did not lead to charges. The patient also filed a civil lawsuit against the hospital and the doctor. As Skip had hoped, the hospital was dismissed from the suit.

The civil case against the doctor was later settled with no admission of guilt.

Did the assault really happen? Who knows? But after the sad episode, Sally accompanied me as a chaperone more frequently.

+++

Beats called me not a week after the primary care doctor had been fired. My heart sank at his news.

"Wave, a nurse is making trouble for me. She has filed a complaint."

"What happened?"

He explained. Beats had been on the general medical ward checking on one of his patients. He'd approached a nurse sitting in the nurse's station, walked up behind her, and started rubbing her neck and shoulders.

"I also made a few comments, just joking around, and she got all bent out of shape," Beats added.

"What were your joking comments?"

"I joked about her nice rack." He guffawed. "She didn't like it and got up from her chair to leave. As she walked away, I said she had a nice ass, too, and gave her rear a couple of harmless smacks."

Oh, my God. This is a huge problem. "Skip just fired a doctor for a sexual assault accusation," I told him. And in Beats's case, it was no accusation; it was a free admission of guilt.

"I heard."

"Good, so you know the stakes. What happened next?"

"She got all worked up and started crying. I guess I did crack her ass a little too hard. It echoed through the nursing station." Beats started laughing again.

"That sounds terrible."

"What should I do?"

Start packing your bags and call a lawyer.

"I think you should report it to Skip yourself, personally, right now. Talk to him, face-to-face." *This time around, let Skip do the dirty work.* "I will, of course, have to file an incident report with the medical staff office."

"I'll tell Skip. I'll talk to him in the next day or two. You go ahead and file your report. I know you gotta do that. No biggie. They can add it to the pile." Beats chuckled.

The pile?

"Talk to Skip now. Right now. Go there immediately. The longer you wait, the more trouble you'll face."

"You know, that sounds like good advice. I'll walk over there right now."

A call from Skip informing me of his termination, no doubt, would be forthcoming. But after filing my reports, hours passed with no call. Calling Skip's office, a little after four, was fruitless. He, of course, had already left for the day. The secretary reported he had met with Beats earlier, but she knew nothing else. What happened the next day was appalling but, knowing Skip, not surprising.

Skip quashed the issue. He transferred the complaining nurse to a different unit, and she quit soon after. Beats told me he'd apologized to Skip and had told him he didn't mean anything by his actions in the nurse's station. Skip had accepted his apology, had given him a talking-to, and had placed my incident report in Beats's secret file.

It was obvious at once why Skip had responded so differently to the two reports of sexual assault. The fired doctor worked in a small clinic with low revenues that Skip wanted to close anyway. It was a great opportunity for Skip to shut down that office and lighten the payroll. Beats, however, was a specialist and generated millions in revenue for the hospital. He was, in Skip's mafia-like words, one of the hospital's biggest earners.

It was the money. With Skip, it was always the money.

32
PHYSICIANS' MEETING

The fall meeting's agenda was full, but the meeting room wasn't. Fewer than twenty physicians showed. Given the value of these meetings, I couldn't blame the doctors for not attending and took no action to enforce attendance.

Skip started the meeting by emphasizing the importance of the Get Crabby program. He addressed the doctors directly. "Doctors, I have received numerous reports that some physicians are not taking the program seriously. Therefore, everyone will be required to take a test on the content of the book." Scattered chuckles followed. Skip flushed. "This is important. I expect everyone to get crabby." More giggling. Skip was reaching for his goatee when Slenderman spoke up.

"Skip, this program is stupid. No one is going to take it seriously. I'm not reading that damned book or taking a damned test. Fire me if you want. I don't care. I won't do it."

Several doctors spoke up in agreement.

"Do you seriously expect us to dance?"

"The book and video are childish."

"No one has time for this new-age junk."

More whispered derogatory comments.

Skip sat down, dejected.

No puppet show or pantomime today.

Skip flashed an angry glance toward me as though he could read my mind. Time to move on to the next item on the agenda.

"As to the next topic," I stated loudly, "it has come to administration's attention that some physicians have been wearing Cobra pins on their lab coats." This statement triggered renewed chuckles.

"Is that a pledge pin on your uniform?" one doctor said, quoting the line from the movie *Animal House*. His imitation of Mark Metcalf was excellent.

Skip's face darkened with growing fury.

"What's a Cobra pin?" another doctor innocently asked.

"It's a pin in the shape of a cobra," Skip suddenly shouted. He then jumped up from his seat and stood erect. His voice rose as he continued speaking. "This is not appropriate professional attire and must not be worn. Doctors who continue to wear the Cobra pin will face disciplinary action."

Another doctor asked, "What's the big deal? What's wrong with the pin?"

"It's a hateful, anti-administration pin!" Skip's face betrayed his rage, but all he got was the doctors' laughter. "This isn't funny! This pin has a sexual connotation, and wearing it will not be tolerated. It represents a penis! An erect penis!"

I felt embarrassment at the spectacle Skip was making of himself. Finally, he sat down with a look of fury on his face.

"Penis?" Dr. Lyssa suddenly added. Like gasoline to fire, the room exploded in laughter. Lyssa continued repeating the word. Then, surprisingly, she said, "Oh, I'm sorry. I should not have said that." She said nothing the rest of the meeting.

Her counseling might be helping.

"Next topic," I said. "Let's talk about the computer system." Several new items relating to the electronic medical record were presented. Each item required more doctor time and data entry.

"Can we get scribes to help us with all these data requirements?" Dr. Wurst asked.

"No!" Skip answered at once, sounding totally annoyed. "That would be an extra expense we don't have in the budget."

"It would increase productivity if we had scribes."

"I said no. You would have to see double the number of patients to break even on a scribe. Double!"

"That's crazy," Dr. Wurst said, a bit bewildered. "My average billing is four to five patients an hour. Are you saying I would have to see ten patients an hour to break even on the hiring of a scribe?"

"At least." Skip folded his arms and pouted.

"My average office charge is one hundred to two hundred dollars. And that doesn't factor in the extra revenue from testing or referrals."

"That other revenue doesn't count."

"Just listen for a minute. Let's say I bill a hundred dollars a visit. You're saying that I'd have to generate an extra five hundred dollars an hour to cover a scribe? Scribes earn thirty to forty dollars an hour, tops."

"Well, you also have to take into account benefits and extra administrative costs."

"Seriously? You're going to tell me that for a forty-dollar-an-hour salary, there are four hundred sixty dollars in extra costs?"

"Around here, there probably are. Mars Hospital has more middle managers than you can count," Slenderman interjected, which infuriated Skip.

"I don't expect you to understand." He was quivering with anger. "You are doctors. This is finance." Even the beet-red skin on his hairless head was trembling. "I'm telling you, we don't have it in the budget. No scribes. Next topic."

"What about our bonuses?" Dr. Wurst continued. "Those were due to be paid out months ago. When are we getting paid?"

"We're working on it. Bonuses will be coming out soon. We're doing the calculations."

"They were due exactly a hundred and thirty-two days ago."

"The contract allows appropriate processing time."

"In the contract, it says bonuses are due April thirtieth. It further states that all checks have to be issued within thirty days of that date to allow for processing." Dr. Wurst was well-prepared.

"That means thirty business days."

"The contract says days, not business days, but even so, it has been more than thirty business days. Are you going to pay us what we're due?"

He cast a stern look at Dr. Wurst. "Some of you are being overpaid." Dr. Wurst was very productive and received enormous bonus checks. "We have to take a look at total compensation from a corporate compliance standpoint."

The room erupted, this time not in laughter.

"Overpaid? What are you talking about? We're supposed to receive the amount agreed to in each of our contracts!" Dr. Wurst did not look happy.

"Well, I was going to wait until I had finished all the calculations. Some of your bonus checks are too large. Some bonuses are six figures. I need to adjust the payment as we can't pay out that kind of bonus money. It isn't right. We can't pay any doctor more than the seventy-fifth percentile of what doctors nationwide make in their respective specialty."

"Says who?" Dr. Wurst said. "That's not what the contract states."

"Well, that's the law. We'll give everyone a contract addendum before the bonuses are paid. Our lawyers are working on this."

Dr. Wurst seethed. "I am not signing any contract addendum." A cacophony of voices agreed with him.

"You have to sign it." Skip's head was as red as fire. "I run this hospital, and what I say goes."

"But the hospital bylaws state—" another doctor began speaking.

"Bylaws? My law trumps the bylaws or any other rule or regulation in this hospital. I am the law!" Skip shouted, pounding the table. Following this outburst was silence. Even Dr. Slenderman, for once, was speechless.

"Wow," another doctor finally said.

"Skip." Dr. Wurst spoke slowly and calmly. "You can give me a contract addendum if you want. But listen very carefully. I will sign *nothing*. I am going to contact my lawyer and have him send a demand letter for the bonus."

"The contract addendum is very reasonable." Skip sounded calmer, and his voice had an edge of concern. Dr. Wurst's threat had no doubt intimidated him.

"It reduces our pay to a reasonable level?" Slenderman helpfully suggested.

"Yes," Skip quickly agreed, not seeing the trap.

Dr. Slenderman pounced. "Ha! That is the stupidest thing I ever heard. A deal is a deal. If the hospital didn't want to pay each doctor what is stipulated in their contract, they shouldn't have signed it. Dr. Wurst is right. No one in their right mind would sign a contract addendum to cut their pay."

"But you *have* to sign. I'm in charge and say you have to," Skip whined. "Our lawyers say you have to sign."

"You better get new lawyers," Slenderman stated flatly.

It's time for me to end this. "I think we should move on. We aren't going to resolve this issue right now. I suggest Skip talk further with hospital counsel and address the matter again later."

"Good idea, Dr. Wave," Skip quickly agreed. He sounded relieved. "We have other, more important business to cover." These more important topics would not include anything related to sexual harassment. Skip had vetoed my plans for a seminar on the topic. He was afraid "it would give the doctors ideas."

Skip announced a bake sale to raise money for charity. He also announced a retirement party for a middle manager. Finally, he reported the parking lot was going to be closed for a couple of days. It was getting a new coat of blacktop!

"What about improving our computer reliability or internet speed?" a doctor asked when Skip had finished.

"We are looking into that."

"You say that every meeting. Nothing ever happens."

Other doctors brought up other outstanding issues. They got the same non-answer.

"Dr. Wave, I think we have run over our allotted time." Skip had had enough. He was pulling the plug on the meeting. "We'll continue this discussion later. Meeting adjourned." Skip shot out of the room like a bullet. Even running, he moved with his odd little prance, as several rude comments pointed out after he was gone.

The doctors, mostly grumbling, left the room slowly.

Dr. Lyssa cast me a wary look as she walked out of the room.

Did I just hear her say "penis" in the hallway?

+ + +

After the meeting, the doctors' lounge was in an uproar.

"You see now why Stercus took a shit in front of Skip's door?" Beats commented when he saw me enter. "Skip will be getting even more steamers if he hands out a contract addendum."

Several doctors agreed, and some even went so far as to volunteer for duty.

A wry smile involuntarily crossed my face, but this was no way to act. "Defecating in front of his office won't help."

"Probably not. But Stercus sure had it right," Beats added.

Several doctors in the lounge were now sporting Cobra pins on their lab coats. Slenderman was handing them out from a cardboard box. "I will salute any doctor who shits in front of the door to administration," he said. "Hey, Wave. What did you do with your pin?"

"I won't wear one. When I went into administration one day, Skip patted me down looking for it."

"No way," Slenderman shook his head.

"He hates those pins. What they symbolize, even more so."

"I like the pins even more after today's meeting," Slenderman said as he pinned a cobra to Dr. Wurst's lapel.

"Skip should be worrying about paying the doctors and addressing real issues," Dr. Wurst said, proudly displaying his new pin. "He shouldn't waste his time worrying about Cobra pins." He took an extra pin for Sally.

Great, that's just what she needs.

Beats began the "Crap dance." Wurst and a couple of other doctors immediately joined in.

That's my cue to leave.

33
OFFICE INTERLUDE

"You better come see this," Sally announced one morning while looking out the front office window. She was wearing a Cobra pin.

"What is it?"

"Look." A man was riding a lawnmower down the middle of the street, a long line of cars and trucks following him, vigorously honking their horns. "That's your next patient."

The patient, a fifty-five-year-old gentleman, was coming in for "trouble sleeping." The patient parked his lawnmower, and after Sally put him in an exam room, she returned to inform me, "This guy is *loaded*."

Sigh. "And it's not even noon," I said.

"Not even nine-thirty! He can barely stand."

"Terrific."

The smell of booze hit my face the moment I opened the exam room door. The patient was sound asleep on the exam table. He snored loudly and required vigorous shaking to wake him.

"Are you okay, sir?"

"Doc, I'm fine. I want some sleeping pills. I can't sleep." The irony of his comment didn't register.

"You were sleeping just now."

"I was tired from the drive. The sleeping pills are for nighttime. I can't sleep at night."

No way. Sleeping pills, when mixed with alcohol, can be fatal.

"Why were you riding down the road on a lawnmower?"

"I don't have a license. I got some DUIs."

"How many?"

"Three or four, maybe five. I'll never get a license again." That was certain. In Nebraska, having multiple DUI convictions precluded a driver's license and could land you in prison.

"You shouldn't even be driving a lawnmower when you're drunk. Did you know you could get another DUI for that?"

"No, you can't. It's not a car."

"Yeah, but it has a motor. And you were driving down the street."

He became agitated. "Impossible!"

"I think we should talk about your drinking problem."

"I don't have a drinking problem."

"Sir, you have multiple DUIs, and you're drunk right now. You have a problem." In this town, he wasn't the only one.

"I haven't been drinking today, except for a few beers for breakfast I drank over at Sal's."

"Beer for breakfast means you have been drinking today."

"Just a few." He hiccupped loudly. Clearly, I needed to wait until he'd sobered up to discuss his drinking problem.

"I'll make you another appointment. Let's reschedule. Do you have someone we can call to come pick you up?"

"What about my sleeping pills?"

"Sleeping pills can interact with alcohol and kill you."

"I take sleeping pills all the time."

Who is prescribing this guy sleeping pills? The records, unsurprisingly, revealed it was Dr. Do.

"You shouldn't take these while drinking," I advised. "That's extremely dangerous."

"You're not going to give me the pills?"

"As I said, I can't."

"I knew I shouldn't have come." He cut me off. "My bar buddy told me you probably wouldn't write for the pills."

I felt pride hearing my reputation in town. "Do you have someone we can call for a ride?"

"Already got a ride."

"I can't let you leave on that mower. You're drunk."

"You can't stop me." He made a menacing glare, got up, and walked out of the exam room and the office. He climbed onto his lawnmower and started driving. *Time to call the cops.* While bound by patient confidentiality, medical ethics require a doctor to act if a patient is doing something that puts other lives in danger. Driving drunk down the road on a lawnmower was a clear example. Sally heartily agreed and handed me the phone.

But the call wasn't necessary. The moment he turned onto the road, sirens blared and squad car lights flashed red. The Mars police, having undoubtably been called by angry motorists, were waiting for the lawnmower man. As soon as he pulled into traffic, the police stopped him and arrested him for DUI.

He was convicted of DUI and driving on a revoked license. He received prison time. And he blamed me. Before going to prison, he wrote a scathing review, accusing me of refusing to treat him as well as calling the police. He also threatened to sue, but he never did. But his negative review and a one-star satisfaction rating were as bad as any lawsuit. The review and rating would float around the internet to haunt me forever.

And Crabby, always watching, would be angry, while Skip, always waiting, would cut my pay.

+ + +

Later that week, there was an even more serious drunk driving incident. It happened on a Saturday morning. Once a month, Saturday clinic was held for patients who couldn't make regular office hours. That morning, a car sped into the parking lot. The driver, a man, parked the vehicle parked sloppily and staggered out of the car and into my office.

"Where's the doctor?" he asked, slurring his speech. He could barely walk.

"What is going on here?"

"You the doctor?"

"Yes. What may I do for you?"

"I need these pills refilled." He handed me an empty methadone bottle. Dr. Do was the prescribing physician.

Methadone has two primary uses. First, to detox and treat heroin addicts. This requires a special license Dr. Do didn't have. Second, it's used in specially licensed pain clinics for the treatment of chronic pain. Dr. Do's clinic wasn't licensed for this either. A special license is required because methadone is a synthetic opioid in the same family as heroin and Oxycontin. Although it has less potency than the other opioids, outside of a treatment protocol, it can be very addictive and subject to abuse.

I handed the empty bottle back to the drunk man. "I didn't write for these pills."

"I know. My doctor's in rehab. I lost my pills and need a refill." He explained he'd accidentally dropped his full 100-tablet bottle of methadone into the bathtub. All 100 of the tablets had rolled right down the drain. It was an unbelievable story told through slurred speech.

"I didn't write for these pills, which means I can't help you."

"But my doctor's out and I need more."

"Sorry, sir. I can't refill them."

"Then who can?"

"You can't get them here. This clinic doesn't have the required license. And, in any event, you're drunk. This medicine shouldn't be mixed with alcohol. I'll call a family member, friend, or cab. You're in no shape to drive."

"You goddamned piece of shit." He gave me the finger as he left the office. Tires squealing, he sped out of the parking lot. He did not, however, turn on to the road. He turned onto the sidewalk where children might have been playing. It was a beautiful, sunny Saturday morning. Sally handed me the phone with neither of us speaking.

I dialed 911. Police sirens came in screaming moments later, and two squad cars flew past the office. The drunk pill-seeker was arrested just a few blocks away, still driving on the sidewalk. His blood alcohol level was three and a half times the legal limit.

Fortunately, he'd harmed no children.

Bushes, trees, and garden gnomes hadn't been so lucky.

+ + +

"The ankle sprain is ready, Wavesticks. She's really hurting. She's in the room with her dad." Sally's appeared deeply concerned.

The father of the patient, an eighteen-year-old girl, had called earlier begging for his daughter to be seen. Sally had told him to come right in. A review of the records showed his daughter had been in the emergency room the night before and had been diagnosed with a sprained ankle. The reports were unremarkable. The patient had been given an x-ray, which came back normal, and she was given an ACE wrap, crutches, and ibuprofen before being sent home. Standard treatment. But Sally's face made me suspect something wasn't right.

"Do you think she's faking? Maybe looking for narcotics?" I asked. The sprained ankle trick was just behind back pain as the most common reason used by drug seekers.

"I don't think so. This one looks legit." Sally had a good nose for drug seekers, and I trusted her judgment.

"Good morning," I said, entering the exam room.

The patient, a stocky young lady with long, blonde hair and wearing a team uniform, was crying. Her father was close to crying too. He spoke right up.

"Doctor, I think she broke her ankle. She's miserable."

"The x-ray was negative for fracture, but I can take another look at her ankle." Just removing the ACE dressing caused the patient to gasp in pain.

While I worked, the patient explained she'd been playing in a softball game. She'd slid into second base and had immediately felt intense pain in her ankle and lower leg. She couldn't walk. The ankle wouldn't bear weight. And any movement caused severe pain. She had been up all night with the pain and hadn't even changed out of her uniform.

"I'm no doctor, but I was in the ER with my daughter last night," the dad added. "And I saw the x-ray. The bones were definitely apart. It was broken! And the emergency doctor didn't even see her. A nurse practitioner came in and told her it was a sprain. She put the x-ray on a screen to show us. I pointed right to the spot where the two bones were apart, and she said it was just a shadow." The father's description of events was very troubling.

"Are you sure the doctor didn't come in at some point?"

"No. We never saw the doctor." The emergency room notes reported a detailed exam by the emergency physician. In addition, he had signed off on the x-ray as having "personally reviewed the x-ray with the patient." This documentation is important as it allows the doctor to charge for the service. If what the father was saying was correct, this was yet another clear case of billing fraud, not to mention gross malpractice.

"Oh my." A gasp escaped my mouth once I'd removed the ACE bandage. The bones were clearly broken. While it wasn't a compound fracture, a situation where the broken bone tears through the skin, it was close. I could see the broken end of the bone tenting upward on the skin, and the entire foot had turned black and blue. The patient gasped for breath and almost fainted from the pain.

"Doctor, I told you it wasn't normal." Dad was right.

"She needs surgery immediately. I'll call an orthopedic surgeon at the University of Omaha and arrange ambulance transport."

"Why didn't they do that last night?" His voice was angry.

"I have no answer for that. But we should focus on what to do right now—get her to the university hospital for emergency surgery." After she left by ambulance, I called the Mars Hospital radiology department.

"Has anyone seen the ankle x-ray yet?" I gave the patient's name.

"No, it's still in the pile of x-rays from last night."

"Well, put it on the top of the pile and get the radiologist to look at it now." Ten minutes later, Dr. Theia, the radiologist on duty, called back.

"They totally blew this x-ray. The ankle and leg are broken in several places."

Dr. Theia was aghast when he heard the story of what had happened to this poor girl. "We should have twenty-four-hour radiology coverage," he said. "Emergency doctors don't have sufficient training to read x-rays. But Skip says it isn't in the budget."

Of course Skip says it isn't.

The patient did well with surgery. Pins were placed, and after a long course of physical therapy, she recovered. Naturally, I forwarded reports of this gross malpractice to the state medical board and appropriate hospital departments. I warned that a lawsuit was likely, in hopes this might trigger action, but it didn't.

And she never sued the hospital, despite having what would have been a slam-dunk malpractice case. Only a small fraction of patients with legitimate claims of malpractice ever sue.

34

THE HOSPITAL

Dr. Demeter called one afternoon for advice on his pending malpractice case. Litigation had been dragging on for years, but the case would soon go to trial. The case centered on a patient who presented to the emergency room and was assigned to him, as he was on call that night and this patient had no doctor. The patient was admitted, treated for an acute issue, and discharged in good health. A week later, the patient died at home from an unrelated cause. The family sued the doctor and hospital for $8 million, but it was a very weak case. After all, the patient had died long after discharge and from a different problem.

"So what's the issue?"

"Skip demands that I settle." The doctor explained that the hospital had first tried to claim he wasn't a hospital employee, disavowing him even though he had a contract and received a regular paycheck. They made this claim in hopes that the hospital would be dismissed from the lawsuit. The hospital is jointly liable for any malpractice judgments against any employee, just as any company is jointly liable for its employees' actions in the performance of their professional duties. That ridiculous attempt to get out of the lawsuit had failed. Now Skip wanted the doctor to settle.

"They've offered to settle for five hundred thousand. The judgment would be split equally between my malpractice insurance and the hospital's. Skip says it's a good deal, and that I should take it. But I didn't do anything wrong. And if I settle, it'll go on my record."

All malpractice settlements against doctors are reported to the National Practitioner Data Bank. This is a national repository for all malpractice settlements and judgments in the US. Anything reported to this repository follows doctors for life, impacting their ability to get hired at reputable hospitals and clinics, which is why the Dr. Dos of the world come to places like Mars Hospital. And it affects how much future malpractice insurance will cost. Hospital administrators, on the other hand, suffer no such consequences from insurance settlements.

"You aren't required to settle," I said. "If you feel you didn't commit malpractice, you *shouldn't* settle." Mars Hospital's malpractice carrier for employed physicians didn't have a forced settle clause. More and more hospitals were using forced settle policies for their employees. In these policies, if the insurance company demands that you settle, you have no choice. It's an abhorrent policy for doctors. Skip must have been unaware these policies existed, or he'd certainly impose them on Mars physicians.

"Skip told me that if I lose the case, the lawyers will come after my assets. He says if I have a judgment over my one-million-dollar malpractice coverage limit, I'll lose everything."

"That's not true. They'll take any excess judgment amount from the hospital's insurance. The hospital carries thirty million." Doctors rarely had their personal assets at risk.

"They do? Skip didn't tell me that."

Skip was trying to bully this doctor into settling because he feared a large judgment would raise the hospital's insurance premiums. Of course he wouldn't tell the doctor the truth.

"Skip also said that if I didn't settle, the malpractice insurance company would cancel my insurance. And he said if I lost, I'd never get insurance or work as a doctor again."

Skip had really piled it on.

"That isn't true, either. If you lose the case, your premiums will go up. But doctors rarely lose their insurance." This was the doctor's first malpractice case. Doctors with many of them—such as Dr. Do—still managed to qualify for insurance. And it was the hospital, as the employer, who paid the premiums anyway. Skip's whole "you'll lose your insurance and never work again" line was just a bluff. But that hadn't been his only threat.

"He also said I'd have to use vacation time if I went to court. I don't have much to begin with, and Skip said he wouldn't pay me while I was out."

"He said that?" This was preposterous as well as infuriating. Defending a malpractice case was part of a doctor's regular duties. It's certainly no vacation.

"Yes. What do you think I should do?"

"That's really your decision, but this is what I'd do. If I didn't provide proper care, I would admit it and accept whatever damages were claimed. If, however, I knew that I *had* provided proper care, I would never admit otherwise. I'd take the case to trial and let the chips fall where they may."

"That sounds like an honest approach."

"Besides, if you admit malpractice, you must make a statement in court. If you don't really believe you committed malpractice, stating so is perjury. And anyone trying to force you to perjure yourself is committing subornation of perjury. That's a felony. As for vacation,

I'd tell Skip that if he charges you, you won't attend the trial, settle, or show up in court. This is a civil case. You aren't required to show up. If you don't, a default judgment is entered, and the hospital would be stuck paying anything your malpractice policy won't cover, so that would fall right back into Skip's lap. You have the real power here."

The doctor took my suggestions to heart. He threatened to tell the judge that Skip and his insurance-assigned lawyer were trying to make him commit perjury. And he threatened to no-show at the trial if charged vacation time. Skip backed down, and afterward stormed around the hospital for a few days in a rage. Fortunately for me, as I didn't need the extra headache, the doctor never mentioned who had advised his course of action.

The case went to trial, and the jury was out all of five minutes. They ruled in the doctor's favor, and the plaintiffs received nothing.

35
THE END OF FALL

"Doctor, we have a problem. More complaints are coming in about you!"

My final fall meeting was off to a wonderful start.

"Oh? What complaints?" I asked. *Had it been the lawnmower man, the methadone guy, or both?*

"A patient called and said you called the police on him. He said he was driving a lawnmower, and you called and reported him."

Looks like we have a winner! "That isn't true. Someone else did."

Dead silence.

After about a minute, Skip spoke. "But he called and said it was you."

Silence.

I looked directly at Skip. Another minute passed. He finally broke.

"He wouldn't say it unless it were true."

"Are you calling me a liar, Skip?"

"Now... Dr. Wave, I'm not saying you're lying." His tone was flustered, he broke eye contact, and his right hand started seeking out his goatee. Despite the bluster, at his core, Skip was a coward.

"Good. He arrived drunk on a lawnmower. He wanted a refill of controlled substances, which I refused. He left the clinic against my advice, drunk, on a lawnmower. The police were waiting for him, probably because of angry motorists' complaints. When he turned his riding lawnmower onto the road, the police arrested him. I don't doubt he thinks I called the police, but I did not. You can check with them."

"Did you go out and talk to the police on his behalf?"

"No. I'm glad they arrested him."

"Dr. Wave! That's not good customer service. That's exactly what I've been talking about for the last few months. That's why we tried the crab program."

Tried? My heart rate soared. "He was drunk," I reiterated. "He was a threat to public safety. I did not report him, but I was about to." *No need to mention the methadone guy if Skip hasn't already heard about him.*

"Maybe if you had refilled his medication, none of this would have happened."

"Skip, it was a controlled substance that interacts with alcohol. It was not indicated, and it could have killed him."

"You seem to think prescribing controlled substances is never indicated. Do you ever write for narcotics?"

"Occasionally. But I'm careful. As you know, doctors can lose their licenses over prescribing narcotics."

"The reports I'm getting are that you are too strict in your prescribing. You should reflect on loosening up your habits."

"I will reflect on it." *Doctors don't go to jail for reflecting. But I am not going to loosen up.*

"Good. Now, let's talk about the crab program. The doctors are still refusing to participate. Due to their irrational behavior, I'm dropping the program." Skip droned on about how great the program was, how regrettable it was that the doctors had refused to give it a fair chance, and how much money it would cost the hospital to pull out. As he talked, I did my best to keep my face blank. But my heart was full of glee.

"I also want to talk about the Cobra problem. We've told doctors not to wear the pin, but they still are." He proposed various possible solutions to crack down on Cobra pins, my favorite one being random checks performed by nurses. Half the nurses on staff wore Cobra pins themselves.

"I don't think that solution will work. Nurses work closely with doctors. They would be unlikely to report them."

Skip reluctantly agreed. "The nurses are as much of a problem as the doctors around here. They're threatening to join a union!" The thought of a unionized nursing staff terrified Skip more than anything. Any nurse participating in activities to form a union was fired immediately. This, of course, is illegal, so Skip would always come up with a flimsy pretense to justify the termination. Sadly, in an at-will employment state such as Nebraska, these terminations are both expensive and hard to fight in court. Few people even try.

"Skip, how should we address the issues brought up at the physicians' meeting? Especially bonus pay."

"Legal counsel says we can't force doctors to sign a contract addendum." Skip's voice was filled with sadness. "They say we could fire the doctors, but we can't force them to sign a contract addendum."

"So what does that mean for us?"

"It means I might have to pay them after all. I'll still cut the amounts if patient satisfaction scores aren't perfect. I just can't write six-figure bonus checks."

Hopefully, he hasn't seen my online reviews. "If a doctor earns a six-figure bonus, the hospital makes many times this in revenue,"

I pointed out.

"That revenue doesn't count."

Why?

Skip suddenly changed topics. "Doctor, I haven't received your application to stay on permanently as medical director."

My right eyebrow rose in suspicion. *He wants my application?*

"I won't be applying for the permanent job, Skip." My new job search was well underway.

"Good, because I'm eliminating your position at the end of your contract. It'll save money."

"Who will handle physician matters?"

"I'll personally take care of all medical director duties."

That's not going to go over well.

"What about the clinic? Who will staff it?"

"Oh, I don't know. I'll find somebody."

Hopefully, for Sally's sake, not Dr. Lyssa or Dr. Do.

"In my opinion, Skip, this hospital needs a medical—"

"It's done. Do you have anything else for me today?"

"I should inform you of some issues pertaining to the emergency room." I had collected and reported to the state and federal government many issues relating to malpractice and illegal billing. As medical director, it was my duty to inform Skip of these matters despite the fact I suspected he would do nothing. I had delayed this report to Skip long enough.

"Yes, I know about your little investigation." Skip frowned.

"Here's a copy of my findings." I set a large file in front of Skip containing the misdiagnosis and fraudulent billing on the ankle sprain, the stroke diagnosed as alcohol intoxication, the patient who'd fainted and was diagnosed with low blood sugar when in fact the sugar was sky-high, the patient with a reported normal pelvic exam who had a long-forgotten tampon stuck inside her, causing a horrible infection, the patient diagnosed with a toothache who had a serious case of oral herpes, the patient who'd cut his arms with a knife in a misguided attempt to relieve high blood pressure and had been committed to the Mars mental hospital, the patient who'd arrived covered in nicotine patches, which weren't removed, and subsequently had suffered a heart attack from nicotine poisoning, and many other similar cases. Sprinkled in with the malpractice, numerous cases of billing fraud were also documented in detail.

"These cases must be formally reviewed, and action must be taken," I said. "I have of course reported these to the department chair, but nothing has been done. And the billing fraud needs to stop immediately."

Skip took my file. He didn't even pretend to look at it.

"I'll handle all this personally." He pranced over to the file cabinet and started placing the reports in various secret files.

"A formal case review and disciplinary hearing—"

"Dr. Wave, this meeting is over."

The rest of the day, between patient visits and with Sally's help, I mailed off innumerable packages again reporting the malpractice to the Nebraska State Medical Board and the billing fraud to the Office of the Inspector General and Department of Justice Health Care Fraud Unit. Although I had already reported all these cases, this time I included both Skip's and the medical staff departmental chairs' inaction with the reports.

I finished the fall season smiling.

Winter is coming.

WINTER

36
THE NURSING HOME

One winter afternoon, Saloon Sally called the office regarding the Mars Nursing Home.

"Doc, a nursing home patient is walking down the middle of the street. He walked right past the saloon. I figured I'd give you a call, even though you've told half my customers to stop drinking." She chuckled. "Lucky for me, the dumbasses don't listen."

I grinned. "How do you know it's a nursing home patient?"

"The home's a block away and some old man just walked by in a red gown open at the back with his ass hanging out."

Sounds like a nursing home patient to me.

"Did you call the nursing home?" Dr. Bacchus is the Mars Nursing Home medical director, so it was unclear why she was calling me.

"That was my first call. I talked to a nurse. She said he couldn't be a nursing home patient. I cussed her ass out, so she transferred me to Dr. Bacchus, one of my morning regulars. He said I was crazy and must be drunk."

Calling Dr. Bacchus a morning regular was disturbing but not enough to report. And given the lax security at the nursing home, not to mention all its other problems, Sal's story didn't seem crazy to me. Unfortunately, despite my complaints, the state had taken no action against the facility. Other than complain, all I could do was refuse to send patients there.

"Thank you for letting me know. I'll call the fire department."

They dispatched a crew. An elderly nursing home patient was found wandering down the road just as Saloon Sally had reported. He suffered from Alzheimer's disease and had no idea where he was going. The fire department took him straight to the Mars Hospital emergency room. An hour or so later, my office phone rang again. It was the ER doctor.

"Dr. Wave, I have a report on the nursing home case."

"I'm happy to take it, but why are you calling me? The report should go to the nursing home director. Dr. Bacchus is the attending physician for this patient, not me."

"Yes, but I thought I should call you. This patient doesn't just have Alzheimer's disease and mild hypothermia from walking outside in the cold. He's drunk. His blood alcohol level is 0.11. The nursing home chart shows Dr. Bacchus has been regularly ordering him beer."

My jaw dropped. "Beer?" It's unheard of to order alcohol for nursing home patients. *Why would anyone give a nursing home patient beer?*

"That's right. I couldn't believe it myself. But there's a written order. And this isn't the only patient he prescribes beer to. Apparently, it's a habit."

"Thank you. I need to report this at once." Dr. Bacchus, while not a hospital employee, was a member of the Mars Hospital medical staff. Thus, the fact that he'd personally ordered beer—an act of clear malpractice—could be held to account by the Mars Hospital medical staff, at least in theory. Nursing home actions, on the other hand, such as subjecting patients to the hose room and serving frozen food, while horrible, weren't specific acts of malpractice by this doctor and therefore weren't under the medical staff's purview. All I could do in those cases was report the behavior to the state.

And though I had seen, reported, and complained about plenty of malpractice in the last nine months, this time I was going to *insist* on a formal medical staff department review and not just mail letters and file incident reports that would be ignored. But first things first. Dr. Bacchus, quack or not, deserved a courtesy call from me before I acted. This call infuriated him.

"There is nothing wrong with ordering a patient a beer! Nothing. Beer is legally available for adults. I drink it myself. There's nothing to report."

"He's an elderly patient with dementia," I said. "He's on multiple medications. He has an array of other serious health issues. Don't you think those are good reasons to avoid ordering beer?"

"No, I don't. Beer is good for health."

"I disagree, as most doctors would. He was wandering down the street, drunk and confused. It's freezing out. He could have died."

"That's the nursing home's fault for losing track of him."

"It's your fault he was drunk. I've been told beer prescriptions are a habit for you."

"I can't believe you're reporting me to the medical staff."

"I'm giving you the courtesy of—"

"Fuck you." A loud click followed, and the line went dead.

That went well. I filed for an emergency disciplinary hearing, which I scheduled for the next day. The hearing would consist of Skip, myself, and three senior physicians who were the chairs of different departments. I hoped Skip wouldn't use his power to cancel the hearing. After the date was set, I called Skip.

"Dr. Wave, he's the only critical care doctor on staff!" Skip whined. "Having a critical care doctor generates revenue."

Dr. Bacchus was trained in critical care. Occasionally, he managed ventilators and various medical problems in Mars Hospital's small intensive care unit. But he had a reputation as a quack, too, so few doctors ever consulted him.

"Yes, I am aware of that."

"We have to be careful. He sends many patients to this hospital, and that's also an important source of revenue. I wish you had talked to me before reporting him."

Then the report would have been buried in your secret files.

"I've been handling all the complaints against him personally," Skip added. His voice was flustered.

"All the complaints? I haven't heard of any others."

"I keep them in the secret files."

I knew it.

"And just what are these complaints?"

"Well…" Skip hesitated.

"Skip. I *demand* that you tell me. I'm the medical director, and I insist on hearing the other complaints."

The first complaint had occurred a few months prior. Dr. Bacchus was working in the ICU and ordered adjustments to the ventilator settings for a patient. A respiratory technician trained in operating the complex breathing machine was called to make the adjustments, but Dr. Bacchus was in a hurry. It was documented that he had yelled, "I know how to work these damned machines," and had begun adjusting the ventilator. But instead of inputting the new settings, he'd accidentally turned the ventilator off and had no clue how to turn it back on. Alarm bells screamed. The patient, already needing life support, went into cardiac arrest. A code blue was called. The patient survived but was braindead.

The second complaint was from just last week. Dr. Bacchus tried inserting a breathing tube into a patient prior to surgery, but he was having a hard time. One of the surgical nurses certified in the insertion technique asked if she could give it a try. Enraged at her request, he'd ripped the tube out of the patient's throat, had thrown the bloody tube in her face, and had stomped out of the room. She'd inserted a new tube easily in spite of the patient's throat being bloody and swollen, and had then filed a formal complaint.

"Why hasn't he been suspended?" I asked. "This is malpractice at its worst." These reports were horrifying. They shouldn't have been in Skip's secret file but used to remove this doctor immediately.

"Now...Dr. Wave, he's the only critical care specialist we have. And he sends us a lot of patients."

"These reports must also be reviewed at the hearing tomorrow. You agree, *don't you?*" I held my breath during the long silence that followed.

"Alright. Fine."

When the hearing began, the nursing home doctor didn't even bother to attend. It was self-evident, based on the incident reports as well as his no-show, that all his medical privileges should be suspended immediately. Skip disagreed. He felt the doctor deserved a second chance.

The other doctors at the meeting, including Dr. Slenderman, who was there on behalf of the surgery chair, sided with Skip. They were also concerned that the doctor would sue if he was suspended.

"That's why we have insurance and lawyers," I countered. "And our first duty is to protect patients."

Slenderman's eyes rolled. "Give me a break, Wave." He then stated his real concern. "We have to give him a second chance. What's happening today could happen to any of us." Slenderman's eyes narrowed and focused on me.

My eyes focused right back. "If any of us commit gross malpractice, we should face a review."

The vote was four to one against suspending the doctor. Instead of expulsion, a strongly worded letter was mailed suggesting he take some classes in continuing medical education. No further action was taken.

Slenderman later reported that the doctor had wadded up the letter and thrown it in the trash. This, Slenderman added, was "where it belonged."

I subsequently mailed a copy of the incident reports, along with a summary of both Skip's and the medical staff's inactions to where they belonged: the Nebraska Medical Board as well as other various state and federal agencies.

I also attempted to report Skip, again, to the mayor. His coverup of malpractice was more than enough to justify his immediate removal.

The mayor hung up as soon as she recognized my voice.

37
OFFICE INTERLUDE

A new patient presented for the reason, "the doctor cut me wrong." When Sally came to tell me he was ready, she was visibly upset. "This is a sad case. He's a young guy, and he's in there crying. The surgeon messed up and cut some nerves, and now he's wearing a diaper."

My heart sank. "Which surgeon?"

"Slenderman."

Of course. As I entered the room, the patient—a clean-cut, fit, and otherwise healthy twenty-six-year-old with brown hair cut short on the sides—immediately begged for help, tears rolling down his cheeks.

"Doctor, you have to do something. I had surgery, and now look at me. I'm in a diaper!" He pointed to the diaper sticking out along the sides of his jeans. "I shit myself. I piss myself. And I can't get it up. You got to do something. You got to fix me."

"Tell me what happened."

He relayed the following story: He had developed back pain after lifting weights and had gone to see Dr. Do who had prescribed him narcotics. They helped a little with the pain, but he had developed constipation, a common side effect. He had then developed mild abdominal discomfort, so he'd gone back to Dr. Do, who had sent him to Dr. Slenderman to evaluate the abdominal discomfort and constipation. Slenderman had scheduled exploratory surgery to figure out what was wrong, and the patient had awoken from surgery impotent and incontinent.

"The doctor said some nerves got cut. 'It happens,' he said."

Like hell it happens.

"You gotta do something. Can you help me? Dr. Do isn't working. I heard she's hooked on dope. Please, you got to help me. I can't wear a diaper all my life."

My heart went out to this poor fellow.

"I'll look into the matter, but if nerves were cut…" I thought better of finishing that sentence. My mouth snapped shut. No point in being too grim. Time to look a few things up.

The medical record showed that he'd seen Slenderman for constipation and mild abdominal discomfort—clearly narcotic side effects. *Given these facts, why had Slenderman performed surgery?* Nothing in the record supported an operation. The patient had even been given an abdominal scan, which had come back normal.

Even less clear was how the nerves had been accidentally cut. The surgical report was bland. It read like a form letter. "Abdominal pain" was the indication for surgery, and the report mentioned nothing going amiss and no nerves being cut. Everything looked great on paper.

"What's going on?" Sally asked as she joined me at the computer. "Why is this guy in a diaper?"

"It looks like nerves were cut, but there's no record of how it happened."

Sally pointed to the name of one of the surgical nurses on the report. "I know this nurse. Let me call her."

Sally heard a remarkable story. During the operation, Slenderman had become upset with a new surgical nurse. It was her first day, and she was slow and timid. He began cursing at her, swearing, and stomping his feet, none of which helped the situation. He then asked for a particular surgical instrument, but the nurse handed him the wrong one, and he exploded in rage.

"She told me he started throwing instruments around the room. He kicked over a surgical tray, then started kicking the wall."

"Unbelievable, even for Slenderman. What did the anesthesiologist do?"

"Nothing. He was reading a newspaper. She said the patient's abdomen was left wide open while Slenderman cursed and screamed. A new tray of surgical instruments was prepared, then he angrily got back to work in the patient's abdomen. He was working extremely fast, not paying attention, and cursing and yelling the whole time. When he finished the case, he reported the new nurse for incompetence. She quit the next day."

"No wonder nerves were cut. I can't believe this happened."

"Slenderman and the surgeons at Mars Hospital yell, curse, and throw surgical instruments all the time. Everyone knows it."

Everyone except me. "They don't all behave like this, do they?" I asked.

"Maybe not every surgeon, but a whole lot of them do, especially the general surgeons."

It sounded like this was a serious and widespread problem. After the patient visit and an emergency referral to the University of Nebraska for a neurological consult, it was time to talk to Slenderman directly about this.

And I know right where to find him.

+++

"You performed surgery on someone who came to me as a new patient." I said to Slenderman the moment I entered the doctor's lounge.

"Lucky me. So what?"

I placed a printed copy of the young man's electronic chart on the table in front of Slenderman. "What happened to this guy in the operating room?"

"I don't like your tone. Are you accusing me of something?"

"I just want to know what happened."

"Nothing. The surgery went fine. Everything was normal."

"He wears a diaper. He is incontinent of stool and urine, and he's impotent. That's not fine. He says nerves were cut."

"He's lying. I didn't cut any nerves."

"And the diaper?"

"Look, sometimes these things happen. It's a known complication of surgery, and sometimes nerves or blood vessels get damaged. Don't make a big deal out of this."

"Did you get upset during the surgery? Did you curse, scream, and throw surgical instruments?"

Slenderman's face turned red. "Who told you that?"

"I'm asking you."

"No, I didn't. If someone said I did, it's a fucking lie."

"The report said everything was normal with no mention of complications. Clearly, this was not a normal operation."

"Look, like I said, these things happen. At the time of the surgery, everything looked fine. It wasn't until afterward that I found out he had a little problem."

"A little problem? You have destroyed this young man's life. Why did he even have exploratory surgery?"

"He had abdominal pain."

"I reviewed the workup. Scans were negative. Nothing was acute. It obviously was the narcotic pain pills that caused his constipation and mild abdominal discomfort."

"Are you second-guessing me, Mr. Board Certified? I'm the surgeon. I felt he needed exploratory surgery."

"This is a catastrophic case. He's a young guy, and this will affect him for the rest of his life."

"Tell him not to sue. Tell him he has no case. I don't want another lawsuit." Slenderman had several. "And don't go making a big deal out of this. I've told you before, if you're not careful, you'll find people looking through your charts, and before you know it, there'll be a disciplinary hearing against you. You better watch your step."

"That sounds like a threat."

"It's not a threat. It's a fact."

The discussion ended on that sour note.

✦✦✦

"Skip, I need to talk to you about Dr. Slenderman." A couple of hours later, after sending a full report to the Nebraska Medical Board begging for emergency action, I marched into Skip's office. I didn't expect much, but I had to try to get Slenderman suspended for this horrible act of gross malpractice.

"Funny," Skip said. "I was thinking the exact same thing."

I was immediately full of suspicion. "What did you want to talk about?"

"It has come to my attention that you are not using Dr. Slenderman for referrals."

No shit.

Skip rattled off the names of a few of my patients referred to university surgeons. Slenderman had no doubt previously researched this to use against me. He must have run to Skip with these names right after I'd confronted him in the doctors' lounge. "These are patients Slenderman could have seen, but you sent them to a university surgeon. I'm genuinely concerned about this. The hospital cannot afford to lose business to other institutions. And as medical director, it's especially important you use the service lines and specialists we have at Mars Hospital. Sending patients to the university hospital makes me look bad."

"I sent those patients away because I thought it was in their best interest. Dr. Slenderman is a lousy surgeon. His complication rates are horrendous. I did what I thought was best for the patients." *I'd rather send patients to the local butcher than to Slenderman.*

"Now...Dr. Wave, what is best for the patients is keeping them right here in town. Having folks drive all the way to Omaha is a huge burden. It's a long drive."

"Now, Skip…" I couldn't resist the urge to mock him. "As their life is on the line, a drive to the best possible surgeon with the lowest complication rates, most experience, and best outcomes seems well worth a couple hours' drive." Omaha was far, but it wasn't *that* far.

"Dr. Slenderman is a fine surgeon. He has full privileges on our medical staff."

"He shouldn't. I've come here today to report a sickening case of his malpractice. In the middle of an operation, Slenderman flew into a rage—yelling, cursing, and throwing surgical instruments. As a result of his behavior, a young man will be impotent and wear a diaper for the rest of his life. Slenderman should be tossed off the medical staff, along with any other doctors who behave this way."

I'm pulling no punches today. This case in an outrage.

"That is unfortunate, but Dr. Slenderman assures me he provided the absolute best treatment. He just told me about the case. He says the diaper thing was an unavoidable complication. And as for his behavior, what you reported isn't true. There is no yelling, cursing, or throwing of things in the operating room. I asked the director of nursing myself."

She must be covering for Slenderman and the other surgeons.

"This 'diaper thing,' as you call it, must be reviewed," I continued, "as should every claim of inappropriate behavior."

"I disagree. One unfortunate outcome doesn't warrant a big fuss."

"A big fuss? This kid is in a diaper due to a surgery he didn't even need! The patient's symptoms were all from narcotics inappropriately prescribed by Dr. Do. It is a travesty that surgery was performed."

"Now...Dr. Wave, you're speculating."

"If the case is investigated properly, the truth of the matter will be determined."

"I have investigated. There are no issues of merit here. You have reported the case, and rest assured, I'll put a report about this into his secret file."

My voice rose. "Unacceptable! Slenderman is an incompetent quack and a menace to our patients. You *must* suspend him immediately."

"I will take the matter under consideration. And you know, Dr. Wave, you have had plenty of complaints yourself." Skip walked to the cabinet and pulled out my secret file. It was thick. "It would be easy enough for me to have you reviewed. You wouldn't want that now, would you? Especially since your job is ending soon, and you are applying for new ones. You need my reference." Skip smiled slyly.

"Is that a threat?"

"Of course not, Dr. Wave. You know, I could be a great reference for you. If you drop this matter right now, I'll write you a glowing letter. But if you don't…" The threat hung in the air. Job interviews were heating up. Without a strong reference from Skip, there would not be another medical directorship, and my administrative career would be over. What to do?

Threaten Skip right back.

"Skip, I expect any reference given to be truthful. If it isn't truthful, I'll sue you and the hospital for everything I possibly can. And a story like that would be big news. Even with calls to your contacts on the newspapers, you wouldn't be able to keep it out of print. And believe me, a story like that, whether I win or lose, would *make you look bad.* Talk about bad-mouthing!"

"Now...Dr. Wave, you need to calm down." Skip's voiced trembled, his cheeks turned ruby red, and he quickly grasped his goatee with both hands. Drops of sweat that looked like dew drops on a rose petal suddenly glistened on his bald head. "No need to talk about lawsuits. I'll write you a fine letter, but there will be no hearing. This case is closed." He frowned, let go of his goatee, and crossed his arms. The dew drops continued to glisten.

"I'm still filing for an emergency hearing. Block it if you want. And I am reporting this horrible malpractice."

"Fine. This meeting is over." Skip pounded the table once for emphasis.

I filed for the emergency hearing. Skip canceled it. But, somewhat surprisingly, he gave me good references when future employers started checking. My threat had worked.

I also called the mayor one more time on the off chance she might do something, but she hung up on me once again. So I went to her office to confront her directly. After presenting the case to her and adding in numerous examples of Skip's incompetence and corruption, she bluntly stated, "I put him in charge of the hospital for those very qualities."

My only hope now was some state or federal agency, and even that seemed slim.

38
OFFICE INTERLUDE

"Take a look at the schedule, Wavesticks." Sally had on her mischievous smile as she handed me a clipboard holding the day's schedule. "I need new knuckles" jumped right out. Unlike knees and hips, prosthetic knuckles, for the most part, did not exist. While I was pondering the imminent visit, Sally offered the patient's background.

"This guy is known around Mars. He has gotten into a lot of fights, mostly at Sal's Saloon. He likes to drink. He likes to fight. He probably needs new knuckles because of too many boxing matches."

"Great. Another beauty." Meeting the town ruffian to discuss knuckle transplants was going to be interesting.

Later that day, the patient arrived. He was a young man of twenty-five, but he looked much older. He had brown, dry, and unusually wrinkly skin and was covered in tattoos. He had a recent black eye that was healing but still very visible.

"Hey, Doc. How you doin'?" He sounded amicable enough.

"I'm fine. Thanks for asking. What seems to be the trouble today?"

"It's my knuckles, Doc. They hurt. Take a look at these." He spread both hands before me. The knuckles were swollen and had clear signs of arthritis, which was surprising at his young age.

"Have you broken bones in your hands before?"

"Oh, a bunch of times. I've gotten into a lot of fights over the years." He explained that he'd started in early elementary school and had never stopped. He'd ended up in the county jail on several occasions, but had never done hard time. He also proudly claimed he usually won, and that the people he fought always looked way worse than he did. In fact, he feared no one, he said, except Saloon Sally and her ball bat. Lucky for him, Saloon Sally didn't hold grudges. She always let him back into her bar after fights, and she was also his tattoo artist.

"You probably have early onset arthritis."

"From all the fighting?"

"Yes. I think it's long past time for you to retire."

"Ah, Doc. I don't try to get into fights. But if someone gives me shit, I slug 'em."

"Maybe the next time someone gives you shit, you should just walk away. You know, turn the other cheek." *That's my helpful Biblical lesson of the day.*

"Can I get some new knuckles? Like artificial ones? And while you're at it, can they be made of brass? I can't use brass knuckles fighting. If you do, you get hard time. But if I had 'em transplanted inside, that'd be legal."

Clearly, he had given this matter a lot of thought.

"There is no such thing as brass knuckle transplants."

"Damn. Maybe someone can invent them for me?"

"No one does joint replacements for all the knuckles. You're going to have to make do with these ones."

"For the rest of my life? They're worn out already."

"Yes, for the rest of your life. I'll run some tests to make sure there isn't another condition present." It was doubtful any other medical condition had caused his arthritis, but it's important not to jump to conclusions. As I expected, testing came back negative.

"You need to stop fighting. Those are the doctor's orders. You should also make other lifestyle changes. No more smoking." He smelled like an ashtray. "And no more drinking." He certainly wasn't a teetotaler if he was familiar with Saloon Sally's bar and her ball bat.

"Damn, Doc. You want to kill all my fun," he said as he walked out of the office.

+++

"You better take a look at Powder." Sally looked dead serious, opposite from how she usually looked when coining a patient nickname. "Something isn't right with this guy." Her brows were knitted with worry. Sally had some rough edges, but she was an excellent nurse and if she said something wasn't right, there was likely a major problem.

"Why do you call him Powder?" The reason for the visit was, "I am sleepy all the time."

I'd have guessed Sleepy as a nickname.

"He's pale, like that guy in the movie Powder you recommended I watch. You better check his blood count." Powder was a movie from the nineties where the main character was ghostly pale. As Sally knew, patients with low blood counts were often very pale. While walking to the exam room, I considered the various tests he might need.

"Hello," I said. "I understand you're fatigued."

The patient was in his early thirties and had muscular arms and shoulders and a square jaw. Other than a slight beer belly, he seemed to be in good shape. But as Sally's sharp eye had observed, his skin tone suggested anemia.

"I'm tired all the time. I'm sleeping twelve hours a night, and I'm still worn out. I feel weak, and I have fevers and chills at night too. I think I got the flu permanently or something."

"I'll run some tests right away." *This is worse than the flu.* His blood pressure was low. His heart was racing. And he had a low-grade fever. "In fact, I'll check you into the hospital overnight."

"Whatever you say, Dr. Wave. Feel like I could use some more rest."

Sally called the insurance company for approval, but she had bad news. "The insurance company doctor says no dice. He says without any testing, he won't approve hospitalization. He says it isn't medically necessary." Her eyes radiated anger. "Asshole."

"Is he still on the phone?"

"Yes. I thought you might want to talk to him." The next half hour was spent trying to convince the insurance company doctor to at least allow my patient overnight admission for observation, but he adamantly refused. It wasn't medically necessary.

Asshole.

The patient went to the hospital on my order anyway. When he arrived, a blood count was drawn, stat. The results confirmed my worst suspicions. The patient had a red blood cell count of four, one-quarter the normal amount. He was profoundly anemic and lucky to be alive. He also had an elevated white blood cell count with abnormal cells and low platelets. This looked like leukemia.

Sally got a blood specialist on the phone for me. The specialist agreed to see the patient in the hospital at once. The specialist ordered an immediate blood transfusion as well as a bone marrow biopsy. She also suspected leukemia and further agreed hospitalization was in order. But when the insurance company was called back, the answer was still no. The insurance company doctor, this time a case review specialist, didn't think a critically low blood count in a newly diagnosed leukemia patient warranted hospitalization, even just overnight.

Asshole.

The only things the case review specialist agreed to cover were the transfusion and bone marrow biopsy, and then only if they were done on an outpatient basis. The patient was lucky to get even this. Insurance companies use puppet doctors who throw around terms like "medically necessary" to cover brutal hardball cost-cutting tactics. It's a disgrace to the profession that any doctor would participate in this sort of criminal enterprise.

Insurance companies and their puppet doctors do not care one whit about what is in the patient's best interest. They only care about the bottom line. If sick people die, all the better. Dead patients don't cost a penny, and insurance companies and their puppets are immune to malpractice claims. All malpractice liability rests with the patient's doctor, even when insurance company negligence is the direct cause of death. It's a crazy, inefficient, and heartlessly cruel system.

The patient received his transfusion and biopsy, and he was discharged home later that afternoon. Sadly, despite aggressive chemotherapy, the patient died a few weeks later.

39
SKIP MEETING

Medical directorship search committees around the nation, in response to my job applications, inquired as to what kind of projects I'd undertaken during my tenure as medical director at Mars Hospital. Reporting Mars Hospital to various government agencies and fighting with my CEO didn't count as projects, but my Every Day Is Monday initiative did. Given my relationship with Skip, I doubted he would be interested. But I needed to try. Not only would this project greatly improve patient care at Mars Hospital, it would also show future employers that I'd taken the initiative in addressing problems.

The slogan was catchy. Any consultant would be proud. This program was designed to solve a major problem at Mars Hospital. On Friday afternoons, the inpatient and outpatient testing facilities shut down. No testing, except in the direst of emergencies, was performed until the following Monday, or Tuesday if Monday happened to be a holiday. And as a result of this lack of testing, no consultations could be performed. This was unacceptable patient care. But knowing Skip, he would turn a blind eye to my concerns. So I planned to emphasize money. The hospital, because of this scheduling policy, was losing a fortune.

My plan was simple. Any test, service, or consultation available on Monday would also be available any day of the week, including weekends and holidays. There would be no more waiting for services at Mars Hospital. Unfortunately, but not unexpectedly, Skip immediately went on the defensive.

His first response was to deny the problem. "Now...Dr. Wave, patients don't wait for tests. We do all testing quickly."

"That is simply not the case." I presented data including specific examples where inpatient testing had not been done over the weekend. And I showed that outpatient testing was lost to other sites because Mars Hospital refused to schedule weekend testing. After glancing at the data, Skip became even more defensive.

His second response was blaming the doctors. "If a doctor says the test is an emergency, it gets done. This is a doctor problem."

"None of the tests I listed in these examples were emergencies."

"The doctor can still call it an emergency and get the testing done."

That's unethical, impractical, and illegal.

"But it isn't an emergency," I said. "A better solution would be for testing to be available every day."

Skip's third response was concern over cost. "That would require more staff. It would be too expensive." But I'd predicted cost would come up.

"It would require more staff. But the increased testing done as a result would more than cover this cost." I provided a detailed cost-benefit analysis, proving that testing revenue far outpaced staff costs. He barely glanced at the analysis.

Skip's fourth response included concern for staff—a first. "The staff doesn't want to work on the weekend. The tests can just be done on Monday." He had also directly contradicted his first response, that patients don't wait for tests.

"But as I point out in the documents, we lose millions due to increased inpatient lengths of stay and lost outpatient testing."

This argument is compelling if Skip would only listen.

"Again, that's a doctor problem. We must insist our doctors cut the length of stay. If there is a test required to discharge a patient, doctors must call it an emergency and get it done. And they are not to use other facilities for outpatient testing. Period."

Back to blaming the doctors.

"Sometimes testing is done at other sites because we don't have an open MRI scanner or other modern equipment." Freestanding testing sites not affiliated with Mars Hospital were springing up everywhere. They offered the latest technology as well as convenient scheduling with weekend and evening hours.

Skip folded his arms. "Our technology is fine. Those new scanners are too expensive. It's not in the budget. Our equipment is modern enough."

"I have data showing purchasing this new equipment would be paid for in under a year from revenues generated." I presented another detailed cost-benefit report, but again Skip ignored it.

"It's just too expensive." His lips curved downward in a deepening frown.

"As to consultations by doctors on the weekend—"

"Fine, make the doctors work on the weekend. They should work on the weekend and do consultations, but they won't like it. They're lazy."

"What I was going to say is that doctors cannot perform consultations if testing isn't available. Consultants typically order tests. If the testing isn't done, the consult can't be completed, whether the doctor wants to work during the weekend or not."

"This is the way we have always done things here."

"The current system we have is a relic, Skip." Decades ago, most hospitals shut down on the weekend. Those days were long gone, except in Mars.

"Doctors and staff would quit if we made them work weekends."

How sweet of Skip to be so concerned for the doctors and staff.

"Suppose a doctor or hospital worker quits. Then what? Wherever they go to work, they will be required to work weekends." My logic was undeniable. All hospitals require weekend work now, except in Mars.

"It's just not in the budget."

Round and round we go.

"This meeting is over." Skip placed an exclamation point on the statement by tugging his goatee.

I mailed copies of my project along with my job applications. Mars Hospital scheduling never changed.

After the meeting, I proceeded to the doctor's lounge.

As soon as I entered the lounge, Beats called me over to a table.

"Hey, Wave, come here and take a look at this." He, Rumpsmith, Slenderman, and a couple of other doctors were looking at documents spread out on a table.

"What are you looking at?" A variety of documents and flow charts were in a wild disarray.

"I hired an accountant. He's setting up a system where I legally won't have to pay income taxes."

"That sounds fishy. Everyone who earns income has to pay income taxes, especially when it's a doctor-sized income."

"Not with this plan. It's foolproof. My accountant has set up an offshore company where all my income will be routed. It's tax-free."

"That doesn't sound legal. And if the money is offshore, how do you use it to buy stuff?"

"That's the coolest part. I have a credit card linked to the offshore account. I buy stuff with the credit card and use the money in the account to pay the bill. And if I need cash, I have an ATM card. They don't even charge ATM fees. Can I sign you up?"

No ATM fees. How wonderful. "I don't think so."

"Why not? Do you like paying taxes?"

"I don't particularly like paying taxes. But I like the idea of going to prison for tax evasion even less. That's how they got Al Capone, you know."

"This is perfectly legal. These documents prove it." He pointed to a stack of legal papers.

"I recall hearing that several doctors at Mars Hospital lost money on Lehman Brothers bonds when the company went bankrupt. Some shyster sold doctors those bonds just before the bankruptcy, and the salesman also had a bunch of legal documents. How did that work out?"

"I got killed on those bonds," Beats answered, "but this is totally different. You in?"

"No, thanks."

"Give it up, Beats. You're wasting your breath. He's too stubborn to take advantage of this." It was Slenderman. For once, he wasn't eating. But he did have a package of Twinkies loaded in his right hand and ready to go. The fact that he was still on staff and practicing made me grit my teeth.

"Dr. Slenderman, are you signing up for this too?"

"Sure am. I'm going to save a fortune in taxes."

Several other doctors signed up that day.

The IRS later cracked down on this tax-cheating scheme. It was nationwide, targeting mostly doctors and lawyers. The operators of the scheme went to prison. The participants—which included Beats,

Slenderman, and several other Mars doctors—were hit with massive tax bills, fines, and interest. It was a major financial setback. They're probably still making payments to the IRS.

40

OFFICE INTERLUDE

"There are two men out front who want to talk to you." Sally sounded, and looked, very worried.

"Patients?"

"I don't think so. They're wearing suits." Suits are not typical attire in Mars. My mind raced as I headed to the front door alone. *Who could they be?* The waiting room was empty except for the two men.

"Dr. Wave?"

"Yes."

"I am Agent Themis, and this is Agent Naso." They flashed their badges. "We're from the FBI."

Agent Themis continued while I began to sweat and couldn't think of a response. Although I knew I had done nothing wrong, the unexpected arrival of the FBI made me nervous. "We have a few questions for you. May we speak with you privately in your office?"

"May I see your credentials again?"

The agents handed me their badges as well as a second ID card with their photos and names. Everything looked legitimate, but I was no expert. "Gentleman, give me a moment while I call and confirm your identity at the local FBI field office."

"Of course, Dr. Wave. Take your time."

I went to my office, called the FBI in Omaha, and quickly confirmed their identities.

"May we speak in your office now, Dr. Wave?" Agent Themis asked when I returned to the waiting room.

"Sure." Never talk to the FBI. If you lie, even unintentionally, it's a crime. And even with a lawyer present, talking to the FBI is perilous. Just ask Martha Stewart. If you're ever confronted by FBI agents, ask for their card and tell them your lawyer will call them. Then shut up. Of course, that's easier advice to give than to follow.

"What may I do for you gentlemen?" I asked when we arrived in my office.

The agents waited until the office door had clicked shut. Agent Themis replied, while Agent Naso opened a notepad and began writing. "We have some questions about the numerous letters and documents you've been sending to the Inspector General and other agencies regarding Mars Hospital billing practices."

Yes! Someone has finally taken notice.

"I'd be happy to answer any and all questions."

He started with basic identifying data, such as my name, address, and Social Security number. Then he got to the serious issue of billing fraud.

"We have reviewed the billing records of a Ms. Geras in particular. They are highly suspicious." Agent Naso handed Themis a thick folder. It contained billing records from an array of departments as well as from individual consulting physicians. "Can you verify for me that these billing records are false?"

"Yes. Ms. Geras relayed to me personally that she never received most of the services listed in those bills. Furthermore, the consulting physicians admitted they'd never seen her. Dr. Slenderman, and I quote, stated he 'might have stuck his head in the room once' and that 'this is the way we do things around here.' He and other consultants waived their bills after I confronted them with their fraud."

Agent Naso spoke for the first and only time. "They didn't waive the Medicare billing. Only the patient portion." He did not look up from his notepad but continued to write.

"And will you verify that the CEO of Mars Hospital was *personally* aware of these billing irregularities?" Agent Themis continued.

"Yes. I reported the irregularities to him personally after going to the billing department. Indeed, I discussed the matter with Skip on numerous occasions. He refused to take any corrective action. Not only that, but he also referred the bill to a collections agency, and they currently are trying to take this poor, elderly lady's home." Agent Themis's face lit up in surprise. Agent Naso didn't look up. "I made efforts to try to obtain charity care for this indigent woman, as Mars is a tax-exempt, not-for-profit hospital required to give free care to the poor. But my attempts were rebuffed. I even set up a payment plan and mailed a check to the hospital on behalf of Ms. Geras using my own money. They cashed the check but still sent her to the collections agency. It's a disgrace."

"And you are aware of other instances of improper billing, correct?" Agent Themis frowned deeply while he spoke.

"Information on specific cases is hard to come by. But I can tell you this. Dr. Lyssa, whom I also reported, doesn't have the documentation to support her level of office billing. And it gets worse. Skip pressures doctors to inflate charges. He has bred a culture of illegal billing in this hospital. Doctors are rewarded if they have high billings, and all manner of unethical and illegal actions are overlooked."

"What exactly do you mean by that, Dr. Wave?" Agent Themis's eyes were wide.

"Two doctors were accused of sexual assault, one by a patient and one by a staff member. The doctor accused by the patient had low billing and was fired at once. The doctor accused by the staff member had high billing and the assault report was buried.

"Then there's Dr. Slenderman. Not only is he a fraudulent biller but a quack and a danger to patients. He recently flew into a rage during an operation and as a result cut the nerves in the abdomen of a young man, resulting in his incontinence and impotence, probably for life. When I reported this to Skip, he ignored the report and criticized me for not referring Slenderman more patients.

"And again regarding Dr. Lyssa, she has mental health issues. But she has high billing, so Skip refused to address her mental health problems despite her receiving court-ordered counseling after she assaulted me."

Agent Themis's jaw dropped at that tidbit.

"Oh, it gets worse. Skip refused to act when a critical care specialist brain-damaged one patient and seriously injured another, because this doctor refers patients from the local nursing home and is 'the hospital's only critical care specialist, and this generates revenue.' Moreover, he allowed another doctor with advanced Alzheimer's to perform surgeries because he didn't want revenues to fall."

Agent Themis shook his head in disbelief. Agent Naso, even with his head turned down, had a clearly visible frown. He continued to record my every word.

"And then we have the emergency department. I reported several cases of fraudulent billing as well as gross malpractice, but Skip did absolutely nothing. He steadfastly refuses to address the malpractice and the fraud. Based on his attitude, I can only surmise that this sort of thing is tolerated in *every* department in the hospital.

"Next, there's the issue of inappropriate narcotic prescribing. As both of you know, the DEA has already investigated at least one physician on the medical staff." Agent Themis's face lit up in surprise; perhaps he *didn't* know this. "Dr. Do was allowed to practice despite strong evidence of drug addiction. And she's written *thousands* of inappropriate narcotics prescriptions despite not having a controlled substance license. Before being shipped off to rehab and getting her office raided, she had the doctor with Alzheimer's disease cosign these narcotics prescriptions, even though his dementia was so advanced, he didn't know the year.

"And there are other doctors, once again including Dr. Lyssa, who prescribe narcotics inappropriately. Not only does Skip know all of this, he also actively encourages this behavior. On numerous occasions, Skip has pressured me to write more narcotics prescriptions. I resist, but not every doctor does. Skip ties a doctor's pay to patient satisfaction. If a patient is angry because you *don't* write for narcotics and then gives you a bad review, Skip cuts your pay—a fact he enjoys pointing out. You can guess the results of this policy. Many doctors now dare not refuse a patient's request for narcotics.

"And, speaking of drugs, I have one more thing to report. Despite my numerous complaints, Skip allows drug reps in the hospital. They're giving doctors all kinds of free gifts to entice them to prescribe new and costly drugs. It's unseemly, not to mention illegal."

Here, my rant ended. Agent Naso finally looked up from his notepad. Both agents sat quietly in stunned disbelief.

"Dr. Wave, these are profoundly serious allegations," Agent Themis said. "And I'll tell you that frankly, they're hard to believe. How can you possibly authenticate all of these accusations?" His eyes narrowed.

"Skip will authenticate them."

"What?" His head popped back and face wrinkled.

"Skip documents everything very well in what he calls his 'secret files,' which he keeps to use as leverage against physicians. If a doctor gets out of line in any way or questions Skip's authority, he threatens to use that information. The files are locked in a cabinet in his office. Everything I told you today and much, much more will have supporting documentation."

Agent Themis and Agent Naso both smiled broadly.

"That's amazing. Dr. Wave, your information today has been extremely helpful. Is there anything else you'd like to say?" agent Themis asked.

"Check the hospital books, especially pertaining to inventory. A patient reported to me that a theft ring has been operating out of Mars Hospital for years, robbing the place blind. Also, you should investigate the retirement plan. The fees charged to enrolled employees are criminal. I suspect, but have no evidence to prove, that Skip is involved in some way with both of these schemes and is possibly getting kickbacks.

"And in addition to the hospital itself, there are terrible things going on in this town. I suspect the mayor of Mars is somehow involved in Skip's various schemes. She's Skip's boss, and I have reported his actions to her on more than one occasion. In response, she told me she 'Put him in charge of the hospital for those very qualities.'"

"Then there's the local judge—the 'hanging judge.' He sends mentally ill patients away for decades on trumped up charges. And he uses the power of the court to aid the hospital in their illegal collection practices. He's a disgrace.

"Finally, there's the Mars Nursing Home. The treatment of patients there is criminal. I have reported this nursing home several times for a variety of horrors, but so far nothing has happened."

Agent Themis began again to shake his head slowly. "Amazing.

Anything else?"

"That's all I can think of for the moment, but if more comes to me, I will absolutely let you know."

"Thank you." Agent Themis gave me his card. "Feel free to call me. It also goes without saying, avoid speaking to *anyone* about this meeting."

"Understood."

Silently, the agents left.

Sally began asking questions the moment they were out the door.

"So what's the story? You were in your office a long time with those guys. What did they want?"

Think of something fast.

"They were trying to convince me to set up an offshore company so I wouldn't have to pay taxes. I heard them out then told them no." My face flushed red.

"Good move, Wavesticks. That's a scam for sure. It would have landed you in the slammer."

"Yes, it would have."

+ + +

Not long after the FBI interview, a call came into the office from Ms. Geras's lawyer. The case against Ms. Geras wasn't going well.

"Dr. Wave, since you paid my retainer and with Ms. Geras's permission, I want to update you on the situation." He sounded ominous.

"Sure. What's going on?"

"I argued to the judge that my client's bill wasn't merely incorrect but fraudulent and that she was an elderly, indigent lady being strong-armed by the hospital and their collections agency."

"And?"

"He ruled in favor of the hospital and gave a summary judgment of foreclosure."

"Doesn't surprise me. He sent one of my mentally ill patients away for fifty years."

"Yeah. He gets every kind of case. Being a small county, we don't have many judges."

"So what's the next step?"

"There's only one thing left to do. Declare bankruptcy. Bankruptcy is a federal proceeding, so it's outside the jurisdiction of the hanging judge. If we file for bankruptcy, the foreclosure will stop. Nebraska has a homestead exemption of sixty thousand dollars in bankruptcy, and her home is small, old, and in disrepair. It's not worth sixty thousand, so this exemption alone will save her house. The hospital debt will then be discharged. All her other debts would be discharged too, but all she has is the hospital bill." This wasn't surprising. Two-thirds of US bankruptcies are due all or in part to medical debt.

"That sounds like a good plan." *Now to the real reason you're calling me.* "How much is this going to cost?"

"A standard bankruptcy is seven hundred and ninety-nine dollars all-in. I file them all the time. But her case has Mars Hospital as a creditor. I have dealt with Mars Hospital and their collections agency before. So I require a two-thousand-dollar retainer to file the bankruptcy. And as you know, Ms. Geras doesn't have that kind of money."

"Why is your retainer so much more in a case with Mars Hospital as a creditor?"

He took a breath. "Here's what Mars Hospital and their collections agency will do. They'll claim fraud. They'll fight the discharge and say Ms. Geras is lying about her assets, has hidden income, or other such nonsense."

"But such a claim is obviously false. She has no other assets and is indigent."

"Mars Hospital knows a claim of fraud raises the cost of the bankruptcy. Nine times out of ten, when they claim fraud, the bankruptcy case gets dismissed because the debtor, being broke, can't afford to fight the false claim. Plus, in Mars, we are dealing mostly with simple, uneducated folks. Many of them already feel shame and guilt over a bankruptcy filing. When Mars Hospital starts claiming criminal fraud, they become terrified. Most fold immediately."

"That's awful." My throat tightened in rage.

"Yes, and illegal. But this is Mars. It happens all the time."

"I'll write the check for your retainer at once. Don't let this happen to Ms. Geras." Two grand is a good-sized chunk of money, even for a doctor. But the hospital's behavior was outrageous.

"Doctor, let me tell you, Mars needs more doctors like you."

Mars Needs Doctors, once again the terrible movie I am still in.

"Thanks. I'm going to ask you a favor. With Ms. Geras's permission, there's someone I'd like you to speak to."

"Who?"

"His name is Agent Themis. He is an investigating agent with the FBI."

"Holy shit, Doctor. Are you kidding me?"

"I am dead serious." A long pause followed.

"Sure, I'll talk to him. Ms. Geras will certainly agree."

"Thank you."

"Hell, I have stories about Mars Hospital and our hanging judge that will turn his hair white."

"Excellent. Here's his number." I smiled as I read off the digits. *Justice cometh, and that right soon.*

+ + +

"Horny is ready."

The nickname surprised me. This visit reason was "sore throat."

"Does he have a sex issue?" Men are sometimes too shy to give the real reason for their visit when scheduling. A visit planned for a sore throat can turn into lots of different things.

"Nope. You'll see. And let me know what's going on," Sally said.

The patient, a fifty-five-year-old gentleman with thinning gray hair and a scruffy beard, sat on the exam table. He looked normal, except for the large horn growing off the side of his head. The horn started on the right upper aspect of his forehead and stood eight inches tall. It was thick and irregular in shape.

I've never seen anything like this.

"Hi, Dr. Wave. Nice to meet you."

"Nice to meet you too. So what seems to be the trouble today?" My eyes were fixated on his horn. I couldn't help myself.

"No big deal. I have a sore throat and need some antibiotics."

"A sore throat?" my voice weakly parroted.

"Yeah. I usually see Dr. Do, but they said she's out until next week."

She's returning? That's news to me.

"Any other symptoms or problems? Anything else going on?" *Like a giant horn growing out of your head.*

"Nope."

"Are you sure?"

"Well, there is one more thing."

Here it comes.

"I have a slight cough." He absentmindedly scratched his horn.

"Have you noticed anything different or unusual? Any skin changes or growths?"

"Nothing I can think of."

"Well, what about that?" My index finger pointed to the horn.

"Oh, this?" He scratched his horn again. "I've had this a couple of years."

"Is it growing?"

"Yeah, it's getting bigger all the time."

"Have you seen a doctor about this?"

"Dr. Do. She said it was acne. She told me not to worry. She gave me some pain pills in case it hurts."

How could she call this acne? And does she give narcotics for everything?

"Does it hurt?"

"No, my throat is the only thing hurting."

The patient had a mildly red throat and no other abnormalities on exam—except the horn. An urgent evaluation was needed.

Could this be some sort of cancer?

"I'll give you some antibiotics for the sore throat." A rapid test had confirmed strep. The patient smiled in response to my statement. "But I want to run some tests to figure out why you are growing a horn."

"Is Dr. Do wrong? People have been telling me it ain't normal to grow a horn."

People were right.

"It sure isn't acne. I'll figure out the cause."

"Okay, Dr. Wave."

The test results came back quickly. It was kidney cancer. The cancer had spread to his skull, and this is what had formed the horn. Cancer had also snaked through his blood vessels from his kidney all the way to his heart. Aggressive chemotherapy was started at once, but by this time, it was far too late to do any good.

The next Monday, at my meeting with Skip, he confirmed Dr. Do's return. I stated my concerns about her incompetence, prescribing habits, drug addiction, and licensure issues. Skip brushed them aside. Over my firm objections, he was bringing Dr. Do back. Skip even had the audacity to ask me to cosign her narcotic scripts as "Dr. Essex was not currently practicing."

After I declined, Skip found someone else to sign the scripts.

The state medical board received a letter regarding Dr. Do's malpractice and return.

And Agent Themis received a call.

✚ ✚ ✚

One winter afternoon, during a snowstorm, an emergency call came into the office.

"Wavesticks, pick up line two. It's one of your patients. She's worried about her kid."

I quickly picked up the phone. "How may I help you? My nurse says your child has a problem."

"My daughter is having severe stomach pains." A girl moaned in the background. "I think I should bring her to your office." The daughter had never been to the office, but her mother had been a patient. Given that fact plus the raging snowstorm, an alternate plan seemed appropriate.

"No. I think you should take her to the emergency room immediately, especially given the weather. This sounds serious. I'll call the ER and tell them you're on the way."

"Okay, Dr. Wave."

My next call was to the emergency room to warn of the incoming patient. About two hours later, the emergency room doctor called back.

"You're not going to believe this." The emergency room doctor explained that the mother and her daughter had arrived in the emergency room not long after my call. The daughter was in labor.

"When I told the patient's mother the cause of her daughter's abdominal pain, she struggled to understand exactly what I was say-ing. She then stated pregnancy was impossible as her daughter was a Christian and had taken a chastity vow." These were common in Mars churches. As this case demonstrated, they rarely worked as intended. Instead of preventing premarital sex, the vows had encour-aged the hiding of unplanned pregnancies.

"Luckily, the delivery was without complication and the new-born was in perfect health. When I returned with her new grand-daughter, the grandmother fainted. We put her in a gurney next to her daughter and new grandchild. When she woke up, she kept asking how this happened. I told her it happened in the usual way." The ER doctor chuckled.

"Thank you for the update. I'm glad that despite no prenatal care, the baby was healthy."

Alas, this was not the first case in Mars, Nebraska, of a young lady hiding a pregnancy all the way to delivery.

And it would not be the last, chastity vows notwithstanding.

✦✦✦

An elderly lady presented for "jail follow-up." She was in her late sixties, older than the typical Mars inmate. Sally told me what had led to her arrest.

"Story goes she was walking out to her mailbox. She was only wearing flip-flops, her Depends, and a bathrobe, which was wide open and flapping in the breeze. The neighbor saw her saggy boobs and complained."

"She was arrested for indecent exposure?"

"No, the cops told her the neighbor complained, and after the cops left, she went to the neighbor's house and started pounding on the door, yelling that she would kill everyone in the house. She stuck a steak knife in the door to make her point. The police were called back, and they arrested her. They took the steak knife as evidence." Sally smiled.

"She doesn't have a steak knife with her now, does she?"

"Nope, but she is wearing her Depends and bathrobe. Oh, and fuzzy pink slippers."

"Seriously?"

"Seriously. She's the fashion queen of Mars, Nebraska. Have fun."

As I nervously opened the exam room door, the patient spoke right up.

"Hey, sexy!" She had a big, toothless grin on her face. As Sally reported, she wore Depends, a skimpy bathrobe, and fuzzy pink slippers. She was also covered in numerous old tattoos that had stretched and faded over time. "You're looking good." She giggled and blew me a kiss.

"What brings you in today?"

"I just got out of the can. My lawyer gave me this form for you to fill out." She handed it over. It was from her public defender requesting information on any medical conditions present.

"I will happily fill out the form." Although I had never seen this patient before, she had been cared for in the clinic in the past. Detailed records on her medical history were in the electronic system. While I was reviewing a printout of her medical records to obtain the information I needed, she began talking about her case, and descended into blameful rambling.

"Everyone is out to get me. My neighbors are jackasses. All they do is complain about shit. If I had a shotgun, I'd put them in the ground. The fucking hanging judge is nothing but trouble. He's out to get me. He's been out to get me for years. My lawyer is a kid who looks like he's twelve years old. He doesn't have enough brainpower to blow his fucking nose."

The form only requested medical history, but for good measure, I gave her a physical exam and ordered some tests. When everything was complete, her mood had noticeably improved.

"Thanks. Did you know I used to dance down at Aladdin's Lamp?" Aladdin's Lamp was a seedy strip club just outside the city limits in an unincorporated part of the county. The Lamp, as people called it, had been around forever. If she'd worked there as a stripper, it must have been decades ago. The city fathers occasionally complained about the club's threat to the town's morality. Mars, after all, was a religious town. But nothing was ever done to close the Lamp, and the same city fathers who occasionally complained were also frequent patrons.

"No, I did not know that." *Always be polite.*

"Yes, I was their best stripper for years. And believe me, I learned a trick or two down there. If you ever want a piece of ass, you come knocking on my door." Cackling, she grabbed my rear. She cackled even more as she watched me jump and cry out.

"Hey! That's inappropriate." My face blushed deep red. *She reminds me of Dr. Lyssa.*

"Sorry. You've got the kind of ass a girl can't resist." She winked, got up from the exam table, and walked out of the clinic proudly holding her form.

Sally chortled after hearing the story. "Don't you go sneaking over to her house, Wavesticks. You might just have to marry her like good old Dr. Himeros. Hey, why don't you see if she can get you a VIP card to the Lamp, and we can go? You'll get some cobra action for sure. Those Lamp strippers are knob slobs!"

I can guess what knob slobs are.

My face, blushing once again, delighted Sally.

No attempt was made to get an Aladdin's Lamp VIP card.

41
SKIP MEETING: FIRECRACKER!

Skip was excited and welcomed me into his office with the statement, "I have some big news for you, Dr. Wave." This sort of welcome was never a good sign.

Does he know about the FBI?

"What's the news?"

"I have enrolled the hospital in a new program. This will replace the crab program. It's much, much better."

"Really?" My heart sank and my face undoubtably flashed disappointment. "What's the program?"

"It's called Firecracker." When he said firecracker, he clapped his hands. "This is going to be great. I enrolled Mars Hospital in it at a seminar I recently attended." At these seminars, consultants wined and dined hospital administrators as they pitched whatever fad program they were peddling. These consultants were like drug reps, only for administrators.

"What does this program entail?" Preparing for the worst, I

gritted my teeth.

"Well, we want our employees to be firecrackers." Again, he clapped his hands. "What that means is someone who is hardworking, devoted to patients, and always thinking outside the box."

The term "thinking outside the box" made me cringe.

"Firecrackers also come up with new ideas." He clapped his hands again.

Great. It looks like every time he says the word firecracker now, he's going to clap his hands.

"It's this coming up with new ideas that is the heart of the firecracker program." Clap.

"That sounds… interesting." *That sounds ridiculous.*

"Each month, we will award a Firecracker of the Month." Clap. "The winner will get to park in a special parking space."

"We already have an Employee of the Month award rewarding a parking spot."

"We're changing the special parking space sign from Employee of the Month to Firecracker of the Month." Clap.

"You don't have to clap every time you say firecracker." It was already annoying.

"That is a key part of the Firecracker program." Clap. "We clap to emphasize the importance of the word *firecracker*." Clap. "But there's more. Every person who gives a firecracker idea gets a reward." Clap.

"What's the reward?" At some institutions, a cash reward was given if a money-saving idea was suggested and adopted.

"They get a stick of gum."

"That's the reward?"

"Yes, for each *extra* idea they give, they get a stick of Extra gum. This is for the extra effort they are making." Skip seemed incredibly pleased with this childish concept.

At least he didn't clap his hands when he said extra.

"We also are getting rid of the suggestion box out front."

Since time immemorial, a suggestion box had sat in the front lobby of Mars Hospital.

"We are replacing it with the firecracker box." Clap. "Firecracker ideas can be placed in the firecracker box." Clap.

He clapped once but said firecracker twice. Should I call him out?

"And we'll be putting up the ten Firecracker Pillars of Fire." Clap. "These will be large, beautiful Greek-style pillars made of marble. They'll go in the lobby. Each pillar will represent one of the ten Firecracker Pillars of Fire." Clap.

He then started listing them: service, initiative, innovation, technology…" Great. *He's already memorized them.*

"What about our doctors?" I asked. *How will this latest nonsense impact them?*

"There's a book to read. It's called *Be a Firecracker!*" Clap. "And a torch is coming. He will attend the next physicians' meeting."

"What is a torch?"

"That's what Firecracker advisors are called." Clap. "They are named torches as they light the firecrackers." Clap.

This is a nightmare.

"Do you think that is a good idea, Skip? The last time an advisor came to the physicians' meeting, it was an unmitigated disaster."

"Torches have a different approach. There will be no movies, pantomimes, or puppet shows this time. These torches mean business and will tell the doctors the new protocols being implemented in the clinics."

"What kind of protocols?" *This is getting worse by the second.*

"Did you know some doctors are still writing prescriptions? A firecracker doesn't do that." Clap. "One pillar of fire is technology, so our first firecracker protocol will be removing prescription pads and requiring all prescriptions be prescribed electronically." Clap.

"Yes, I did know that some prescriptions are still being handwritten. Eighty percent of prescriptions ordered by Mars doctors are sent electronically, but in some situations, the prescription can't be sent electronically. For one, some pharmacies still don't accept electronic prescriptions. What do we do in that case?"

"The pharmacy will have to start accepting them electronically or lose business. We'll only deal with firecracker pharmacies." Clap.

That would be hard to enforce. Some patients are required to use an insurance-approved mail-order pharmacy. They have no option to use a different pharmacy, and prescriptions to some mail-order pharmacies had to be handwritten. And the Mars Hospital pharmacy, used by all Mars employees, was still in the Stone Age.

"Skip, our pharmacy is one of the pharmacies that does not accept electronic prescriptions."

Skip seemed taken aback. "Now... Dr. Wave, that can't be true."

How can Skip not know this? Doctors complained about this embarrassment constantly.

"It *is* true. The Mars Hospital pharmacy accounts for over half of all handwritten prescriptions."

"That will have to change."

Right. The pharmacy always fights any kind of change.

"What if a patient requests a handwritten prescription? Are doctors supposed to tell the patient no?" *Crabby never says no.*

"Doctors must innovate and figure out a solution. Innovation is a pillar of fire." *That was a vague non-answer if there ever was one.* "Here's your copy of the book, *Be a Firecracker!*" Clap. Skip handed me a hardcover book with a dancing cartoon firecracker on its cover.

Terrific.

"This program is going to be a game-changer," Skip said.

Game Changer was another universally hated consultant term.

It was doubtful this dumb book would change any game. It would only waste more hospital money and doctor time. Handing out sticks of gum and renaming the suggestion box as well as the Employee of the Month program would not go over well. Doctors would see right through this nonsense.

Here we go again.

But my tenure as medical director was ending in just a few weeks. After that, no more firecrackers!

Clap.

42

OFFICE INTERLUDE

Sally had big news. She shouted it the moment she saw me.

"Wavesticks, last night, the managers went to all the offices and took the prescription pads. I almost called the police when I arrived this morning and found them missing. I thought they were stolen. But an email said they'd been confiscated."

Opening my desk drawers confirmed that all the pads were gone.

"Lucky I have a secret stash," Sally said. "I keep them hidden in the ceiling above a saggy tile."

"Why do you do that?" Skip had secret files on doctors, doctors had secret charts on patients, and nurses had secret prescription pad stashes. *Can you say dysfunctional hospital?* "And why do you even *have* prescription pads?"

"It takes months for an order of pads to get filled around here. These are my reserves." It wasn't surprising that it took months to get an order filled. The hospital had significant inventory and supply problems.

"Unbelievable. I'm calling Skip."

He picked up on the first ring.

"Skip, have you heard that all the prescription pads were confiscated?" I asked.

"I have! Like I told you, it's part of the Firecracker program." His hands clapped audibly over the phone.

Good grief.

"Initiative is a pillar of fire. Firecrackers don't wait, they implement." Clap.

"You didn't even tell the doctors."

"I sent an email."

"Doctors also use prescription pads to write return-to-work and school notes. They use them to order medical equipment and devices. They use them for physician referrals and many other purposes."

"Oh? I didn't know that."

"That's why this shouldn't have been implemented so quickly. Those prescription pads need to be returned."

"I'll speak to a torch. One of the pillars of fire is technology. The torches want everything done electronically. No more paper."

Silence.

Where's the clap? Oops, he didn't say firecracker. He got me!

The call to Skip ended, and I resigned myself to a wave of angry phone calls and emails from doctors. Hopefully, all doctors had their own secret stashes of prescription pads.

Angry phone calls and emails flowed in all day.

43

THE DOCTORS' LOUNGE: JOKER

One morning in the doctors' lounge, Beats posed a riddle: "Hey, Wave, why do undertakers nail coffins shut?"

"Why don't you tell me?"

"To keep the oncologists out." Beats always made fun of the cancer doctors. At Mars Hospital, they were known for giving chemotherapy no matter what—even in the most incurable of cases.

"Hey, Wave, how do you know who the oncologist is at a code blue?" That's the medical term for a cardiac arrest.

"How?"

"They're the ones pushing chemotherapy." One oncologist sitting in the lounge did not look amused. Beats started talking directly to him. "You guys will give chemo to anyone. You guys would give chemo to a mummy. How's King Tut's chemo coming along?" Beats giggled. "Last week, I saw a ninety-year-old patient with incurable cancer whom you had started on chemotherapy. Ninety years old!"

"You put a stent in that patient's heart," the oncologist countered.

"You put in stents. I give chemo."

"And everyone makes their car payment," Dr. Slenderman chipped in. Today he was eating popcorn out of a giant canister divided into three sections. Crumbs from white, orange, and brown popcorn kernels were stuck in his beard.

"Hey, Wave, did you hear they canned Dr. Bacchus from his job at the nursing home?" Beats asked. He was a great source of gossip.

"No. What happened?"

"He showed up drunk and pissed in a hallway. The guy is a lush."

"That seems like a pretty good reason to let him go." *So is gross malpractice.*

"You want to know the funny part?"

"Sure."

"It was his third time getting caught drunk at work and pissing in a hallway. The other times, he just got a warning. But three pisses, and you're out." Beats laughed loudly.

"Unbelievable."

Who will they get to run the place now? Not me!

"I warned him. Did you know he would piss on the floor right here in the doctors' lounge?"

"What? Repulsive!"

"Yeah, I told him to keep out of the lounge if he was going to piss on the floor every time he was here."

"There are bathrooms just outside the lounge. Why would he urinate on the floor?" *What a crew at Mars Hospital. A doctor who urinates on the floor. A doctor who defecates in front of administration. And a host of other doctors with a mix of mental illness, incompetence, and criminal behavior.*

"I don't know." Beats slowly shook his head. "Probably because he was drunk. He'd show up here every morning smelling like a brewery."

"I guess he's not a firecracker," Slenderman commented between handfuls of popcorn.

Beats, on cue, clapped his hands.

"You've heard about the new program," I said. That wasn't surprising. Torches were all over the place. The doctors' lounge was kept locked for the first time in memory to keep them out.

"Yeah. They stole my prescription pads," Slenderman moaned. "These fucking consultants or torches or whatever the fuck they're called turned my office upside down. They're worse than the crab people."

"Well, you signed the hospital contract to become an employee," Beats observed. "Slenderman, you ever watch *The Twilight Zone?*"

"What?"

"*The Twilight Zone.* You remember that old TV show." He started humming the theme song.

"Sure, I remember it."

"In one episode, a guy sold his soul to the devil. He signed a contract like you did. And you know what? Things didn't work out well for him either."

Beats sure is on a roll today.

"Contract or not, this is bullshit," Slenderman said. "These new consultants need to be reined in."

"I fully agree," I interjected. "I've raised objections to Skip. So far, he refuses to contradict the torches. I'll discuss the matter more at the upcoming physicians' meeting, which we're finally having."

+++

The winter physicians' meeting was long overdue, and it seemed like my job might end before it was ever held. Skip had delayed the meeting time and time again due to holidays, due to weather, due to conferences in Florida, Mexico, and other warm and sunny locations, and due to an array of other flimsy excuses. Clearly, he'd prefer not having a physicians' meeting at all. But, finally, at the behest of his torches, he had relented and called a meeting. So here we were.

As the usual dozen or so doctors filed in for the meeting, they were pleasantly surprised with a sumptuous spread of food. My first thought was that the food was from drug reps. It had the look of a kickback meal. But no. The torches had provided the food—at the hospital's expense, of course. Hopefully, the food would put the physicians into a good mood.

A line formed. I grabbed a plate and got in line behind Dr. Slenderman, and my eyes locked onto a large pile of shrimp. The shrimp looked delicious, and my mouth watered. But to my dismay, Dr. Slenderman, using his hand, scraped the entire mound onto his plate, which required both hands to support its weight and prevent shrimp from spilling to the floor.

I couldn't believe it. "You're taking *every* shrimp?"

"First come, first serve."

After filling my plate with other food options—there was some grilled chicken he didn't seem interested in—and returning to my seat disappointed, I began counting Slenderman's food plates. *One, two, three…*Slenderman made several trips back and forth to the food table, cutting the line each time and filling plate after plate. *God, this guy can eat.* As Slenderman completed his fourth trip, Skip called the meeting to order.

"I'll begin by introducing our chief torch, Mr. Siriso. He leads Firecracker." Skip clapped his hands, and the snickering began.

I grimaced. *Off to a bad start.*

"Is this the guy who took all our prescription pads?" Dr. Slenderman immediately mumbled from the back, his mouth stuffed with shrimp.

"And a lot of other stuff," Dr. Wurst said. "Toys, batteries…" He rattled off other items the torches had removed from offices. The list was growing daily. As the hospital clinics were all owned by Mars Hospital, Skip felt free to send torches into the clinics to confiscate banned products. Skip felt the doctors, as mere employees, had no say in the matter.

"Toys!" Dr. Lyssa blurted out. "Toys!" She started clapping her hands.

Her firecracker word must be toys.

Dr. Lyssa looked at me, covered her mouth with both hands, and quieted down.

Good.

"Yes, I ordered the prescription pads confiscated," torch Siriso replied. "To be a firecracker"—his hands clapped together loudly over his head—"you must use the latest technology. Technology is a pillar of fire. That means no more prescription pads. And to be a firecracker"—another exceptionally loud clap—"you must make safety priority number one. Safety is also one of our ten pillars of fire. Therefore, we removed toys, batteries, and several other things from the office."

"Toys are dangerous?" Dr. Wurst sounded confused.

"Yes. A child might be injured."

"And batteries? Those are dangerous?" Dr. Wurst continued. "Without batteries in the office we have to call the freaking IT department whenever anything needs a new battery. Talk about inefficient, not to mention slow."

"Yes, batteries are also dangerous. They are a choking hazard."

Doctors immediately began cracking up at the ridiculous statement.

"What if I promise not to put batteries in my mouth?" Dr. Wurst replied dryly, shaking his head. Laughter continued.

The torch ignored his comment and kept talking. "I will now pass out the book Skip requires you to read. It's called *Be a Firecracker!* and it describes the firecracker program in detail." Clap. He handed out books, and as soon as doctors saw the dancing firecracker on the book cover, their laughter intensified.

"Not again," a doctor said. It wasn't clear who spoke.

"What's with the clapping, torch man?" Slenderman asked when the laughter had quieted down. His shrimp plate was now clean.

"We clap when we say firecracker to emphasize the merit of the program and remind us of the ten pillars of fire." He clapped again, prompting more scattered giggling.

Skip frowned.

"If we clap while making crab claws, can we call it a crabby cracker?" Dr. Wurst made crab pinching motions with his fingers, which caused a soft clap. "That way, we can combine the crab program with the firecracker program."

Other doctors made crab pinches in concert with Dr. Wurst. Skip's hairless head took on a reddish hue.

"Or what if we clap with the book?" Dr. Wurst made a much louder clapping sound by opening and closing the front and back covers of his *Be a Firecracker!* book. "Does that work?"

"This is serious. It's no joking matter." Skip yelled. "We have eliminated the Get Crabby program due to lack of support from you doctors. This time, you will support the Firecracker program!" He clapped. After clapping, he grasped his goatee with his right hand. His voice full of rage, he continued, "Torch Siriso, tell them about the next step in the program."

"We are getting rid of desk chairs. As part of the Firecracker program, all physician desks will be converted to standing desks." Clap. "Firecrackers don't sit." Clap.

A moment of dead silence was followed by howling protests.

"You can't take our chairs!"

"I won't stand all day!"

"That is insane!"

Protests continued, but Skip was unmoved. A smile of smug satisfaction crossed his face. "It's already done. Torches removed all chairs last night. We also removed the desks and put in standing desks."

Great. Time to head to Walmart and buy a folding chair for the office. And what the hell is a standing desk anyway?

As the protests continued and Skip sat with his arms folded, Slenderman asked an interesting question.

"So you took our desks and replaced them with standing desks, whatever those are. Skip, were the expensive mahogany desks and fancy chairs in administration also replaced?"

Skip blushed, looked annoyed, and dodged the question. "Let's move on. The types of desks and chairs used in administration is irrelevant. We have other important things to discuss."

The torch quietly slinked out of the room.

"Sounds like a no to me. What a bunch of hypocrites." Slenderman shook his head and frowned.

"There will be a sale in the gift shop…" Skip began rattling off his other "important things to discuss." Dr. Lyssa clapped and blurted the word "toys" twice while he was speaking. The other doctors brooded. At the conclusion of his important announcements, Skip suddenly ended the meeting. "This meeting is now adjourned."

"Skip, we haven't had the open discussion yet. Doctors have several issues—"

Skip cut off my protest. "There's no time. I have a plane to catch."

"Where are you going?" Slenderman asked. Empty plates surrounded him, which appeared to have been licked clean.

"Grand Cayman. There's an important conference there."

This revelation was met with groans. Slenderman frowned and shook his head.

I tried again. "Skip, there are outstanding issues from the last meeting that we—"

"Sorry." Skip leaped from his seat and high-stepped it out the door as fast as his little legs could move him. No issues from the prior meeting had been addressed. And, as everyone knew, they never would be.

44
THE END OF WINTER

Doctors hated the standing desks. Not only did they look ridiculous, they also had no drawers for storage. All items normally stored in the drawers had been unceremoniously dumped into cardboard boxes and shoved under the standing desks. Doctors were outraged over this violation of their space and privacy.

To sit, doctors smuggled in chairs. A cat-and-mouse game then developed. Torches occasionally found the illicit contraband and confiscated them. But new chairs were purchased. Rinse and repeat. Skip kept track of all illicit chair use in his secret files.

Torches next banned all food and drink from the office, which included coffee. And coffee pots were then smuggled into the offices just like the chairs. Whenever a torch arrived at an office, an alarm to hide the coffee pot was called out. Someone would then run, grab the pot, and place it in the trunk of their car until the torch had left. Occasionally, a pot wouldn't escape in time, and it would be confiscated. Illicit coffee pot usage was also documented in the secret files.

Mini fridges for food storage were banned, smuggled in, hidden, and retrieved in similar fashion. It just took longer to hide the mini fridges. They were larger and heavier. Still, most offices got the hide-the-fridge drill down to under two minutes.

Words were also banned. A list of forbidden words, which seemed to grow daily, was posted in each office with the instructions that all word-use violations must be immediately reported. The word *hospital* was on the banned list. *Medical facility* was the approved replacement. The words *physician* and *doctor* were both outlawed. We were now *providers*. Doctors despised this demeaning term. *Patient* became a forbidden word as well. *Client*, that hated lawyer word, was to be used instead. Employees stubbornly refused to follow the word proclamation—at least when torches weren't listening—and they also refused to file any word-use violations, much to Skip's chagrin.

Finally, cell phones were banned. They distracted employees from work. This was undoubtedly true but hard to enforce. Everyone awaited a banning of pockets, as this is where cell phones went at the first sign of a torch.

The torches, who were universally hated, never made any rule or regulation that improved patient care. Caring, in general, seemed something they neither understood nor were interested in. Their edicts only made patient care more difficult. Consultant groups are major contributors to the expense and inefficiency of the US health-care system.

Little did I know at the time, the Firecracker consultants would soon lose their lucrative deal with Skip—knowledge that would have eased my final, anxious days on Mars—I mean *in* Mars—quite a bit.

+++

On my last day in the clinic, Ms. Geras arrived with another delicious pie. She also gave me a thank you card. *What a lovely lady.*

"The pie and the card are for being a good doctor. And to thank you for helping me." She had declared bankruptcy. As predicted by her lawyer, the hospital had objected, claiming fraud. The bankruptcy trial judge quickly dismissed the claim of fraud as unfounded. The debt was discharged, and the federal bankruptcy judge sternly admonished the lawyers for the collections agency for making such an absurd fraud claim. "My house is now safe, and the debt is gone."

Until the next time you get sick. Bankruptcy can only be filed once every eight years.

I helped myself to a slice of pie and took a big bite. "Sally, the torches have declared it against the rules to eat in the clinic." My mouth was Slenderman-full of pie, and my words were muffled.

"The torches can go fuck themselves," Sally dryly replied. She wore her Cobra pin, which perfectly summed up her opinion of administration, torches, and their rules.

After we had efficiently devoured the pie, it was back to work. And, as though for a grand finale, some of the oddest cases yet were arriving.

✚✚✚

The reason for the patient visit was, "adult baby."

"So why exactly is he here, Sally?"

"He's here for disability. He brought forms." Sally face-palmed.

"Adult baby? Is that a thing?"

"He's even wearing a diaper. And a bonnet." She started laughing and could barely get the words out.

After using Google to search the question before seeing the patient, it turns out "adult baby" as an identity is indeed a thing.

There's a condition called paraphilic infantilism, where adults think they're babies. A man in California had been granted disability for the condition, and this had been in the news. That's probably how this fellow got the idea for this interesting way to make a disability claim.

"Good day. I understand you're here for an evaluation for disability?" My hand went to my mouth to prevent chuckling. A heavy-set, middle-aged man in an adult diaper was sitting on the exam table. He wore a bonnet, sucked on a pacifier, and had a stained Winnie-the-Pooh t-shirt. He even held a rattle.

"I'm an adult baby. I need disability." He explained his baby routines. His wife dressed him, fed him, changed his diaper, and powdered his bottom.

What a lucky lady. But his wife wasn't here. She was at work.

"How did you get here today?" I asked.

"I drove."

"Babies can't drive. How does that fit with your syndrome?"

"I had to drive. My wife couldn't come. But I am a baby. Look at me."

"And how long have you been an adult baby?"

"Oh, um, for a long time," he stammered.

"Are you working? Do you have a job?"

"Yes. I work in a factory outside of town."

"And you go to work like this?" I pointed at his bonnet.

"I can't go to work dressed like this! The guys at work couldn't handle it. But I change into baby clothes as soon as I get home."

"To qualify for disability, whatever the disabling condition may be, it must prevent you from working. The fact that you go to work means you don't qualify for work disability regardless of whether or not you are an adult baby."

"Wait, you mean I have to stop working first?"

"It's not about stopping work. A medical condition must prevent you from working."

"How could I pay my bills if I didn't work?"

"That's the point of disability. People who are medically unable to work receive disability because they cannot earn money to pay their bills."

"That's ridiculous. Just look at me! You have to fill out the forms." Waving the forms in one hand, he shook his rattle slightly in the other.

My eyes teared up and a giggle inadvertently slipped out. "I'm sorry, but I can't fill them out," I said. "It would be fraud. I'm happy to refer you to a psychiatrist. Your adult baby syndrome should certainly be evaluated. Psychiatric treatment is in order."

"Fuck that. If you aren't filling out the forms, I'm leaving." He stood up and walked out of the room. Passing a trash can on his way out, he tore off his bonnet and angrily threw it away.

+ + +

"This is a day to remember, huh?" Sally announced that the next visit reason was, "I'm allergic to horse semen."

Yikes.

The patient, a skinny young fellow in his twenties, got right to the point the moment he saw me enter the exam room. "I have a rash over my body from head to toe." The patient was indeed covered with a red, splotchy rash that looked allergic. There are many possible causes of such rashes. Typically, horse semen is not the first thing that comes to mind.

"And this rash is from horse semen?" I asked.

"Yep, that's what I'm thinking."

"Do you work on a farm? Do you raise or breed horses?"

"No."

"How were you exposed to horse semen, then?"

"What do you mean?"

"You think this rash is caused by horse semen, so you must have been exposed. I'm asking how."

"That doesn't matter, Dr. Wave. You don't need to know that." He blushed deeply as his eyes focused on his shoes.

"Did horse semen contact your skin?"

"Yep. Drenched head to toe, and the very next day, this rash started coming up."

Yuck.

"Very well, I'll give you a course of some anti-allergy medication. Also, I must advise you to avoid further exposure to horse semen. Future exposure could lead to an even worse reaction."

His expression was pained with disappointment.

"I also suggest allergy testing to confirm this is indeed the cause of the rash and not something else."

"Do they test for horse spunk with this allergy testing?"

"No. That's not part of the standard panel." *Nor any panel for that matter.*

"Forget it. It's horse spunk. I'm sure. Just give me the medicine." Prescription in hand, the patient left, his face beaming happiness.

"So what's up with this guy, Wavesticks?" Sally asked when he was gone. "Is he screwing farm animals?"

"He wouldn't say. All he would tell me is that he was drenched in horse semen head to toe. He gave no further details."

"Oh, God! What a freak."

I shrugged. "He was just horsing around." I blew a horse-like raspberry.

"I am going to miss you, Wavesticks."

+ + +

Sally informed me a new patient had been added on at the last minute.

"We just had a guy walk in for evaluation, and I'm pretty concerned."

"Why's he here?"

"He thinks he killed his wife."

"What?" My eyes widened in surprise. "Grab the panic buttons. I'm going right in to see him. Please accompany me." Sally put a panic button around her neck and handed another one to me. She was so concerned, she didn't even moo. Both cowbells in place, we entered.

I hope I'm not murdered on my very last day.

A middle-aged man with frontal baldness and brown hair on the sides sat on the exam table. "I'm going crazy, Doctor." He trembled as he spoke. "I thought I killed my wife! I have a clear memory. My wife was cooking dinner. I opened my closet, took out my shotgun, and shot her dead." Blood drained from his face. "I woke up this morning in a panic. I love my wife. Then she walked into the bedroom and said, 'Good morning, sleepyhead.' I started screaming. Doctor, I remember shooting her. I remember seeing her brains splatter against the wall. I remember the sound of the shotgun and the smell of the gunpowder. I remember! I am totally going crazy. My wife told me to come see you." He began to cry.

Sally's eyes were wide, and the color was draining from her skin.

"Do you use any drugs or alcohol?" I asked.

"No."

"What about prescriptions? Are you on any medications, especially anything new?"

"Yes." He reported he had recently been started on Chantix for smoking cessation by another doctor.

That's it. "That medication sometimes causes intense, unusual, dreams. Sometimes they are so vivid they are confused with real memories." A study published in 2015 in the medical journal *Sleep* showed vivid or unusual dreams occurred in 12.4 percent of all patients taking Varlenicline, the generic name for Chantix.

"So that's what made me think I killed my wife? You're saying it was all a dream?" Doubt filled his voice.

"Yes. It's the medication. It was just an intense, vivid dream. Stop the medicine immediately. You aren't crazy. I once had a patient who wouldn't speak to her husband for a week. In a dream, they'd had an argument. But it never really happened. This is a well-known side effect of this medication."

"Damn right I'll stop it. Why wasn't I warned?" A tone of anger replaced the patient's doubt.

"The drug company does put a warning in the package insert." Of course, those are rarely read by patients. In 2009, the FDA had placed a black box warning—their most serious and high-level warning—on Chantix for its neuropsychiatric side effects. But in 2016 the FDA removed this black box warning. Doctors should warn their patients about serious potential side effects of medications, but often they don't.

"They should ban this drug if it does shit like that!"

"Well, it isn't common to have side effects as severe as yours. And the medication does work well for its prescribed purpose." *And makes buckets of money for the pharmaceutical company.*

I sent the patient home with instructions to take it easy for the rest of the day. He was deeply shaken by the experience. Some patients develop PTSD after such an intense dream. And, just to be sure, Sally called and checked on the wife. She was fine.

"Check up on this guy, will you, Sally? I'll be gone, but we should make sure he doesn't have long-term psychological issues from this."

"Will do. I'm just glad he didn't actually kill his wife."

"Me too. Any word yet on which doctor you'll be assigned to after I'm gone?"

"Around here, it could take them months to figure it out. I'm going to interview for a job at the university in Omaha. I'm going to escape this shit show just like you."

"What sort of position?"

"It's a job in their intensive care department. Would you mind being my reference?"

"I'd be happy to."

"I might also take some advanced classes at the university while I'm there."

"That's a great idea. You're smart and can do so much more than be a nurse at Mars Hospital. Of course, this means you'll have to move."

"Gee, that breaks my heart." Her words were dripping with sarcasm. "Mars should be called The Land of Misfit Toys, as only a misfit would stay here. Or maybe Mars should be called The Career Burial Ground. Anyone who stays in this town can kiss their upward mobility goodbye." Sally sounded fed up, but her insight was accurate. The Mars medical staff was certainly full of misfits. Sally was too smart and too talented to have her career buried in Mars.

"Well, it's time to say goodbye. I'm off to meet with Skip, then I'm out of here. Sally, it has been terrific working with you. I hope you get that job. And your advanced degree."

"Thanks, Wavesticks. Here's a little going away gift."

Sally handed me a gift-wrapped box. Inside it was a shirt that said, "What happens on Mars stays on Mars." Attached to the shirt was a Cobra pin.

It's now my favorite shirt, pin and all.

+++

"We have to ban Facebook!" Skip shouted when he heard me enter his office, but he didn't look up from his PC screen. One hand was locked around his goatee and the other clutched his mouse. His bare scalp glistened with sweat, and his lower lip trembled.

"Why?" My face broke into a wry smile. Whatever Skip was staring at on his computer screen wasn't my problem.

"Employees are making hateful Firecracker posts." Skip was so upset, he'd forgotten to clap.

Should I call him out?

"Look at this." He nudged the computer screen toward me. A variety of posts mocking Firecracker as well as good old Crabby the Crab were on a Facebook page. The page, titled "The Cobra Club," hinted at who might be responsible.

"And they are bad-mouthing me." Skip scrolled down to a section devoted to mocking his walk.

"It's childish," I said. "You shouldn't give them the satisfaction of even noticing it."

"We have to make every employee delete their Facebook."

"I don't think you can do that."

"In that case, I want someone to inspect and review every employee's Facebook account." He looked up at me.

Don't look at me. I'm out of here.

"I don't think you can do that either." But some employers around the country had done just that, demanding passwords to employees' social media accounts.

"We'll see about that." Skip turned off his computer with a hard slap. "Is this our final meeting?"

"Yes. I start a new position in two weeks." A major medical center in Boston had offered me a directorship. It was a big step up from The Land of Misfit Toys.

"Congratulations. I also have some good news. We've just received a certificate of need from the state of Nebraska. We are approved to start a one-hundred-million-dollar expansion of the hospital." Skip smiled broadly, unrolled some big blueprints on his desk and gazed at them lustily.

In Nebraska and many other states, hospitals must go to a central planning agency for approval of expansion projects. These central committees are not only inefficient and act to increase the monopoly powers of hospitals, they also are often rife with corruption. Both the Federal Trade Commission and Department of Justice have issued statements against these state committees stating they increase costs, stifle innovation, and reduce consumer choice. But thirty-five states still have certificate of need laws on the books.

How did he get the state to issue him their prized certificate of need? I don't want to know, but I bet Agent Themis does.

"These drawings are impressive." *Ridiculous is a better term. Does the hospital really need a giant new administrative wing?* "Can the hospital afford this?"

"Of course. We'll be issuing bonds. We can cover the payments easily." Mars Hospital was doing alright financially, but this was a massive outlay for a small hospital.

"The hospital is doing well, but if anything disrupts revenue, it'll be sunk."

"Nothing will disrupt our revenue." Skip brimmed with confidence. "Nothing ever does."

A fraud investigation might.

"Be sure to come back and check things out."

Silence.

No way I am ever coming back here.

"Skip, I should relay the concerns and complaints from the doc-tors to you one last time," I said. I began my litany of complaints, but Skip didn't lift his eyes from his building plans. My concerns about the hospital were met with silence, but my complaints about the torches drew a reply.

"The torches stay. The Firecracker program will continue as planned. Dr. Wave, I think this meeting is over. Good luck with your career. Bye."

You forgot to clap again!

Walking out, my smile stretched ear to ear, and I clapped my hands loudly for Skip.

I also called Agent Themis. He didn't pick up, so I left a message regarding the new building plans and the hospital's certificate of need.

✦✦✦

"So you're done here?" Beats asked the second he saw me enter the lounge. It was my last stop on the way out. He, Slenderman, and Rumpsmith were all sitting together. Slenderman was eating a sub sandwich that looked to be at least three feet long, but it was shrink-ing rapidly.

"I just finished my final meeting with Skip."

"Who's replacing you?"

"No one. Skip has eliminated the position. He'll be handling all medical matters directly."

"Skip could fuck up a cup of coffee, but he'll still do a better job than you did," Slenderman cut in, his mouth filled with sandwich.

"Thanks for the compliment."

"What are you doing next?" asked Beats while Slenderman

chomped on his meal.

"I've taken a directorship in Boston." *Crabby's hometown!*

"Hey, Wave, now that you're leaving and you aren't my boss, we can invest together. I'm investing with a group of doctors. Look at this." Beats's eyes glowed as he pulled out and unrolled a blueprint and set it on the table.

Geez, everyone has blueprints today.

"A group of investors and I are buying the old factory in town. We're going to turn it into condos."

"Condos? From an old, abandoned factory? It's sat empty for years." This was the factory across the canal from Sal's Saloon. "Who would want to live there? Who would want to buy condos in Mars, Nebraska, for that matter, next to Sal's Saloon and a stinky canal prone to flooding? And it would cost a fortune to rehab that wreck of a building. How could you make any profit?"

"We can't lose. The guy running the investment is guaranteeing a fourteen-percent return, minimum. This investment can't go wrong."

"Is the guy running this scam named Ponzi?"

"Don't be such a skeptic. He's giving out written guarantees."

"Yeah, the guarantees aren't worth the paper they're written on. No, thanks."

"Don't you want to get rich? Ninety percent of all millionaires made their money investing in real estate. And with a fourteen-percent guaranteed compound rate, you'll do way better with this than any other investment."

Beats must be parroting the pitch the scammer gave him.

"I'm not interested. As a physician, I make good enough money, and I have an interesting job that I enjoy. That makes me richer than most."

Beats wrinkled his nose in disagreement. "Don't say I didn't invite you in when you see the millions this deal makes."

"I won't. Goodbye, guys."

"Hey, Wave," Slenderman began, but then he paused and his eyes flicked to the door. "Who the fuck are you?" he blurted, spewing sandwich in the process.

I turned toward the door to see who he was addressing. My face lit up with the same surprise, but for a different reason. It was Agents Themis and Naso. A moment after they entered, two uniformed police officers also entered the lounge.

"Hello, Dr. Wave. Glad to see you. Stick around. You'll want to see this." Agent Themis's gaze shifted to Slenderman. "You must be Dr. Slenderman. I have a warrant for your arrest."

Slenderman's jaw dropped, and the partially chewed globs of sandwich remaining in his mouth fell to the table.

Raids conducted by the FBI, in conjunction with other state and federal agencies, occurred at several other locations around town that day, including City Hall, the county courthouse, and the nursing home. Dr. Slenderman, as well as dozens of other Mars physicians, numerous hospital administrators, the mayor, and many others were taken into custody quietly and without incident.

Skip, however, went down kicking and screaming, so I heard. He locked himself in his office when he was alerted to the hospital raid. Then he tried to destroy the secret files using the one small paper shredder in his office, which would have taken days. Agent Themis arrived and began pounding on Skip's door, demanding entrance. In a panic, Skip attempted to climb out a window with a few choice secret files tucked under his arms. His office door was busted down before he'd gotten too far. Agent Themis pulled him feet-first from the window and arrested him.

I wonder if they had to pry his hands free from his goatee in order to cuff him.

The papers never said.